ON THE LINE

This Large Print Book carries the
Seal of Approval of N.A.V.H.

On the Line

Donna Hill

THORNDIKE PRESS
A part of Gale, Cengage Learning

GALE
CENGAGE Learning

Detroit • New York • San Francisco • New Haven, Conn • Waterville, Maine • London

GALE
CENGAGE Learning™

LIBRARY OF CONGRESS CATALOGING-IN-PUBLICATION DATA

Hill, Donna (Donna O.)
   On the line / by Donna Hill.
     p. cm. — (Thorndike press large print African American)
   ISBN-13: 978-1-4104-0644-6 (hardcover : alk. paper)
   ISBN-10: 1-4104-0644-X (hardcover : alk. paper)
   1. African American women — Fiction. 2. Radio personalities — Fiction. 3. Counselors — Fiction. 4. Women authors — Fiction. 5. Large type books. I. Title.
   PS3558.I3864O5 2008
   813'.54—dc22
                                        2008003447

Published in 2008 by arrangement with Harlequin Books S.A.

Printed in the United States of America
1 2 3 4 5 6 7 12 11 10 09 08

This book is dedicated to all
our loyal fans.

CHAPTER 1

Before we get into all the drama that is my daily existence, let me formally introduce myself. My name is Joy Newhouse. Some callers refer to me as Ms. Newhouse, Joy, the doctor or bitch. Take your pick. In any event I'm the Diva of the airwaves with the most controversial, highest rated late-night talk show in the Tri-State of New York. My show *On the Line* is syndicated in thirty markets, not to mention streamed on the Internet. In other words, I'm all up in the house!

Yeah, you're probably wrinkling up your nose wondering why if I'm so bad am I on "late night." The deal is this. The kind of stories I blast on the airwaves are not for the faint of heart. In other words "adult programming," "Rated R," "over the top." Get the picture?

I get all kinds of crazy shit — call-ins, letters, e-mails and videotapes. I've even had instances where desperate listeners have come up to the station demanding my personal attention and had to be dragged away by security. Imagine that! Mind you, I'm not a psychologist or some kind of expert, but I do have common sense and that's what I share with my crazy-ass listeners — a dose of common sense and a reality check. Yes, my voice and brand of in-your-face advice reach millions one way or the other five nights per week.

Needless to say, I love my job. Every night is a new experience. When I first got into the radio game I got so many FCC fines for my potty mouth, that it was either move me to late night or lose my gig. I opted for late night. You see, I'm a straight shooter, no-holds-barred kinda girl. If I think you're an asshole I'm gonna tell you. As a result, my producer and best friend, Macy, works double time on the "bleep" board. And, trust me, I make a sistah work for her paycheck!

Me and Macy go way back from our teen years of growing up in Do-Or-Die Bedstuy in the heart of Brooklyn, New York. So I still have a little hood in me beneath my polished exterior and can get funky with the best of them. But Macy is usually at my side to keep me in check on the air and off.

Truth be told, not only is Macy my best friend, she's my *only* friend. Sad, huh, that a successful woman like myself can count her friends on one finger? But it's cool. I'm not complaining. I have a good life. I live well, eat well, dress well and drive a brand-new Jag. My celebrity gives me entrée to all the hot parties and society events. That ain't half-bad especially for a chick that barely made it out of high school in one piece — mentally and physically.

There's no special man in my life. But I keep my pipes well-tuned — like now. I wish I could tell you what his name is, but for the life of me I can't remember.

"Hey, babe. Time to get up. Rock and roll." I shake his bare shoulder. He groans and squints up at me. A slow smile moves across his mouth.

"Hey," he says, his voice still thick with sleep.

We must have gotten in from the party about five this morning. Screwed until the sun came up then passed out. It was now almost three in the afternoon. Although I didn't go on air until ten, I need my down-time to prepare — preferably alone. I use that time to go over the tons of letters and e-mails that come into the station to see which ones spark my interest, can cause the most eyebrows to be raised and still pass under the FCC radar.

"Come on, babe, I have things to do." I call him babe so he won't flip about me not knowing his name. Plus it sounds like I almost care.

Reluctantly he throws the sheet off and DAMN I remember why I picked him. The brother was hung and even at half-mast he looked lethal. He noticed me staring and grinned.

"Want some more?"

I think about it. "Maybe some other time. You wore a sistah out!" I grin then turn away and head to the kitchen before my carnal nature changes my mind. The sun is beaming in through the windows. I adjust the blinds, turn on the radio and listen to *The Steve Harvey Morning Show.* That man is a riot.

Compared to the rest of my apartment, which is pretty awesome, my kitchen would give Martha Stewart a run for her money. Stainless steel throughout, gray and white marble floors — real marble, not that stick-on stuff — double sinks and a cooking island complete with a hibachi grill. Trust me, it's not that I like to cook or anything, I just love the look.

"Can I call you?" he asks, coming out into

the kitchen while fastening his pants.

My eyes roll over him. "Why don't you leave me your number and I'll be in touch." I give him my best I-promise-to-call-you smile.

"Yeah, sure." He turns and walks away.

A few minutes later I hear the front door slam shut. Suddenly I remember his name. Randy Temple. I shrug and sip my coffee. Don't know why he should be offended — men do it all the time. Some man somewhere is telling a woman right now, "I'll call you." Yeah, right.

I wander into my office, coffee cup in hand, and plop down into my chair. This is my sanctuary. I think it's kind of cozy with its solid wood furnishings. Shelving runs along the wall where I keep photos of me and Macy at the many celebrity events that we've attended over the years, my broadcasting trophies and a picture of the projects. Yeah, the Marcy projects, that's where I spent my formative years. I keep it there to remind me of where I've been and never want to be again.

There is a box at the foot of my desk piled high with letters. Depending on the issue I can usually get to three or four letters, handle the call-ins and maybe squeeze in a few e-mails if there's time. I reach into the box and pull out a random handful, put my feet up on the desk and open the first letter. One of my main criteria for reading a letter over the air is that it must read like a story, all the juicy details and the "he said, she said." See, I run my show like radio of old where folks would tune into *The Shadow* and stuff like that. Only I kick it up a notch. Yeah, reality radio, baby. I spread open the letter entitled, My Dilemma . . .

Dear Joy,

Damn, damn, *damn!*

I consider myself a woman of above-average intelligence. I am well educated, successfully self-employed in a very influential and highly visible position, and financially quite stable.

I have never had a brush with the law. I pay my taxes on time and make regular contributions to several reputable charitable organizations.

In other words, I am in the upper crust of your radio demographic. I am the sistah that your advertisers are dying to reach: I own a home, save and invest my money wisely, have a superb credit rating and regularly enjoy the finer things in life.

I have not one, but two master's degrees from Ivy League institutions, and a bachelor's degree from the finest women's college in the nation, thank you very much.

I remained a virgin until my sophomore year, and though I am now in my mid-thirties, I can count the number of lovers I have enjoyed on one hand. And I swear under oath that I have never, ever, *not one, single damn time, had sexual intercourse without protection.*

So how can something this ridiculous, this stupid, this *low,* happen to me?

I can't tell you how often I've talked bad about the women who call your show for advice because they find themselves pregnant and don't know who the daddy is.

I can't count how many times I've snickered, criticized, rolled my eyes, called 'em stupid, trifling, and some of everything else.

This kind of tacky ghetto farce was never supposed to happen to *me.*

You may have heard of me, Joy. I feel as though I know you because you are part of my life every night, from the time I roll into my California king–size bed until I drift off to sleep, counting my good fortune.

I am Simone Forrester, the nation's leading advocate and most visible and highly respected spokesperson for interracial identity and rights. I am the founding and current president of Multiracial Unity, Love, Tolerance and Identity (MULTI), the largest, most visible and influential network of its kind in the nation.

In that capacity, I appear regularly on national television — and radio — and in newspapers and magazines all over the country, and sometimes in various parts of the world. I have written three successful books on matters related to multiracial identity and earned a reputation as a leading expert on the topic.

I have won awards for my work, which is regularly called "groundbreaking," "powerful," "affirming," "life altering" and "revelatory."

But none of that is helping me now. I peed on that EPT stick and my world turned inside out in less than ten seconds. As I write this, I have just returned home from my doctor appointment, the one where they verify the pregnancy with a blood test and a pelvic exam.

I believe I am the only person in the world who knows that I have been carrying on simultaneous relationships with two men. Two men who are as different as, well, black and white.

My head is spinning, Joy.

My life is so successful because I have organized it to run a certain way, and it has been working just fine. Better than fine: wonderfully.

But now, my breasts are sore and growing

like balloons.

My stomach is heaving.

Everyday scents make me nauseous.

The most ridiculous things are making me cry.

Two months, the doctor said. *Two months along.*

As though that was perfectly normal and understandable, perfectly logical.

Which it might be, if not for my "dilemma."

Let's call it that, okay? My Dilemma.

As if it's not enough that I am in love with two men — and *yes,* even though it may be considered ho-ish behavior, I have been maintaining intimate relationships with both of them — now I am pregnant. Despite the consistent use of both condoms and the Pill.

I could tie my brain in knots trying to figure out how the hell this happened, though we all know the small-print statistical probability with all forms of contraception, and our mama's sage warning: No form of birth control is one hundred percent!

Of course, I realize I have an option about this whole motherhood thing. I can get an abortion since, thankfully, they're still legal in the U.S., at least for the moment. I can carry the child to term and then give it up for adoption.

But since thinking of or referring to my growing, unborn child as *it* turns my stomach and makes me want to cry, I'm facing the fact that I may want to keep the baby. Become a mama.

Which is complicated enough without My Dilemma: *I don't know who the daddy is!*

Is it Andy, the amazing jazz saxophonist of European ancestry, who grew up in the whitest of white-bread suburbs, discovered Coltrane, Miles and Bird in his twenties, and flew the coop of law school for a life fueled by passion and artistic freedom?

Or is it Sam, brothah-from-the-hood who parlayed his athletic scholarship into a Harvard MBA, and is now a rising Fortune 500 company star with killer hours, nonstop demands, and the corner office and perks to show for it?

Joy, my life has never been as simple as black or white. You see, when you're an *AND,* as I am, as all multiracial people are, your day-to-day existence is a balancing act.

Having this baby would obviously throw my life off balance. But I have to know who the daddy is before I decide whether to have or keep the baby. You can understand that, right?

Not knowing? *That* is absolute hell — worse than the sore breasts, the morning sickness, the emotional seesaw.

Because if Andy is the father, my child will

16

be three-quarters white. And if it's Sam, my baby will be black.

Having this baby would knock me off the fence, this place I have called home for as long as I can remember. It would upset my balance. And without my balance, who am I?

But some part of me believes, I mean truly and genuinely *believes* that, since I became pregnant despite two levels of birth control, God wants me to have this child.

I know it's irrational, but that's what this pregnancy has done to me. I feel a bond with the child already, no matter who the father might be. It's just that there will inevitably be a moment of truth at some point, after I tell them I'm pregnant, or after the baby is born, when everything will fall apart.

Is it too much to hope that they'll both stay?

Oh, Joy, I know it's unrealistic. But doesn't love make us unrealistic anyway?

That's why I need *your* wisdom, your advice and your guidance.

I feel stuck, unable to move in any direction. What mess have I created for myself?

Am I a bad person?

Do I have a flawed heart? Or worse, corrupt and depraved morals?

If I tell them, I'll lose at least one of them. I mean, after they learn that I've been seeing (and genuinely *loving*) both of them.

Would both of them leave? Would either of them stay?

Will my child and I be forever alone?

If I get rid of the baby (even typing those words makes me shudder), then there is no dilemma, at least not right now. But what about the future?

HELP!

I think I know exactly when I conceived.

Approximately eight weeks ago, to use the ob-gyn's language, I had an unusual weekend.

Now, as risky, dangerous and possibly ho-ish as it is to be in love with and carrying on full-blown relationships with two men, I never, *ever* slept with them within the same twenty-four-hour period.

I mean, a woman has to have some standards, right? But it was Valentine's Day, and that was the first time I let my guard down.

Is it divinely ordained? Is it the end of life as I know it?

What will this do to my professional reputation? My career? How can I go from a highly respected expert, national figure and spokesperson to a potential candidate for Jerry Springer or Montel or Maury: Who is the father of this ho's baby anyway?

So you see, my sistah, I was obviously not cut out for this life of duplicity and deceit. Sperm hit egg and bam! Pow! Simone has to face the possibility of life off the fence.

Joy, I guess you can see why you're the only one I can possibly confide in about My Dilemma.

So now that I've told you more than I'd ever planned to, please help me as you've helped so many others.

Please offer the light of clarity to guide me through this dark and foggy situation.

I have only one month before my to-have-or-not-to-have option expires, as abortions are not normally performed after the first trimester.

I am pregnant.

I love two men.

One black. One white. Each a part of me, and vice versa.

I cannot choose between the halves of myself. I will not choose one love over the other.

Help me, Joy! My very sanity and the life of my child hang in the balance of your response to me.

Thank you in advance for your kind consideration of this request.

Sincerely,
Simone Forrester
Founding President
MULTI
Seattle, WA

Dayum! This one is definitely show material, I think after I pick myself up off the floor and finish laughing. I put it on the desk just as my front doorbell rings.

I suck my teeth, an Old West Indian habit. Oh, did I mention that I'm part Bajan on my mother's side? It accounts for my high cheekbones, thank you very much. As I push back from my seat and head to the door, I think it better not be "babe," then I wonder how whoever it is got past the doorman. I peek through the peephole. My girl, Macy, is on the other side making stupid faces. Laughing, I pull open the door.

"What the hell are you doing here?" That's my way of saying hello.

"Checking on you." She sniffs the air like a hound dog. "I smell a man." She arches a brow and looks at me.

"Been here. Done it," I offer as an answer.

Macy tsks, tsks me. "Girl, one of these days you're gonna get yourself hurt dragging strange men into your house."

"Makes life exciting. You coming in or you plan to reprimand me from the door?"

She pushes past me like she lives there and I don't. I shake my head and chuckle.

That's my girl.

Macy is what is referred to by the fellas as a "brick-house." She has what women pay for. She's what I call HAT. Hips, ass and tits — with a pleasing personality, of course. She's not all that great to look at in the face, kinda homely if you get my drift. But by the time she hooks up her weave, throws on one of her designer outfits and slashes some lip gloss on her big lips, you'd barely notice that she vaguely resembles a horse.

"So what were you doing when I so rudely barged in?" She tosses her purse on the couch.

"Is that Prada?" I eye the bag with longing.

"Yeah," she answers all nonchalant.

"I'm definitely paying your ass too much."

"Don't hate." She glances around. "So what were you doing?"

"My usual. Going through some of those letters for tonight's show."

"Anything juicy?" Her pop eyes pop even more.

I tell her about Ms. Upper Crust and her dilemma.

"Humph, humph, humph." She shakes her head. "Takes all kinds. I can hear the calls come in for that one. What else you got?"

Macy always tries to get a head start on the show so she'll know in advance how often she's going to have to bleep my ass.

"Come on in the office. You can go through some with me."

She follows me to the back of my two-bedroom condo. "Help yourself," I tell her, pointing to the box. I resume my position.

Macy pulls up a chair and digs in. We're both quiet for a while reading and discarding. Macy is the first to break the silence.

"Girl, you have got to put this one on the air."

"What's it about?"

"Some chick who signs herself as, A Lovely Mess. Listen to this . . ."

CHAPTER 2

I knew my life had unraveled as I boarded my flight to Phoenix with only moments to spare. I made myself comfortable in the window seat I'd managed to nab with the intention of cleaning up some files on my laptop. However, my mind was full with other things. I stared out the window and wondered at what point my life had become so complicated. I was losing myself for love's sake. I was in love with three different men, maintained three different identities, lived in three different homes and owned three different cars. The sex was equally great, but different with all three, believe it or not.

I had heard about nymphomaniacs and did not consider myself to be one. In fact, I was in this situation because, long ago, I had come to the realization that sex outside of marriage was wrong. Each husband had been patient and kind and respected the fact that I was a woman who cherished the sanctity of marriage as well as my body. But the best thing about all three is that they are not the jealous types. They have lives that they are comfortable living with or without me. There is nothing more attractive than a confident, independent man. I married Antoine six years ago. I then met and married James and Mark two years later within the same year. It was hectic, but I thrive on hectic situations.

It seemed that just as I began to doze off, the pilot announced that we would be landing soon.

As I made my way through the terminal, briefcase and laptop in tow, I thought I heard someone call my name. "Maya!" There it was again. It sounded like . . .

"Hey, sweetheart, let me get that." I turned to my right and, sure enough, it was James. He greeted me with a kiss on the cheek. "How was your flight?"

"Ahh, well, it was smooth," I said, a bit surprised to see him.

"That's great. I know your car's here, but I wanted to surprise you and pick you up. I thought maybe we could have an early dinner, and who knows . . ." James smiled seductively.

I was a little perplexed by this. I mean, he never picked me up from the airport and this "who knows" thing. Well, what did that mean?

We hadn't had sex in almost a year . . . at least not in the traditional way. A funny thought came to my mind. I remembered when former President Clinton was going through his Monica Lewinsky scandal. He held fast to his excuse that he did not have sexual relations with her. I thought with a Southern twang, I have not had sexual relations with this man. How crazy. Everyone knew oral sex was also sex.

As long as I had known him, James had had high blood pressure, but within months of going on the medication, he had become impotent. With the occasional creative ways we had developed for him to please me, ours was pretty much a nice companionship. I love James and there is nothing he wouldn't do or buy for me, but as an older, retired, impotent man, there is very little he could do for me physically anymore.

"Well, what about my car?"

"You're flying back out in another two days, just leave it here."

"That's such a waste of money."

"Amaya, since when has wasting money concerned you? You know we can afford it."

I hated surprises like this. I did not like not being in control of things. But I supposed this dear man had to exert his manhood in some way. While we waited to retrieve my luggage I wondered what James was up to.

"So, to what do I owe the honor of this surprise pickup?"

"Well, I have a surprise for you, dear."

"Another one? I'm not sure how much more of this I can take," I joked. "Will it do me any good to ask what the surprise is?" I asked, getting a little irritated.

"Not one bit. You'll just have to wait and see," James responded, grinning from ear to ear. He pulled up to Rio Sabor Brazil, a Brazilian-style steak house and a meat-lover's paradise.

"Wow, I've wanted to try this place for the longest time. Okay, now I'm really suspicious," I remarked, studying James as he held the door open for me to enter the restaurant. The Southwestern decor was impressive with the Sunset over Tuscany and Wall of Ages mural from Provence, France. There was a rustic, romantic feel about the place and the many candles added to the intimacy of the surroundings. After a few glasses of wine, we feasted on a prime rib special, prepared with roasted vegetables and garlic mashed potatoes.

"That was delicious," I said, still savoring the memory of the meal as we drove down the highway.

"You're right. It looks like we'll have a new favorite place," James replied as he turned on the blinker to signal he was exiting the free-way. I noticed it was a different exit from the one we usually took to get home and figured it was another part of this ongoing series of surprises he had in store, so I said nothing. The drive had become quite relaxing, accompanied by the two glasses of wine I'd had during our meal.

After another five minutes of driving, James turned right onto a street leading to the airport, which was where we had originally come from. Perhaps he was taking me back to my car, I thought. But he turned right instead of left and headed toward the hotels. Within minutes, we pulled up in front of the Embassy Suites Hotel. Before I could ask James why we were there, he was out of the car, the valet was in and my door was being opened. This was getting just a little weird.

"James, what is going on?" I demanded.

"Just bear with me a few more minutes, baby!" James replied. "I promise it'll be worth it."

We walked briskly through the lobby, caught the elevator and rode it up to the penthouse suite, where James seemed to magically produce a plastic card key to the room. My mind was racing now. It wasn't my birthday, anniversary or any other special occasion I could think of. Once we entered the beautiful

27

suite, there was no one popping out from behind furniture yelling "Surprise!" but rather, just the two of us. Now, I was really getting upset. I folded my arms and stood in the middle of the living room.

"Okay, James, enough! I have had it up to here," I said, gesturing with my hand above my head. "You tell me what this is all about. I've gone along with this little game long enough."

"Okay, baby! I wanted to make this really special," James said, taking my hand and leading me into the bedroom. "I know I have not been able to be the perfect husband to you for a while now, but that is going to change, starting today." He gathered me up in his arms and began kissing me passionately, while massaging my breasts and buttocks.

"James, what are you . . ." I managed between kisses.

"Let me show you, baby! I just love you so much," James said as he began unbuttoning my shirt and then my slacks. When he pressed up against me, I was stunned to feel his erection. I drew back and stared at him. There was a look in his eye that I had not seen since the first time we had sex.

"What happened? What did you do?"

"That Viagra really is a wonder drug, baby!"

"What? Viagra! But what about your blood-pressure medication? I've heard that you're not supposed to mix medications like that."

"You're right, but my doctor is monitoring me closely. I'm not worried, I'm happy, excited even. Do you know how I feel as a man, wanting my wife and not being able to make love to you? You can't even imagine. I feel like less than a man."

"But, baby, you do give me pleasure and our marriage is about more than sex."

"Amaya, I'm not crazy. You're a young, beautiful woman who is full of life and most likely at her sexual peak. Without this Viagra, it's just a matter of time before I lose you."

"But . . ."

"No buts, it's true. You can say what you want but I know the real deal. I haven't lived this long and learned nothing. I'm seventeen years older than you and I'm going to do whatever it takes to keep up. Allow me this," James said as he began kissing me on the neck.

I had to admit it felt good. James and I had had many passionate nights while we were dating and through our first year of marriage. While I had been very content with the way things were, there was a part of me that missed our bonding the way a husband and wife should. For him to go to these lengths for me endeared me to him more than words could ever explain.

I tore open his shirt, kissed him passionately as we made our way to the king-size bed and hoped with the help we now had, nature would take its course. As luck would have it, it did, again and again and again.

On my way from LAX to the restaurant the following day, I thought about Mark. It was not unusual for me to lay everything out for him whenever he had an important meeting. Today he was to host his company's annual fund-raiser. Having started out as the assistant grant writer for the organization, he was proud to have worked his way up to executive direc-tor, which was being announced today. But, it seemed that for most of the important mo-ments in his life, I had not been there to share them. And today, not unlike many other days, my flight from Phoenix had been delayed. I had promised I would meet him at the event, but I was sure that after so many promises he had no faith that I would be able to make it before the event was over.

I squeezed my Mini Cooper into the only available parking spot within a two-block radius off of Melrose Avenue. There would be another two blocks to walk once I reached Tommy Tang's. I suppose I could have taken advantage of the valet parking, but I didn't want to wait. Catching a cab would have been my best bet, but I was pressed for time. As I walked briskly along Melrose Avenue, a thin layer of sweat covered my forehead. I was praying I had not missed too much of the event. When I walked through the doors, there was still a good crowd formed in the private dining area, but I knew I had missed the announcement. I made a quick dash to the ladies' room to freshen up. This was a grazing ground for celebrities and I wanted to look my best. After maneuvering my way through the crowd, I reached the private ballroom just in time to hear Mark thank everyone for their contributions and bid them farewell. I stood off to the side and watched as the crowd thinned out. I could see Mark scan the room and, without blinking, his gaze caught mine. I could see his face register disappointment and then in the very same instance he smiled that dazzling smile that always made me melt. I walked toward him, but before I reached him, a man came up, shook his hand and congratulated him.

"John, let me introduce you to my wife. Amaya, this is John McNeil, my new boss."

Extending my hand, I said, "Very nice to meet you. We are so excited that you have extended this opportunity to Mark."

"Oh, well, I can't think of a better person for the job. Mark is very passionate about his work and working with the community. He's also made a lot of connections with the entertainment industry and that is invaluable. Mark, you have a wonderful weekend. You did a great job tonight. We will have a busy week next week, so try not to party too much," he said jokingly.

"I will, John, you do the same." Mark then turned to me. That dazzling smile had been replaced with hurt that flickered in his crystal-blue eyes. "I'm glad you were able to make it," he said somberly.

"Mark, I did my best. I have no control over the flights," I responded in my defense, but it was lost on him.

"But you do have control over your life. Look, I don't want to argue. I just want to talk about this when we get home. Where did you park? I'll walk you to your car." He placed his hand in the small of my back and gently guided me toward the direction of the front door.

Although we walked in silence, once we reached my car and I was all settled in, I rolled down the window and said, "I'll see you at home, honey." Mark just nodded and walked back toward the direction of the restaurant.

Mark was Caucasian with black hair, blue eyes, a very nice build and stood approximately six feet, two inches. Any woman would be lucky to have him. But I really didn't have time for attitude or an argument. Sure, I was disappointed that I had missed his promotion announcement, but he would just have to understand that my career was important to me, too.

Once I reached our apartment near the Hollywood Hills, I hurriedly went upstairs and began removing my clothing. I wanted to shower and get comfortable before Mark got home, but just as I stepped into the shower, I heard the garage door open and within minutes Mark entered the house.

He didn't make a sound as he slipped out of his clothing. I had my arms outstretched and pressed against the shower wall. I leaned toward the spray of the water with my eyes closed. The water flowed down my face and hair. I never even heard Mark open the shower door to enter, but before I knew it, he had joined me in the shower and was behind me, hands reaching around to fondle and massage my breasts. He began to grind me from behind. I moaned in anticipation, moving back on Mark's groin as he pressed even harder until gaining entry.

Although Mark had been angry with me, it would seem that all was forgiven, for now.

I was so glad to be back home in San Francisco that I could have run from the airport once the plane landed. Instead, I went through my normal routine of picking up my luggage and taking the shuttle to my car. I couldn't wait to see Antoine. He had seemed pretty distant the last time I talked to him. I was sure it had something to do with talks of budget cuts at UC Berkeley where he was associate head coach for the men's basketball team. I was fortunate enough to have caught a much earlier flight, putting me at home half a day earlier than anticipated.

I figured I would go home, take a long hot bath, get comfortable and wait for Antoine. Who knew, maybe I'd even surprise him and make dinner. Instead of pulling into the garage, I parked in the driveway and just grabbed my laptop and toiletry bag out of the car. Antoine could get the big suitcase out of the trunk for me later.

This time, I didn't fumble with the keys. When I entered the foyer I noticed the lights were on. I called out to Antoine but received no response. I set my purse and keys on the little table right next to the door and stepped out of my pumps. As I walked down the hallway to the bedroom, I began removing my blazer and unbuttoning my shirt. That bathtub had my name on it. But I was rooted mid-stride when I heard sounds coming from my bedroom. My mind was playing tricks on me, because even though I knew what the sounds were, I told myself it was the television. Willing my legs to move, I managed to make it to the bedroom door that was ajar. There it was again. *"Oooooh, Toiinnnne, don't stop, baby, please!"* the voice said breathlessly.

I actually stood outside the door wondering how I should make my entrance, if at all. My mind was racing. Should I barge in mid-orgasm? Wait for them to finish? Or, go back to the kitchen and microwave a large bowl of water to boiling? I could even go for the bat in the hall closet, but that might make too much noise. Just as I had mustered up enough courage to storm in, I guess Miss Thang had reached the pinnacle of her orgasm. She began mewling like a wounded animal. *"Ooooooh, baby, it's so, soooooo, good. Pleeeeeze."* I could hear the springs in the bed creaking in rhythm to Antoine's pace and his heavy breathing. I had to admit, Antoine was great in the sack, but I was not as vocal during sex as this whore. Standing there, thinking of all the times we had made love in this very same bed made me physically ill. I turned and ran to the hall bathroom and fell to my knees in front of the toilet. I must have thrown up everything I had eaten for the past two days. I felt so sick and weak. But now my cover was blown and the element of surprise gone. I could hear scrambling and then bare feet running on the hardwood floors in the hallway. I composed myself enough to get my head out of the toilet and prop myself up with my elbow. I had to have a little bit of dignity. I also wanted to see the expression on Antoine's face. When the running stopped, I looked up and there he was, standing in the doorway clad in only his boxers with her, whoever she was, right behind him with my top sheet draped around her like she was posing for some Roman advertisement. She was about my height and build, a shade lighter with a short, trendy haircut. Attractive, but she didn't have anything on me, except for Antoine, I guess.

I flushed the toilet, still trying to keep my dignity intact. A little wobbly, I stood watching the expressions on both their faces.

"Baby, I wasn't expecting you until later this evening. What's wrong?"

I really couldn't believe he had just asked me what was wrong as he stood three feet away from me with the woman he had just had sex with.

"Are you joking?" I managed to reply. "Antoine, who is this ho and why is she still standing here?" I screamed, getting stronger by the minute. By now, I was standing and making my way over to them. I lunged at her, but Antoine blocked the doorway while she ran back to my bedroom. I was blind with rage as I pounded Antoine's chest and struggled to get out of his grasp.

"I'm sorry, Amaya. Baby, I'm sorry. I would give anything to take this back," he said, keeping me locked in a bear hug. Just then, the tramp walked down the hallway, half-dressed, and opened the front door. "Call me when you get your life together, Antoine," she yelled, and slammed the door.

"Why, Antoine? Why?" I screamed.

"I know it might sound cliché, but it just kind of happened. I mean, you're gone so much." I broke free from his grasp and walked into the living room.

"She must really be something in the sack for you to bring her to our home and into our bed," I said, more to myself. But his silence spoke volumes. "So, how long has this been going on?" I asked, almost afraid to hear the answer.

"Almost a year," he said quietly as he took a seat on the sofa.

I walked back down the hall to the bedroom before the tears could reach my cheeks and began packing another suitcase. This time I would not be returning.

As I made my way from Los Angeles back

to Phoenix from yet another client meeting, my head remained in the clouds. I hadn't been able to focus at work nor when I was with James or Mark. When at work, I used the excuse that I was having problems at home, which was no lie. When at home with Mark or James, I said it was very hectic at work. During the weeks that followed my discovery of Antoine, I sent for the rest of my things, of course making sure they were sent to a hotel. I changed my cell phone number, had my mail forwarded to a post office box and filed for divorce. I could not forgive Antoine for his infidelity no matter how hard I tried. Perhaps, if it had been a one- or two-time deal, but it had been a relationship that spanned nearly a year, which meant there were feelings involved. Also, when I thought back to that evening and the following conversations, Antoine was not really all that remorseful. Of course, he was sorry that he had been caught, but the fact is that he was in love with me and Sheila. That was her name. He told me that himself. The funny thing was, he had no idea how much I understood that part of it. But I needed to be number one. I needed him to be monogamous. I was faithful to our marriage just as I was faithful to my other two marriages. Just because I was not around as much as he would like was no excuse for him to have an affair. The saddest part of this was that I had been with Antoine for a total of seven years, the longest I had been with any man. It would take some time for me to fully recover from this, but I had to keep up the image of being in control of my emotions.

Fortunately, there would not be much for us to divide as part of the divorce settlement. We had no children. Of course, there was the condo and our cars, which were both paid for. But, in order to expedite things, I was giving him the house. My car had been sold back to the dealer and in addition to our separate bank accounts, we had a little over one hundred thousand dollars in a joint account.

I didn't see that as a problem. Split down the middle . . . a clean break. That was all I wanted.

It had been a little over two months, and Antoine and I would be officially divorced in another three weeks. I had been so drained during this time and it seemed that everything just required too much energy. I could not even remember the last time I worked out. Before flying out, James made me promise to be seen by the doctor, just to check things out. I managed to squeeze in an appointment before leaving. On the surface everything checked out, but Dr. Shipley was thorough.

She drew blood, suggested I take more iron and get more rest.

The following Monday afternoon, I had the rare occasion to have a few hours while in Phoenix to run some errands. Later that evening, I was scheduled to fly back to Los Angeles for my weekly client meeting.

Just as I pulled up in front of the post office, my cell phone rang.

"Hello," I answered.

"Hi, Amaya. It's Dr. Shipley," the voice on the other end responded.

"How is everything?"

"Just fine."

"I'm sure you have good news for me!" I said excitedly.

"I sure do. You're nine weeks' pregnant," she said.

Five months later . . .

I smoothed my hand along the duvet and stood back, taking the room all in. It was beautiful. So much had changed since I found out I was pregnant. At that time I had been blindsided, but my need to be in control over-rode good judgment and I made an appointment the following week to terminate the pregnancy. I even went so far as to go to the appointment and get prepped for the procedure, but just could not go through with it. It dawned on me that the baby growing inside me was the only thing that was truly mine and that would love me no matter what, even with all my flaws.

After traveling two to three times a week for the past five years, the time had come for me to slow down. I took a leave of absence from my job with no real intention of returning. I could not possibly keep the schedule I had kept in the past. I gave the room another once-over, admiring the neutral, pastel green-and-yellow pattern that colored the room. The nursery was perfect. I sat in the rocking chair near the window looking out over the busy hustle and bustle of the city.

Although I was filled with joy and looked forward to what the future held and what type of mother I would become, I missed my old way of life. There was a void because my divorce with Antoine had been finalized and, soon after learning I was pregnant, I filed for a legal separation from James. I never went back home to Phoenix, because I just couldn't bear to see his face. He had to have been devastated, and yet I didn't file for divorce because a part of me felt the need to leave the door open . . . to what? I didn't know. Perhaps it would be perceived by James as less cruel. I just couldn't deal with either of them right now.

Mark and I had settled into a nice rhythm. Since I wasn't working, life was great for him, but even carrying the baby, I was still hollow inside. I believe you will always in some way be connected to a person you've been married to.

"Honey, you ready?" Mark asked, appearing in the doorway.

"Yeah, just let me get my sweater," I said, lifting myself out of the rocking chair.

"We don't want to be late for your doctor's appointment. Although I'm sure little Mark Jr. is as healthy as a horse," he said excitedly.

I smiled lovingly, wondering how long this wedded bliss would last after Mark Jr. or Antoine Jr. was born.

By the time Macy is finished, tears are rolling down my eyes from laughing so hard. "How do these crazy broads get themselves into these messes?"

Macy wipes her eyes. "You got me. What's crazier is that they actually write in."

"True." I snap my fingers. "Tonight's first topic will be Women Who Cheat and Get Screwed."

Macy gives me a high five as we laugh some more.

"Whew. Look, I'm going to jump in the

shower and get myself together. Fix yourself something to eat or whatever, then we can head over to the studio."

"Cool. I'm starved." She heads to the kitchen and me to the bathroom.

At about eight we pile into my Jag and drive to the WHOT studio, which is located in lower Manhattan.

"So do you think there's going to be many changes with the new management in place?" Macy asks as we pull into the employees-only parking garage.

I shrug. "Who knows? Anytime some new suits take over, there're changes. As long as they leave me alone we're cool."

We get out and I hand my keys to the valet. We walk to the underground elevator and up to the tenth floor.

The studio is buzzing with activity as usual. We wave to the night owls who hold the station down and head to our booth. Macy goes into the control room to get set up and I begin organizing my letters for the show. I adjust my headset, draw in a deep breath and wait for Macy's signal.

She gives me the five-second countdown. And it's showtime. . . .

CHAPTER 3

"Hold on to your seats, it's Joy Newhouse in your house. Forget that easy listening music, put the love songs on hold. This is WHOT and you're *On the Line*," I sing in my trademark falsetto. "We have another hot show lined up for you and we're going to kick it off with Women Who Cheat and Get Screwed. Yeah, you heard me. Put your feet up on the table and check out these tales from two of our devout listeners. We'll be taking calls."

I read the letters with all the drama the stories entail, complete with sound effects. By the time I'm finished, the board is lit up like the Fourth of July. I take a few calls then I notice Macy signaling me from the booth. Her eyes are wide and she has both thumbs up. Her signal for a "hot" one.

"We have a call on the line, folks, and it sounds like a good one." I depress the button.

"You're on the line!" I chime in with sassy flavor.

"I don't want," the caller whispers, "to do this anymore."

I smile inside. I have a sixth sense when it comes to the callers with real dirt to dish. I subconsciously adjust my headphones, touch the microphone more out of habit than to reposition it and sit up a little straighter. "What can I call you?"

"Daphne R—"

"Just your first name, Daphne. And what is it that you want to tell me?" I probe.

With a great sigh the caller begins. "I've been living a lie."

"Come on, Daph, who among us doesn't have a secret or two?" I pause for effect. "So what makes your secret so special?"

"It's not just a secret." Daphne inhales with great emphasis. "It's a secret life. Almost like double jeopardy."

My ears perk like a championship German shepherd beneath the headphones. "So you're having an affair. Unfortunately, that doesn't make you so special these days. Every minute of every day someone is cheatin' in the next room."

The caller begins again slowly. "I'm living a double life. I mean two homes, two husbands, two sets of children."

"Say what?" Another one, I think. What the hell . . .

"You heard me. I have two lives."

"Aiight, I'll bite. How in the hell can *you* have two sets of children?"

"I met my first husband when I was in college and he was in medical school. We fell in love and were married the Saturday after I graduated. I took a government job and he continued with medical school. When he took an internship in another state, I stayed at home because I loved what I do."

"You're snoozing me here, Daph."

"You said to start at the beginning!"

"Can we fast-forward to the juice?"

"While he was off learning to save lives, I delved into my work and got promoted twice. With the second promotion came the opportunity to travel to foreign countries to work for weeks, even months, at a time."

I begin making a snoring sound.

"Okay. Okay. About six months into one of my assignments I met Salvador. He was charming, handsome, fun and there."

"So you had an affair, not headline news, like I said in the beginning."

"At first it was an affair to end all affairs. Only he never knew, because I told him I was single. Meanwhile back at home my husband finished his medical training and got a job near our home.

"He wanted me to change my job so I could be at home more, but I refused. He reasoned that I had patiently waited for him to do his thing, so he felt he had no right to ask me to give up what I loved. He didn't know it was Salvador that I was loving!"

"Can we get to the two-husbands, two-sets-of-children part?"

"Things were fine for a year or so. I'd go off to work in Brazil for weeks or months and my husband would be at home doing his thing. One night while we were having dinner, Salvador took a little black box from his pocket, got on one knee and asked me to marry him. When I opened the box, the brilliance of the huge rock stunned me. Without giving it a thought, I said yes."

"So Sal baby still didn't know you were married?"

"Salvador *still* doesn't know I'm married!"

"Okay, I've got to admit, you've got me curious. Go on."

"Meanwhile, when I returned to the States the next day, Eric, my *husband,* welcomed me home with open arms. On our way from the airport we take a different route than usual and when I question him he simply says, 'I have a dreamy surprise for you.' He pulls in front of a beautiful house with a huge bow on the front door. At that moment, I knew we belonged together.

"When I looked at him, I saw a man who truly loved me and I couldn't bring myself to hurt him. We'd grown up together. We were both children in adult bodies with big dreams when we met and we had lived those dreams. We belonged together."

"Okay, so now we have to tell Sal this ain't gonna happen?"

"That was truly my plan." Daphne begins to talk faster. "The six weeks I was at home with my husband were wonderful and so busy we didn't even have time to take a deep breath. The night before I had to return to Brazil he looked at me and said I made him complete and that we were going to fill the house with babies that would grow up to be great leaders.

"When I closed the car door I had every intention to break it off with Salvador the minute I landed."

"So, since you're on the line confessing your sins of bigamy, I know that didn't come to pass."

In a defeated tone, Daphne says, "No."

"What *did* happen?"

"When I arrived, Salvador was waiting for me as usual, but grinning brighter and broader than I had ever seen. Since it was our custom to have dinner at one of my favorite restaurants, I thought nothing of his taking me there. Once we stepped inside, the place was packed with cheering friends and family. It was an engagement party!"

"I can see things getting a little more complex. Go on."

"Everyone told me how much they loved me and welcomed me to the family. But when his mother told me that she never thought her Salvador would find a woman to give her grandchildren it ripped my heart out. How could I break the news to them that I wasn't free to marry her son?"

"You set your jaw, part your lips and begin speaking." I do nothing to hide my sarcasm.

"I knew I had to do it. But I had to choose the right time. And in a restaurant with a hundred people wasn't the right place."

"So why didn't you tell him the minute you were alone?"

"I don't know," Daphne whispers.

"Yeah you do. You saw the bling. You blingin' in the U. S. and now you blingin' in Brazil." I laugh at my own quip. "I like that blingin' in Brazil!"

"How dare you pass judgment on me! You make me seem so materialistic."

"If the Prada fits, diva!"

"I don't have to take this! I'm hanging up!"

"No, you're not. You love attention. That's your drug of choice. So you're the wife of a doctor with a government job that takes you to exotic lands and when you get to those exotic lands you're the wife of a Brazilian balla. Now you call me and want someone to feel sorry for you. You may as well get what you came for."

Silence.

"Well?"

"Suppose, and only suppose, you're right. What should I do?"

"Let's not fast-forward quite that far. How did you end up with two husbands and two sets of children? I can't wait to hear how you pulled that one off!"

"I never got up the courage to tell Salvador about my life in the U.S. During my four-month tour of duty, we planned a wedding fit for royalty. With every rose petal ordered, every inch of lace measured for my dress and every hors d'oeuvre we sampled, I told myself I couldn't go through with the charade."

"You said you were in Brazil for four months planning this wedding farce. Did you return to the U.S. before the wedding?"

"My assignment brought me back for two weeks."

"And?"

"I was miserable. I knew I was in too deep. How could I pull this off? I went to my boss and asked to be reassigned, but that would require that I be demoted. I was the leader of the project and there wasn't another assignment available."

"Now if you truly wanted out, you could have taken the demotion or found another job."

"You don't understand, I love what I do. I am the only black woman in the world with this assignment."

"Whatever you say, Mrs. Daphne to the second power! So you marry Salvador, obviously."

"The wedding took place three days after I returned to Brazil. On a hilltop overlooking some of God's most beautiful handiwork, I stood and lied in front of Him and five hundred of Sal's relatives and friends from around the globe."

"How long ago was this?"

"Almost four years."

"And you're still married to both these men?" My tone suggests I felt Daphne was prone to hyperbole.

"Yes."

"And you want out of which one?"

Loud silence fills the airwaves. "You know, this would be the perfect time to pay some bills. We'll be right back with Daphne, who will let us know who she's going to choose."

Off the air, I speak quickly and to the point. "Look, Daphne, if that is your name. I don't know if you are yanking my chain or not, but this is the stuff great ratings are made of."

"I swear to you, this is the truth. I am at my wit's end." Daphne begins to choke back tears. "I just want out."

"We'll be back on the air in forty-three seconds. Hold on to those tears."

I hit the hold button and replace my headphones. I wasn't sure what to make of the story, but I also wanted to know where it was headed. Macy signals I'm back on the air. "Welcome back. In case you just tuned in, we're on the line with Daphne who has a biiiiig secret. Apparently, she's been living a double life for almost four years and counting. Well, we need to know how you pulled off two sets of children. Come on, girl. Tell it, tell it, tell it!"

"You make me sound like such a money-grubbing selfish person."

"And you don't think you are?" I chuckle. "You've really deceived yourself, haven't you, honey?"

Silence.

"You know, if I tried to psychoanalyze you, I would get arrested for practicing medicine without a license. So I'm going to get back to what I'm truly good at, getting people to tell it all. So as I stated before, how in the hell do you have two sets of children?"

"Salvador wanted a baby right away and refused to accept any excuses."

"Honey, you never got the memo *we* are in charge of, Ms. Kitty? Can't nobody *make* you have a baby!"

"You don't understand," Daphne said. "Salvador is very persuasive."

"Yeah, whatevah," I mock. "Go on."

"I got pregnant the first month we were married."

"You don't seem to know how to move this story along, so let me help you out. How in the hell did you keep husband number one from finding out about the pregnancy from husband number two?"

"I left Brazil when I was six weeks. When I arrived home, everything was normal except me. I tried so hard to pretend it was, but I couldn't. I thought of every conceivable scenario to handle the mess I'd gotten myself into without anyone getting hurt. I could have an abortion and tell Sal I lost the baby, though every minute of every day as the baby grew inside me, I loved him a little more. There was no way I could try to convince a medical doctor that the baby was his. Besides, what would he say when I told him I was taking the baby back to Brazil with me?"

"Girl, this is one hot mess! We want to know what you did and we want to know it now! How did you get out of it?"

"I didn't *get out of it,* as you say. After ten days at home I told my husband I had been reassigned in Brazil and that I had to leave right away and I wasn't sure when I would be able to return because my assignment was classified —"

"Ain't that an understatement," I interject. "And he bought this line of steaming buffalo chips?"

"He was reluctant but agreed. I took some vacation time from work and went to a mountain cabin to think."

"So how'd that work for you?" My sarcasm is lost on Daphne.

"When I was there I decided that I'd return to Salvador and have the baby. After it was all over I'd just cut it off with Eric — you know, divorce him. I was in Brazil for almost a year and hardly ever called home.

It gave me the fortitude I needed to make a clean break. When Sal Jr. was six weeks old I returned.

"Eric was distant at best and I told him I wanted a divorce. He was devastated. He told me he knew things weren't good between us, but he was willing to do whatever he needed to do to make me happy. I tried to explain to him that it was me and not him."

"Oh no, not the *it's me* speech! Can we get to the part of the two sets of children?"

"Eric whined and begged. Begged and whined. It was merciless. He finally convinced me to go to counseling."

"How much time has passed and who's taking care of Sal Jr.?"

"Almost two months. The baby was with his father and nanny. I talked to him every day and I took two weekend trips to Brazil."

"So hubby number two is putting up with this madness?"

"Somehow I've made him believe the government won't let me quit and I have to do what they tell me. Go where they send me."

"Okay, so back to the counseling."

"Eric poured out his heart, shed more than a few tears, even begged me to give him another chance." Daphne hesitates and sighs. "I gave in."

"Imagine my surprise."

"We went home and made love like we never had before. I got pregnant."

I whistle through my teeth. "Okay, now we're getting to the good part."

"I'd say it's more like we haven't gotten to the insane part. At this point my life began spiraling out of control. And no matter how hard I tried to hold on I could feel my reality slipping away."

"Honey, your reality was gone long before this. You are so far beyond the point of no return. You've stepped off the diving board and the pool is closed for repairs!"

"Now can you see what a mess this is?"

"I'd have to agree this is quite the *situation*." I don't know whether to ridicule or find a means to rescue Daphne. How self-destructive must a soul be to get this far off the right path of life? "You know, I need to take a break in a couple of minutes, but we're going to do it now so that when we come back you'll be able to finish your story. Back in ninety seconds."

I flip the switch that cut her off from the airways and the telephone. My mind rewinds in warp speed, scanning my mental files for another caller who had intrigued me quite like Daphne in all the years I've been doing the show. I can't think of one. I'd had countless men, mostly long-distance truck drivers, call in with their version of Daphne's story ad nauseam. But this was different.

Macy signals I'll be back on the air in ten seconds. I take a deep breath, adjust the microphone, smile and begin speaking. "And you're back on the line with Joy and Daphne. Daphne is a woman with a biiiiig secret and an even bigger problem. Let's get right to it. Explain to us how you pulled off baby number two."

"I didn't know I was pregnant until I returned to Brazil. Sal was complaining about me being away from Sal Jr. so long and so often and urged me to quit. Of course he harped on that his wife should not be working."

"Yeah, I can imagine how that went over in the Hispanic culture and a rich Hispanic culture at that."

"I convinced him that I was under a military contract and couldn't just walk away. I had to stay at least two more years. But I knew I had to make my trips home less frequent and shorter. I told him I would talk to my boss to see if I could work exclusively in Brazil and only return to D.C. for high-level briefings. It seemed to appease him for the moment. I breathed a sigh of relief."

"And then, Aunt Sadie didn't come to visit?"

"Exactly. I missed my period. And I knew from the timing it was Eric's baby. My first instinct was to take Sal Jr. and run. Just never return to Brazil. Not return to D.C. Maybe get reassigned to Europe."

"But let me guess. You just couldn't do that."

"No."

"I'm sure I'm going to be sorry for asking, but how did you hide pregnancy number two from husband number one? No, wait. Baby number one belongs to husband number two and baby number two belongs to husband number one, or is it the other way around?" I laugh. "I've confused myself!"

Ignoring the latter question, Daphne continues. "It was easy to hide the pregnancy from Salvador. He loved that I hadn't lost the weight from the first pregnancy and when my body made subtle changes he welcomed them. When I was pregnant the first time I didn't even start to show until I was more than five months, so I knew I had time. I returned to D.C. when I was ten weeks and told Eric I was going to have his

58

baby. He never questioned when it could have happened. He picked me up, spun me around and, of course, told me I had to come home. I convinced him it wasn't necessary now and that I was under the care of a military doctor who said everything was fine, which was the truth."

"Damn! How gullible is this guy?"

"Eric is a brilliant surgeon. He's not gullible — he just loves and trusts me."

"And how misplaced is that?" I smirk. "To all you brothers listening to this, there are sistahs who will love you and be faithful to the death. So don't judge all of us by Daphne. There will be brothers looking at their women cross-eyed for years to come if she travels for a living."

"Do you want me to finish or not?"

"Don't get testy with me!" I snap. "You called me, remember!"

"Anyway," Daphne begins with more than a hint of disdain. "Eric called me constantly, which wasn't an issue if I was working. But with the two-hour time difference I had difficulty in the evenings. But somehow I managed to talk to him without Salvador finding out. I finally made it to twenty-one weeks and left for a six-month tour back in the States."

"What about Sal Jr.? How did you explain

not seeing your baby for that long?"

"Sal knew very little about what I do. When I get called on assignment, there are times I can't tell anyone what I'm doing. Though he'd gotten used to it, he never liked it."

"How can any job require you to be away from your family for six months?"

"This isn't a job, it's the government."

"I guess," I murmur. "But how could you, as a mother, go all that time and not see your baby?"

"It was harder than you will ever know and one of the things that drove me to make this phone call." Daphne hesitates, draws in a deep breath before continuing. "I know what I've done is wrong. Wrong for a million reasons that seemed so right not so long ago. Wrong for Eric and Sal. Wrong for Sal Jr. and Erica, but most of all wrong for me."

"How can you think that you are the one most hurt by all of this?"

"Because I am the one who has to walk away from everything. I will lose it all. Everything that I lied and connived to get or hold on to I have to leave now so that no one gets hurt."

"Do you honestly think you haven't hurt anyone by what you've done? I mean, come on now —"

"They will get over it."

"You know, Daphne, at one point of this call I almost felt sorry for you, but now I don't know what I feel. You have two men who adore you and two children who need you. You need to make a choice."

"How can I choose one family over another? I love them all equally. That is why I have to just walk away."

"You're on the line with Joy and Daphne." My tone returns to professional radio talk show host instantly. "We're going to take a commercial break here and when we come back, Daphne, I want you to tell us what you're going to do to fix this mess you've created for yourself. We'll be right back."

I flip the switch. I look at the phone panel and see that every light is lit. Macy has called for an intern to help answer the phones. I've received more than five hundred e-mails since the Daphne tale started to unfold. Instead of scanning the subjects of the e-mails as I normally would, to pick the juicy ones, I close my eyes and lay my head back. Daphne has drained me. I'm so pissed with this woman I don't know what to do, so I do nothing. Rarely has anyone been able to solicit this kind of emotion from me. I use a deep-breathing technique I learned in yoga.

When Macy barges into the studio, I jump involuntarily. "You've got to talk to the caller on line fourteen." Her horsey face is all animated.

I glance at the clock and see I have nineteen seconds before I am back on live with Daphne. "I can't take a call now!"

"He said his name is Eric!"

"Holy shit!" I push the button labeled fourteen and pick up the same time I command Macy to run another short set of commercials.

"You're on the line with Joy."

Silence.

"You've got twenty seconds to tell me why you called or I hang up."

"My name is Eric. And the woman you've spent most of this hour talking to is my wife."

I'm stunned. I'm having a Jerry Springer and Maury Povich moment all wrapped into one. "What did you say?" I ask, trying to buy time to think.

"My name is Eric and I'm Daphne's husband."

Macy signals it's time to return to the air. "Eric, I have to go back on live, *please* don't hang up."

"Why would I hang up without talking to Daphne?"

My adrenaline shoots through the ozone layer and my heart races as I open the microphone. "Welcome back to *On the Line* with your host Joy Newhouse. We spent most of this hour with Daphne, who's been living a double-jeopardy life and says she's sick and tired and wants out. While we were away there was an interesting caller. Our boards have been lit up and if you're trying to get through, keep trying. Daphne, I must tell you I can't remember ever getting as many e-mails for any one caller before you. You've got the world riveted."

"I didn't call for any reason other than to get out this crippling secret."

"So, Daphne, which husband do you plan to tell first and how do you think you'll break the news?"

"I want to tell Salvador that I'm not coming back to Brazil."

"But, by your own admission earlier, you said it's not that easy to just leave your assignment. And what about your son?"

"I've already tendered my resignation."

"Sounds like you've really thought this through."

"Of course I have!"

"And what about Eric and Erica?"

"I still have some time before I talk to Eric. But I can't stay here. Salvador will find me and come make trouble, I'm sure of it."

"So you're not planning to tell Eric until you get around to it?" I toy with her. "Going to weigh your options, as you will. Then spring it on him when it's good for you?"

"I wouldn't put it quite so crass, but yes. Maybe we could move away and I would never have to tell him about Salvador. And even if I do have to tell him, he'd be hurt, but in time he'd forgive me."

"You know, Daphne, you're a pretty cool sistah." I smile both inside and out. "Oh, I almost forgot about the caller I have on hold. Of all the calls we received, I think this one is the most interesting with his opinion on the subject."

I touch the button that opens line fourteen. "Caller, have you been listening to the Daphne saga?"

"Yes, I have." Eric's voice is rich and deep, yet shaky.

"And what do you think about all of this?"

"I just don't understand how she could do this to a man who worships her, would move mountains for her."

"Oh my God!" Daphne gasps. "Eric, is that you?"

I give a high sign to Macy.

"Now that's what I call reality radio, people! And just imagine we have three more fun-packed hours to go. Best of luck, Daphne and Eric. After this commercial break, we'll be back with our next saga." I flop back in my seat, spent. Can't say I don't have fun at my job.

CHAPTER 4

I eye Macy in the control room and she gives me the countdown that we'll be back on air in five . . . four . . . three . . . two . . . one . . .

"Hey, hey, radio-land. Things have been on and popping tonight. If you missed the first couple of hours you missed a helluva lot. But you can catch up online by going to the Internet and downloading the show from WHOTgoJoy.com. Now let's keep it rolling. I'm going to switch gears a little bit. The ladies have been on the hot seat tonight. Now it's a brother's turn to show they can be just as slick as the ladies! I have a letter here from a brother that titles his little saga Confessions of a Baby Daddy. Well alrighty then. Here we go. . . .

Ms. Joy Newhouse, I feel like I know you. I listen to your show all the time. I love your conversations with the public and I really love the jazz and rhythm and blues you play in between your conversations with listeners. It really sets the mood for the conversations. They are all so intriguing. I love jazz, you know. I wanted to call and make a confession. Well, not really a confession, but an apology to the four women that have children by me.

I wanted to do it publicly, so that they will know I'm sincere and have thought about it. I'm not apologizing for my kids, because I love them all. They are my life. But the fact that I have four children by four different women has not been an easy burden. I have three girls and one boy. I have been active in all of their lives since birth. I only married one of the children's mothers, but I'll get to that. I hope you have time for me to tell you the story. I have needed to get this off my chest for some time now.

I'm not a player and making babies was not something I set out to do. It's just a lack of sexual responsibility, but that's not all my fault. Three of the women that have children by me I had been dating for over two years, but if you don't want children, we men need to use a condom at ALL times. The other woman and I both agreed we did not want kids, but I digress back to the condom statement. I hope this story can make a positive difference in some of the younger men who are listening.

I'm an educated man with a master's degree. You can say I was a victim of the Paisley Park Era; Prince, Morris Day and The Time, Sheila E. Sexual freedom was on the rise and as they say, "Gigolos get lonely, too." It was a ridiculous mindset at the time.

My name is Vance Legend and I am a forty-year-old postal worker. I hate my job, but that's another story. It pays the bills and the benefits are great. I met the first mother, Crystal Randall, nineteen years ago in Kansas City, Missouri. I had just finished my freshman year at Benedictine College in Atchison, Kansas, and was working in the summer with my father at Rockhurst University in Kansas City where we lived. I worked with the Upward Bound program. It gave high school students six weeks' experience of college classes on a college campus for college credits and we took the kids on trips to compete against other Upward Bound programs in the area. It was a really cool program and the kids got stipends for the summer.

I was a counselor and tutor at the program and assistant dorm director. We had seventy-five students for the summer. They had classes in math, English, science and reading.

The students had a boys' and a girls' basketball team, and both were very good. I was the coach, along with another counselor, and we practiced every evening. That's where I met Crystal Randall. The All-American Cheerleading Association had their camp at Rockhurst University that same summer and Crystal was an instructor. She had cheered professionally for the Colorado Avalanche hockey team and the Denver Nuggets basketball team.

I noticed her as soon as she set foot on the campus. They stayed in the dorm across a soccer field from where our program dorm was. We first made eye contact in the cafeteria at lunchtime one day. My friend, Hardy Washington, had nudged me and nodded in the direction of her stare. She and a couple of her friends were looking at our table and she was eyeing me. I nodded hello. There was an instant attraction, but after the meal when I approached her she played me off. I liked that. I could tell she was independent and it took more than a hello to get some of her time.

Crystal and I eventually got together and had a great time. For the next few weeks all we did was go for walks, talk, and go around town doing things together. It was really cool. When the time came for them to leave, it was sad. We had grown attached and exchanged numbers. Their next stop was in Wichita, Kansas, about two hours from Kansas City. Crystal asked if I wanted her to come back and visit. Of course, I said yes.

Our students won both the basketball championships in St. Louis, Missouri. We had our summer-ending dinner and gave out awards. It was my last week in the dorm. We had to clean up after the students left. It was just me and Samuel Sharif, the dorm director. I had completed my list of duties three days ahead of schedule.

On Friday evening there was a knock on my door and there stood Crystal. I had been listening to the jazz in my dorm room and drinking wine.

"Can I come in?"

"Sure!" I moved from the doorway.

Crystal put her chocolate arms around me. Her body felt magnificent. She was solid and shapely. I cupped the back of her afro and ran my hands from her neck to her round ass. We moved to the jazz of Grover Washington, Jr. We danced to the bed and we never stopped kissing. I lit candles and we exchanged back rubs and lay in each other's arms caressing each other's bodies. I reached into the dresser next to the bed and pulled a handful of condoms from the drawer.

We stopped making love when the condoms ran out. It was the most remarkable lovemaking I'd had. We had all that pent-up energy and desire. We dated for over two years with plans to marry. Crystal eventually moved to Kansas City with her sister-in-law.

Crystal was studying law and working part-time. We had long stopped using condoms, but she was on the Pill. We made love almost every other day. We were both strong-minded and I was finishing up my senior year in college.

We agreed to take a break from dating each other when we couldn't agree on a date for marriage. We still went out occasionally from time to time. I would see her and her sister-in-law out at the clubs and we always had a good time.

Two months later, Crystal called and informed me that she was going back to Denver. I asked her if she was sure and she said she just wanted to be closer to her family. I understood, because I knew how important my family was to me.

Two weeks later, I got a call that Crystal was pregnant and that we were expecting a child. We argued about whether it was intentional. Though we never came to an agreement about that, I have always loved and admired her. Twyla was born seven months later in Denver, Colorado. I arrived a little after the baby was born. She was a beautiful baby. I stayed for three days and came home to finish school. Crystal and I raised our daughter.

Mostly Crystal. I had her for the summers and went to visit, or Crystal would come to Kansas City to visit with our daughter.

Jessica Simms is the second woman I had a baby by and, the sad truth is, the third woman, Phyllis Charles, was pregnant at the same time. They were one month apart. But we'll talk about her later. Back to Jessica. She and I worked together at the postal service. We knew each other for about three years, but never kicked it together. I would see her all the time at the clubs. She was attractive and all, but she was a wild girl. Smoked weed, drank and did light drugs. I wasn't into that, but she was thick and fine. She had an ass like Janet Jackson.

It was late one night at the club. I got myself a drink and saw her watching me from her table. I walked over and asked her to dance. Four records and slow-dancing later, we were on our way to her house. That was fine with me; I had a three-pack of new condoms and nothing but time on my hands.

Her two-story, three-bedroom house was in the inner city. We reclined on the couch and started watching nothing in particular on television.

Soon the lights were low and we were kissing and exploring each other's bodies. She had on a leather skirt and sweater top with calf-high leather boots and stockings. While rubbing her legs, I soon came to find that her stockings were thigh-highs. Our kisses became more passionate and I soon fell between her bare thighs and served her up. Her moans were loud and her legs straddled my shoulders as she gripped the back of my head and moved my face deeper into her.

She took my hand and turned everything off as she led me to her bedroom. The stage had been set. She let me undress her and I let her undress me. We made love until around an hour before sunrise. I washed up and dressed and was home in bed by the first morning light. That was the beginning of what I called our vampire relationship. I never spent the night and was always in my own bed by the time the sun rose over the horizon.

I was dating another woman at the time named Raven. She and I were at a mutual friend's home at a house party. She wore this tight-fitting burgundy leather outfit that had every man's head in the place turning. She seductively worked the room and I could feel her lustful eyes on me.

Raven and I connected and things were good. I had my cake and ate it, too. It was early June when I got the call that Jessica had missed her period and was pregnant. She promised that she would not keep the baby.

She knew I didn't want children and neither did she and she wasn't trying to trap me. I felt relieved. For the most part we always had used protection and other times I had not pulled out in time, but had been lucky, up till now.

I remember one morning, about a week later, Jessica called to inform me she had talked with her sister and decided to keep the child. Of course, I was furious. I did not want another child, but my thoughts were not her concern. She asked me when I was moving in. I told her she could not be serious. We were just having a fling. I told her I would take care of my responsibility, but there would be no us.

I fell into a selfish depression, never taking her feelings or situation into consideration. I guess that was the day she decided that she would be the closest thing to hell in my life and that's exactly what she was. I never understood, until now, why she hated me, but I thought she understood the rules of our relationship. We had discussed it. But women never understand once emotions and feelings are in the way. I was too foolish to understand it, either.

It was hard as hell working with her at the post office. She soon leaked that I was the father of her unborn child once she started showing, but this did not stop women from wanting to be with me. It's funny now, to think that other women knew I had a woman at the job pregnant and they looked past that and still wanted to give me some play.

Jessica had our child and I was there. She put me through pure hell most of the time. At birth, my son was named Vance Legend Jr. Two weeks later, one of Jessica's fat-ass, no-good, know-I-didn't-like-her, trifling friends came up to me at work.

She placed her large hands on her plump waist and tilted her head arrogantly with disdain. "So, how's Jessica and little Howard doing?"

I looked at her, puzzled. "Who?"

She placed her fat fingers to her lips with a look of surprise. "Ohhh, I guess Jessica didn't tell you that she changed Vance Jr.'s name to Howard. Well, I suppose the cat's out the bag now, huh?" she said as she smacked her contemptuous thick lips, rolled her thick neck and waddled off.

I stood there as my blood boiled. I went to the phone and called Jessica's home phone, but she did not answer. I knew she was home on maternity leave and it was too soon for her to be hitting the streets. I took off sick and jumped into my car and sped to her house. I beat on her door, but she knew not to answer.

I was so mad and had so much hate in my heart that I'm not sure what I would have done to her.

I calmed myself and left her house with a newfound hatred for her. I later thanked God for not letting her open the door, because I'm sure I would be in jail right now. I had never even had the thought of hitting a woman, but only God knows what I would have done if she had answered the door that night. I'm so glad she didn't. I'm sure that God intervened. I went home to my apartment that night and cried.

When Jessica did come back to work, she taunted me, telling me and her friends that I was working for her and I had better keep working overtime in order to support the new car she bought and the hefty child support she kept taking me to court for.

Every time I got a raise, she took me to court to increase my payments. She cursed me every time I went to get my son, but I would not retaliate. I took it. She tried to have me jailed years later for whipping my son because of cursing. She even went so far as trying to get me fired from my job with the same claims.

Jessica has caused me more depression, strife, money and contempt than I wish to remember. But I stood strong to form a relationship with my child and she used him in every way she could to expose every nerve ending in my body. It was one of the most trying times in my entire life.

I often said that if I went to hell, the experience would be like dealing with that woman every day. I often laughed and said that was God's way of giving me hell on earth for being so self-centered and selfish. I never took the time to think if I had just treated her with respect and never had entered into the sexual relationship, both our lives would have been so different. But then I think that if we hadn't had the relationship, I would not have my son. So it was all worth it. My son is my pride and joy and I love him so much. He looks just like me and as I told him before, "Your name might have changed, but it is my blood that flows through your veins and that is all that matters."

My greatest inner fear is that on his eighteenth birthday she will tell me that he really isn't my son. We never had a blood test and it wouldn't matter anyway. I raised him as my son and my son he will always be.

Ms. Newhouse, once again, I'm not proud of my situation, but I've just sat down and realized what a fool I have been to myself and others. As I stated before, while Jessica was pregnant, I was dating a woman named Phyllis Charles on and off. I met Phyllis at my college. I was a Black Student Union alumni representative and she was a sophomore. We met at a retreat. It was an instant attraction.

It was really crazy. We attended the same college, our birthdays were on the same day, and we later found that our mothers had the same name. To make it that much more incredible, if you add up both our birthdays, that's the day our daughter was born, and in the same month we were born. It seemed like a match made in heaven, but I would soon mess that up, too.

I was a roller-skating fool and was one of the best skaters at the rink. I would skate at least three times a week and Phyllis would come with me. But once she became pregnant and started to show, she could not skate anymore. Women loved a brother that could skate and would let it be known at couples skate that they wanted to give up the panties. I was a victim of popularity.

For the longest time, I fought off the temptation, because I was really in love with Phyllis. I would go to her house before and after skating to make sure she was okay and didn't need for anything. She was heartbroken when she learned of Jessica's pregnancy, but overlooked it as best she could.

We got along and I remained true to her, but the rumors and strain of being pregnant at the same time as another woman by the same man took its toll. We were on again, off again for many months, but I would make sure she was okay and had what she needed. Even when our daughter was born I was there. I often had both infants at the same time and would bring them to my parents' and take them to church with me. I would have them every other weekend and my eldest daughter was happy to help with them when she would be in town visiting.

I was forced to work nights and had pretty much no life. I needed the nighttime differential to be able to pay my bills and the child support for three children. Half my check was gone. I often worked part-time in law enforcement to make extra money. I was armed security for several companies before finally working as a security supervisor for a professional football team. I did this for over ten years.

Joy, for the next four or five years, I didn't date much. I had a few relationships, but they didn't amount to anything because I was never fully satisfied. I was not yet thirty-three and had never been married. Out of nowhere I met Regan Childs. She was beautiful. I knew the first time I laid eyes on her that she would be my wife. The only problem, she was married and in an abusive relationship, but I didn't let that bother me.

From talking to her, I quickly learned that she and her unfaithful husband were at the end of their relationship. I remember I had to step to him for pushing her around and finally we moved in together and the son of a bitch threw a rock through the house window. We never had a problem after that. Like I said, I don't have a problem whipping a man's ass over family. Regan and I dated about five months before we were married. I was happy, but was not ready for the baggage that she carried from her relationship. We had communication problems, but I ignored them.

I should have learned a long time ago that when a person has been abused or misused, they need time to heal before they can move forward. I know Regan loved me the best way she could, but she had trouble loving herself. Her relationship with her mother was strained and her sister was self-serving. But we loved as best we could. We had a daughter the first year of our marriage. She is the joy of my life. It seems that we are closer than any of my other children and I know it was the fact that she was in the home with me and her mother for seven years. We communicated and trusted each other.

Regan and I continued to have marital problems and decided to divorce. Sometimes you can't fix two grown people and it's best to separate.

Rita became the love of my life. I never loved another woman the way I loved her. I married her. I think the other women in my life had a problem with that. They are just now getting along, but I made sure our children always were solidified and knew who their brothers and sisters were. We went to family reunions on both sides of the family. I wanted to make sure they knew their roots and their people.

I respect Rita a lot because we came out of our relationship almost as smooth as we went into it. She has a good heart and I truly wish nothing but happiness and love for all my babies' mamas. I have never been one to be jealous. My only concern was that the men they dated understood that I would kill for my children. They have a lot of sick bastards out there and I damn sure didn't want my children to fall victim to any of them.

My children are my life and no matter how much I struggle I have to make sure I take care of them. I'm not perfect and I have done some jacked-up things in my life, but I have always been a loving and caring father and daddy to my children.

Ms. Newhouse, I just want to say to the mothers of my children, thanks for stepping up to the plate when I could not and taking care of our children, and I will continue to support them in their lives and educational quests for college and adulthood. I'm sorry for not being there all the time. I will always give you praise for a job well done. You all have given me my children that are the joy and reason I keep pushing toward my dreams. Forgive me for any pain or tears I have ever caused you and know that it is sincere. Our children came from a love that was true.

Ms. Joy Newhouse, thanks for your show and giving me the opportunity to look inside myself and see the wrongs I have done to these women, but I have been a blessing, too. I love my children and I have a love for all the mothers. What we had was good at one time. I'll never forget. God bless you for all the lives you touch. Continue to be an avenue for lost souls like me, who continue to try and make things right. God bless you and good night.

"Humph! How 'bout that, ya'll, a brother apologizing for being a ho. Now that is a first. But I gotta respect the brotha for trying to do the right thing. And of course I'm cheezing for all the gratitude you tossed my way, Mr. Baby Daddy. Good luck to you and all your babies' mamas. We're going to take a quick break then come back with some calls. Hang on to your seats — it's sure to get bumpy. Back in sixty seconds. . . ."

CHAPTER 5

I pull the headset off and toss it on the table. I hear that bad-ass sister Leela James belting out the blues in her signature voice. Macy always knows what tunes to play. I bob my head to the music, thinking about the calls and letters that have come in tonight. It's been wild and it never fails to amaze me how folks get themselves into the messes that become their lives. The letters I'm pretty much prepared for but you can never tell what crazy mess someone is going to call in and spew all over the airwaves. So I always have to be on top of my game.

When I first started, I tried the sympathetic route, listening and sympathizing, even giving advice that actually made some sense. Trust me, that mess may work on the tube but not in radio-land. With TV you have all the visuals, the tears, the stunned expressions and looks of sympathy. But with radio you have to create the visuals, excite the listeners. And after several months of watching my ratings sink, I knew I had to change my strategy or find another day job. Hence, Joy Newhouse and reality radio was born, and I haven't looked back.

Macy is waving and giving me my count. I put my headset back on and adjust my microphone.

"Hey, radio-land. We're back and you're listening to *On the Line* with Joy Newhouse, WHOT on your dial, reality radio at its best. As promised before the music break, I'm going to take some live calls. And, callers, you better be up to *my* standards or you will get the dial tone. Okay, here we go. Caller, you're on the line."

"I've thought long and hard about what I will miss most after I kill myself. And came up with poetry."

My eyes widen like circles and I signal frantically to Macy and mouth, *"How in the hell did this get past screening?"*

She shrugs all helpless and points to the intern. I turn my attention back to the call.

"I discovered a poem within the past few days that has meant all the difference, spurred me on in this difficult task that lies ahead. It isn't easy to let go, to give up all hope, but this poem has softened the blow of what I'm going to do. It's written by Sylvia Plath, entitled 'Edge,' her last published work before she herself committed suicide. I have to say it is pure genius to me.

"Now, I've got a few options. I could stab myself with these scissors I'm holding. Or I could swallow all the pills in the bottles of Lexapro and Zoloft in my medicine cabinet. For good measure I'd chase the pills with E & J. I'm in a scary place, I know. My period's in its heavy first day and I'm more emotional than ever. I can hear death's call. I can hear my name on death's lips. Death's cry is a song in my ears. But I don't need some radio hack wannabe psychologist to talk me out of ending my misery. I've already made that decision, you see. This is about me speaking some things, letting my voice be heard for the final time. And what better forum than this? I've heard it said everyone has a story to tell. I believe that. Most of the stories you hear don't have the emotional impact of mine. Most are inane. Mine is a real story of heartbreak and pain, like none you've ever heard before."

"What could be so bad that you'd want to take yourself out?" I say, slightly rattled by this caller.

"I'm twenty-nine years old and it's been less than ten years since I graduated from Howard University. I left Howard swollen with hope and high expectations. Got accepted to Princeton. A whole 'nother other, as my mama said at the time. No handsome Greek brothas, but plenty of corn-fed white boys with a taste for chocolate. I graduated near the top of my class from both schools."

"So how did you get to such a dark place? Scissors and antidepressant medicine. That's not a good look." I chuckle lightly.

"Mama'd say I always had this kind of meltdown in me. That my 'constitution' has always been weak, susceptible to fraying. I'd argue her on the point, but you don't argue with my mother and actually win. She's hyperintelligent. A professor of Western civilization at Georgetown University. Beautiful and apparently ageless. We look like sisters. We compete like sisters. She's certainly the more accomplished sister. I never measure up to her. I bypassed Georgetown because I couldn't stand to walk in her shadow for four more years. Some people are born gifted, have so many special capabilities. Mama is one of those people, full of great qualities. But her most admirable quality, the one that shines the brightest, is her toughness. She's not one to play with and people gather that within minutes of being in her presence."

"Well, a lot of people wrestle with standing in their mother's shadow. The best solution is to move away," I reason.

"Mama's a character, like no one you'll ever meet. She loves clove cigarettes. Djarums. And her pack-a-day habit has turned her voice into glass. Growing up, I hated many of her habits. Hated how she escaped to the back porch of our house at night to smoke something a bit stronger than the Djarums. Marijuana in the gut of a Phillies blunt cigar. But no matter how much I hated it, I was still drawn to my mother in ways I can't naturally explain. I'm my mama's daughter, through and through. All told, I'm a healthy mix of both of my parents. To deny that would be to deny something paramount about myself. I tried, for many years, and it came back to haunt me. I am a healthy mix of both of my parents."

"Honey, aren't we all? For better or worse," I interject, eager to keep her talking.

"They've been married for close to thirty-five years, but never shared the same house. Daddy rents a room around the corner from the row house he always paid a mortgage on. Mama, of course, has the house. You see, the Djarums and marijuana aren't Mama's only vices. She has what she's always called an 'insatiable' side. We're like sisters, remember, and so she tells me things. Some things I wish she'd keep to herself. Like the Ben Wa balls. Little round balls, she explained to me that first time, hollowed out and with another smaller ball inside. You insert them in your vagina and rock. Rock and feel the vibration of that smaller ball clacking inside the bigger ball. Rock until orgasm. Does it work? I remember asking her that first off, shocked by her confession but still able to speak. Who's to say? was her response. They did strengthen the PC muscles in her vagina, for certain. They turned her vagina into a fist around any penis lucky enough to gain entry inside it. Got to keep your pussy tight, she told me, if you want to hold any power over *these men* whatsoever. That's my mama's insatiable side, you see. Though married to Daddy all these years, Mama's always been concerned about *these men.* Always had other lovers. Many, in fact. Younger men, always."

"Whoa, Mama is a piece of work." I chuckle in an attempt to lighten the mood.

"And Daddy's loved her so deep for so many years. Sometimes I don't understand it. One of my father's few faults is that he's so judgmental, and yet he's been more than

89

willing to keep his eyes wide shut in that room big enough for a dresser and bed only, just around the corner from his 'hungry' wife.

"I'll get right to it because I know your audience has a short attention span. Daddy was right. I love too deep. And loving so deeply will leave you hurting. Make you want to end it all."

I scribble a note in large print and hold it up for Macy to see. *CALL FUCKING 911. STAT.* I continue listening.

"I've got the scissors in my hand. I've also got enough Lexapro and Zoloft to do real damage. And that bottle of E & J in the kitchen. My death won't be accidental. It'll be well planned. Chasing the pills with E & J is the nice twist, as you'll learn.

"My husband, Nigel, went out for a ride on his motorcycle and never made it back home. His death left me cold, sad and lonely. Oh, how I miss my sweet Nigel. But there is a twist to this tale. A cruel, horrible twist."

"What happened?" I blurt out, anxious to hear the details, but nervous about the path we are headed to.

"I ran across some e-mails on his computer. He was planning on leaving me for another woman. The life I thought I had was a farce. A waste. I've got the perfect ending for my miserable life."

The call disconnects. Panic doesn't describe how I feel. This crazy broad was going to kill herself! Not on my watch.

"Uh, listeners, we're going to break." Glad I deodorized.

I'm generally not one to panic or to let the plight of others become my own. But my hands are shaking and a line of perspiration runs down the center of my back. Damn, what if she does off herself and I did nothing to stop her? Not even offer a kind word. How desperate do you have to be to want to take your own life? My throat tightens. Who am I kidding? I know about that kind of desperation, that feeling of doom and endless nothingness. Been there. That buried feeling of anxiety begins building inside me. I can't catch my breath.

I hear banging on the studio window. I turn to see Macy who has this stricken look on her face and she's motioning for me to turn on my headset.

In a daze, I do as she asks.

"You all right, girl? You look like you've seen a ghost."

More like my past. I draw in a deep breath and swallow over the dry knot in my throat and nod my head. "I'm cool."

That's when I notice all the activity outside the glass walls of the sound booth.

CHAPTER 6

Every member on the studio floor is scurrying around like crazed rabbits. My heart is racing and sweat is running down my back. What the fuck, a suicide! Irving Bledsoe, the new uptight exec bursts into the booth and stops my pacing in mid-step.

"Ms. Newhouse, this is . . ." he sputters and sputters, searching for a phrase that would define what had just taken place. I help him out.

"Some fucked-up shit."

He turns blood red and draws himself up. "The police were able to trace the call. They got there in time."

I fall down in my seat, deflated and relieved. "Good thing I don't do those two-minute calls, huh?" I chuckle and can feel my throat shaking.

He glares at me. "We're reviewing your show," he says ominously, then abruptly turns and walks out.

I roll my eyes. I really am happy though that nothing truly tragic happened. There is so much drama out in the world. The things folks are living through. I shake my head, spin my seat back in place and put on my headset. It's showtime.

"Hey, radio-land. For those who were listening with bated breath to our last call, I'm happy to report that we were able to trace the call and the police arrived in time. Guess we're good for something, huh?" I try to make light of it, but the call really shook me more than I would admit. "Well, we have an hour left and I'm going to read an e-mail that came in a little earlier. I must warn you before I start to get all children and anyone under the age of consent out of the room and away from the sound of my voice. Not only is it hot, it's a bit decadent. So, Macy, get ready with the bleeper. Here we go. . . ."

Dear Joy:
    I am listening to your show on scandalous marital affairs through my wireless connection on my laptop computer. Right now I am sitting upright in my hotel bed writing you this e-mail, because I don't want to call with my confession, because my husband may be listening to your show. My lover is resting comfortably

next to me. He's on his back and his curly-haired chest is a thing of pure beauty. I love the feel of his chest hair on my skin. His nipples are slightly erect and I swear to you that I can't wait to flick on them with the tip of my tongue and feel them get even harder. The bed linen and the entire room, for that matter, are completely soaked with the scent of our passion. Right now I'm looking at his man-hood, which is alive and awaiting more of my affections. He has a pretty and beautiful dick. He has one of those dicks that you just want to suck on. It calls me, it longs for me and I long for it. I've tried to ignore my yearning for him but my desire, cravings and needs were too much for my morality to battle alone. Last night was the first time we made love and I must tell you that he provided me with some of the most exquisite orgasms I've ever experienced in my life. My entire body and soul is still buzzing and no matter how hard I try, I can't shut off the way I feel at this moment. Even as I write this message to you I'm having a difficult time resisting the temptation to toss back the covers, mount him and drain him of his essence. Before I do that I have to tell someone who I think will understand what I've done. I need to confess to someone who will not judge me or think that I'm a bad woman for having an affair as scandalous as the one I've just plunged into.

Joy, I've committed an offensive, spiritually immoral and unforgivable violation of trust. I should be begging for mercy for my sin, but I'm not. I don't really feel guilty or damned, I feel like I did what I've wanted to. And the last time I checked there was no crime against that. Before I get into the details about how I seduced my lover I need to start at the beginning. I've changed the names so that I can protect my husband and my love from each other.

Last week I dropped Charles, my husband of nine months, off at the airport for a two-week business trip to Los Angeles, California. I would like to say he was sad about having to be away from me for so long, but that wouldn't be the truth. He was looking forward to getting away from his son Vince. The two of them just aren't seeing eye to eye these days. Vince is holding a grudge against Charles for leaving him and his mother when he was only twelve years old, as well as for not showing up at his mother's funeral or his college graduation a few months ago. Vince attempted to get his own apartment after graduation but he just couldn't afford one because of his limited income. His lack of funds, the loss of his mother and lack of a job forced him to come and live with his father and me. Vince only planned on staying for a short while until he was able to get on his feet. Charles offered Vince a position in his tele-communications company, but Vince didn't take the offer because as he put it, "he'd rather work in hell before working with his father." I felt sorry for both of them because there was so much unresolved pain between them. Vince enjoyed holding on to his anger and Charles was too stubborn to apologize for the heartache he caused his son. I sup-pose that, by being defiant, Vince was getting back at Charles. And I suppose Charles figured that by being a hard-ass he was show-ing Vince that he wasn't going to apologize even if he knew he was wrong.

Charles is a good man, but he's hard to love and doesn't like expressing his feelings un-less of course he's angry. Sometimes I think he's holding his emotions hostage so that he doesn't appear to be a weak man. Don't ask me the logic behind his thinking, because I couldn't tell you.

I've only known Vince for about a year, which is almost as long as I've been married to his father. I met Vince briefly twice before Charles and I were married. Speaking of mar-riage, that's another sore spot between Charles and Vince. Charles is still raw with Vince for not coming to our wedding, and by some measure I believe he decided to get back at his son by refusing to show up for his mother's funeral. As you can see, the tension and animosity between them is as deep as it is ugly.

After I'd returned home from dropping Charles off at the airport I noticed that Vince had taken the old pickup truck and gone somewhere. I was thankful for his absence because I just wanted to relax and spend my afternoon watching the Lifetime Channel. I figured there would be plenty of time to really get to know Vince since I was on vacation for two weeks. I planned to do some things around the house the first week, but the following week I was flying to Charlotte, North Carolina, for a convention.

I dozed off to sleep watching a Lifetime original movie and was jolted awake by the ruckus the pickup truck made as it was being pulled into the garage. I glanced at my watch and noticed it was well past midnight. I stood up, moved over to the window and saw the light come on in the small apartment that was above the garage. Vince preferred to sleep there instead of the guest room in the house. I was tired, so I called it a night and went upstairs to my bedroom.

The following morning I was awakened by the sound of a basketball pinging against the pavement below my bedroom window. I got out of bed, drew back the curtains and saw Vince shooting hoops. I have to admit, standing in my window watching him turned me on in a way I didn't anticipate. Vince must have felt me watching, because he stopped bouncing his basketball, looked up at me and captured my gaze. I waved to him. He smiled and waved back before continuing his workout. Vince is extremely sexy. He's tall, handsome and has incredible eyes. I watched him for a moment longer before I went into the master bathroom and freshened up. Afterward I headed to the kitchen for something to eat. As I entered the kitchen I was surprised to find that Vince had showered, changed clothes and was preparing breakfast for both of us.

Vince behaved much differently than when Charles was around. He was much more charming and at ease and I liked that.

"I enjoyed watching you this morning," I admitted to him as he began to scramble a few eggs in a pan.

"I felt you watching me," he answered. "What do you like on your biscuits? Butter or jelly?" he asked as he opened the oven door and checked the status of the biscuits.

"Jelly," I said as I took a seat at the island counter. "You didn't have to cook for me, you know," I told him even though I thought it was very thoughtful of him.

"I like to cook. Besides, you can't start your day off on an empty stomach."

"How do you move so gracefully?" I asked, referring to the way he was shooting basketball hoops earlier.

"I've never heard anyone call my movements graceful," he chuckled.

"Well, they are," I quickly responded. He stopped cooking for a moment and then looked at me. Our eyes danced with each other for a moment before he said what he was thinking.

"You sound as if you couldn't pull your eyes off of me." He had a mannish grin on his face. I suddenly found myself at a crossroads. It was clear his words had two meanings and I had the choice of either flirting back or explaining what I truly meant. I don't know why I decided to flirt with him. Perhaps a deep part of me wanted to be daring, or my vanity wanted to know if I could still attract a younger man. Whatever the reason, I didn't use my better judgment.

"It was hard for me to take my eyes off of you," I admitted.

"If you keep on watching me like that you might start to get ideas." He licked his lips like the rapper LL Cool J does. I was delightfully tickled by the sexual undertone that was float-ing beneath his words.

"No harm ever came from having an idea." I paused in thought. I didn't want to go too far with my flirting. I only wanted to go far enough to satisfy my vanity. "If I were you I'd check those biscuits once again." I motioned toward the oven door. "It doesn't take much for them to burn."

"Oh, man," he said, and quickly opened the oven door to remove the biscuits. "Whew, I got them just in time." He placed the pan on top of the stove. "Damn, I burned my finger-tips. The heat went right through the oven mitts." He cringed as he placed his fingertips under some cold water to cool his skin.

Vince finished preparing our breakfast and continued to flirt while we ate. I will admit that I flirted right along with him because it made me feel good. It made me feel desirable and alive when he complimented me on how well I took care of myself and how attractive I was. Charles doesn't express his feelings for me in that way. I tried not to let it all go to my head, but some of it did and that frightened me a little.

The following morning I was again awak-ened by the sound of the basketball pinging against the pavement. I got out of bed, glanced out of my window and what I saw made me study Vince in a way that was dangerous. He wasn't wearing a shirt. I enjoyed looking at his chocolate skin, his long and strong legs as well as his mighty chest. I found myself wanting to kiss and lick his entire body. It was difficult for me not to fantasize about him. Part of me wanted to go lay down on my bed with the image of him on the walls of my mind and release my sexual tension. I closed the curtains and turned my back to the window. I was paralyzed by a dangerous fantasy. I daydreamed about him coming into the house for a cold drink. As he drank, I kissed his shoulders and chest. I pulled off shorts to expose his sexy dick. I imagined that his dick would be long, strong, and render me speechless at the sight of it. I imagined it hanging a certain way before I caressed it and put him inside of my mouth. The idea of having oral sex with him made me wet. *He just doesn't know how much I'd love to suck on him with passion and drink every drop of his essence,* I thought to myself. I knew I'd savor the taste of him because he'd be as delicious and as sweet as he looked. Suddenly, against my wishes and will, my body started to ache for him in a way that it shouldn't have. At that moment, I wanted him as badly as a desert flower wanted water, but couldn't go there with Vince. I couldn't cross a forbidden line just to satisfy my urge and curiosity. I knew that I shouldn't act on my fantasy because it was just too damn crazy and hazardous. I got mad at myself for allowing my mind to take me someplace it shouldn't have.

I began to move away from the window and immediately thereafter the basketball stopped bouncing. I turned back around, peeped out the window again briefly and saw him glaring directly at me. I read his eyes. They were asking questions, dangerous questions that I didn't want him or his eyes to ask. I broke our line of communication and turned my back to him. I knew that the feeling aroused by the presence of Vince was as condemning as Eve telling Adam to bite the apple. My unspoken lust and infatuation with him was strong and no matter how badly my body yearned for him I couldn't allow my desire to guide me into his arms. I was struggling with myself. I knew what was right and morally decent, but another part of me, a bold uninhibited part, wanted to take control and enjoy all of the pleasures that a man and a woman could take delight in.

I had to fight off and get sexual thoughts of Vince out of my system, and the only quick remedy I could come up with was to give myself a quick orgasm and hope that it would gratify me. I went into my bathroom and filled up my whirlpool bath. Once it was ready, I disrobed and slipped inside. I rested my head comfortably on a towel, closed my eyes and began caressing myself. I imagined what Vince's tongue would feel like kissing my breasts and stomach. It didn't take long for me to satisfy myself. Once I was gratified, I relaxed even more and began to think about my life.

I am a forty-five-year-old corporate attorney who works long, stressful hours. I'm also on my second marriage. This time I didn't marry for love. I married for financial stability and wealth. My husband Charles is an excellent provider. He's the president of a telecommunications company and travels often and works constantly. Charles is twelve years older than I am and is more in love with his job and the power he has than he is with me. I knew he was a workaholic before I married him. I reasoned that marrying a workaholic was a bonus, because it meant he wouldn't be bothering or harassing me so much because he'd have other priorities and that suited me just fine. My ex-husband was the type of man who needed to hear "I love you" all the time and stalked me on my cellular phone. At first I thought it was cute, but after three years of dealing with his insecurities and paranoia I'd had enough, especially after he physically attacked me because he thought I was creeping around on him.

I began to feel bad as I thought about Charles and our young marriage. Our intimate life is okay. I'm able to reach a climax with him, but it's not like he's driving me wild. Sometimes I get so hot that I want to break free and get wild and crazy, but I can't do that with Charles, because making love to him is predictable and fundamental. Sometimes I want Charles to take more time with foreplay, but he is a no-nonsense kind of man. He fumbles around until he gets an erection and he's ready to go. If I'm lucky, I'm wet enough for penetration by the time he has a strong erection. Perhaps that's why my interest in Vince is rather strong. Perhaps, in a creepy part of my brain, I want the same man in a younger version. It's sad now that I think about it. I've been married to Charles for less than a year and I'm already having fantasies about other men. The horrifying part is that I'm not just having fantasies about some random guy. I'm having sexual fantasies about my twenty-four-year-old stepson. *Lord, I need help,* I thought to myself. Perhaps I'm not as satisfied with my sex life as I tell myself I am.

After I got out of the whirlpool I stood in front of the mirror and looked at myself. I didn't look bad for my age. I watched my diet and worked out four times a week at the corporate health club. My skin hadn't begun to sag around my chin or eyes yet and I was thankful my breasts still had plenty of perkiness. I was also proud of the fact that I looked younger than my years, or so I've been told on occasion. Whenever I'm complimented about how young I still look I always say, "Baby, black just doesn't crack."

My ass was just that, my ass. No matter how many squats I do, my ass still has an attitude. I suppose I'm like many black women when it comes to my ass. At times I love the fullness of it and enjoy the pleasure it provides me with when it's handled properly. However, at other times the size of it annoys the hell out of me. My ass is determined to be round and plump no matter what I do to tighten it up. I placed some lavender scented lotion on my body then put on my purple thong and bra set before slipping into my black sundress. I went into my shoe closet and found my black sling-back sandals, put on some simple earrings, a little makeup and my sunglasses. I then left the room and headed toward the kitchen. I had to make it to the mall to pick up a few items before I left on my trip.

When I entered the kitchen I was stopped cold in my tracks. Vince was in there wearing only a large bath towel wrapped around his waist. He must have used the shower that was just to the left of the kitchen. His skin was still wet and I noticed a trail of wet footprints coming from the direction of the bathroom. He hadn't noticed me because he was leaning over and searching the refrigerator for something to eat. I focused on his tight ass for a long moment. I allowed my eyes to fall down the back of his long muscular thighs.

"Damn," I whispered softly as the thought of drying his thighs off with my tongue ignited my flame. It took every ounce of strength I had to keep from rushing up to him, removing the towel and smacking his chocolate ass. I cleared my throat to get his attention.

"Oh, shit," he said as he stood up. He turned around to face me and I saw the most magnificent erection trying to break free of its cloth prison. "Sorry. I thought you were still upstairs."

I began randomly scratching my arm while I remained focused on his manhood. "I — um . . ." I had to clear my throat again because my thoughts and words were out of sync. "I'm on my way to the mall," I finally said.

"Which one?" he asked as he rested his behind against the nearby countertop. He knew that I was temporarily mesmorized.

I paused, confused. "Make sure you mop up the trail of water over there." I pointed to his wet footprints.

"I got that. Don't worry about it," Vince said, and then began to touch himself. Normally that type of behavior would have irritated or offended me, but it didn't. It was beautiful the way he massaged himself. I studied his movements and wanted to emulate them. I know it sounds crazy and immature, but I was completely fascinated by what he was doing.

"You're a freak, aren't you?" Vince asked. I refused to answer him. "Sometimes I get so hard that I just have to touch myself. Especially after a good workout."

"Um — I guess it's okay as long as you don't do it in public."

"No, I'm not that bold," he said then stopped. There was a long moment of silence between us and I saw desire in his eyes.

"You look wonderful in your dress," Vince complimented me. "I can smell the scent of your perfume from over here. I love that scent. Sometimes, when you leave your bedroom window open, I swear the aroma of your perfume rides on morning air and floats out to me while I'm shooting hoops. I'm going to be honest, Crystal, I think about you in ways I shouldn't. I try to stop my mind from taking me to intimate places, but it's impossible. I've undressed and made love to you a thousand times in my mind. I've placed soft kisses on your breasts. I've tasted your lips, kissed your neck and caressed your back. I've never felt this type of desire for anyone before. I can't explain why I want you, I just know that I do."

I was speechless. I mean, it shocked me that his words came out so effortlessly. The uninhibited woman within wanted to do him right there on the countertop, but I remained composed.

"Well." I paused as I swallowed hard. "This is an awkward moment."

"Don't you feel it? Don't you feel the same vibe I do?" he asked.

"That's a dangerous question, Vince."

"So you do feel it?" he asked again as he approached me. "I want you, Crystal. I know I shouldn't have feelings for you like this, but I can't help it. There is something about you. There is something about your eyes, your smile and the way you talk to me without saying a word. I love watching the sexy way you swing your hips when you walk and the sexual energy you give off. I'm drawn to you the way a bee is drawn to a beautiful flower."

"Vince, I'm your stepmother. You can't have feelings like this for me. I'm married to your father, remember?"

"Why can't I have feelings for you?"

"It's not right, Vince. Not to mention immoral and a little twisted."

"That's true, it's not right. It's very wrong

109

and very twisted. I'll admit that. But answer one question for me. And don't bullshit me with your answer. I want the truth. Have you ever fantasized about making love to me the way that I've fantasized about making love to you?"

I couldn't believe he asked me that question with a straight face. "Were you watching me?" I asked, but didn't give him a chance to answer before I continued to speak. "This is a dangerous game you're playing, Vince."

"Just answer the question, please."

I focused on a fruit basket sitting on the countertop. "No," I lied to him. "I've never thought about you in that way." I looked into his eyes again.

"Then why does there seem to be some type of energy between us?"

"I don't know what you're talking about," I lied again.

"You mean you don't feel it? That's impossible. The sexual tension between us is thick enough to cut through."

"Sexual tension." I chuckled. "It's very flattering that you want to do me, but that's just not going to happen." I didn't believe the words coming out of my own mouth, because in the back of my mind, I wanted to do him right there. I wanted to murder the erection he boldly stroked in my presence.

110

"Why do I feel like you're running away from the way you truly feel?"

At that moment I noticed how erect his tiny nipples were and I wanted to bite on them. My eyes gave me away, but I tried to cover up my thoughts by clearing my throat. "You should make sure you're dressed when you're around me," I said.

"So, it's like that. We're not going to address this thing that we're struggling with?"

"I'm not struggling with anything and I'd appreciate it if you'd put on some clothes when you're around me. You're not a little boy, you're a grown man, and you should act accordingly when you're around me."

"Okay," he said as he licked his lips. "It appears I've made a mistake. I'm sorry if I've made you feel uncomfortable."

"There is no harm done," I said. Vince left and went into the basement to get a mop to clean up the trail of water he'd left on the floor.

By the time I got situated inside the car my pussy was on fire. I turned the air conditioner on to cool myself down. As I began to accept the fact I was attracted to Vince, I became afraid. I wanted to stop thinking about him, but my mind wouldn't stop projecting images of him fucking me from behind. Doggy style was my favorite position. The images continued to flash. I could see him gently sucking my clit and I could hear his voice inside of my head, whispering to me and repeating how much he ached for me.

"Damn," I said aloud. I wanted to feel him inside me. I wanted to ride him until he begged me to stop. I wanted to make him pay for getting inside of my head so quickly and effortlessly. After what had just gone down, I had to honestly ask myself if I was satisfied with Charles or was I only in love with financial stability?

I don't know why the crazy idea of inviting Vince to fly to Charlotte, North Carolina, entered my head but it did.

"You know, that may be just what I need," he said to me. "A little time to get away and think about what I want to do with my life. Perhaps I'll be inspired to become an attorney like you."

"Honey, there are enough attorneys in the world already."

"So, when are we leaving?" he asked.

"This weekend. I'll take care of your airfare and hotel accommodations."

"What do you think the old man is going to say about this?"

"If you don't tell him, I'm certainly not going to mention it." He smiled at me and I knew that this would be our secret little trip.

■ ■ ■ ■

Once Vince and I arrived in Charlotte, we gathered our luggage and headed over to the rental car desk. The service clerk handed me the keys to the Mustang I'd rented and we packed our luggage in the trunk of the car and headed over to the hotel. We checked in and headed up to our rooms. We had separate rooms, but a door connected them to each other. We opened the connecting doors so we'd have access to each other's rooms.

"So, what do we do now?" Vince asked.

"I'm going to boot up my laptop and do a little work. You can do whatever you want. We'll go out and get something to eat a little later."

"Okay, that's cool. I think I'm going to go see what their gym looks like."

"The hotel has a swimming pool as well," I said. "You could go for a swim."

"That doesn't sound like a bad idea," Vince declared.

Three hours later I'd finished what I was working on and I was hungry. I walked into Vince's room but he wasn't there. I figured he was still in the workout room so I grabbed my door key and headed in that direction. Just as I thought, Vince was inside lifting weights.

"Hey, you hungry yet?" I asked as I stepped inside.

"I'm starving," he replied.

"Well go take a shower and change. Then meet me at the front desk." While Vince was in his room freshening up, I was at the concierge's desk getting driving directions to a restaurant and a good place to go dancing.

Our meal at an Italian restaurant was wonderful. When we left, it was around ten-thirty in the evening. It was a warm and beautiful summer night and the streets of Charlotte were filled with people. I drove over to College Street and parked the car inside a parking garage. Once we exited the garage we merged with the crowds of partygoers heading to various nightclubs. The hotel concierge suggested we go to a nightclub called BAR Charlotte. When we entered the club the music was loud and the dance floor was overflowing with people dancing to a song called "Hips Don't Lie" by a female artist named Shakira. We found a place to sit down and a few moments later a waitress came over to take our drink order.

"I'll have a strawberry margarita," I told her.

"I'll have a beer," said Vince. The waitress walked away then returned shortly thereafter with our drinks. I sipped on my margarita as I swayed to the groove of the music.

"So, do you know this song?" Vince asked.

"Of course I do," I told him. "I may be a little older, but that doesn't mean I don't like the latest music." The next thing I knew, Vince got up and stood in front of me. He spread my legs open while I was still sitting down on a bar stool and began rubbing his hands up and down my thighs. I quickly slapped his hand before he reached my paradise. Vince looked at me, surprised that I stopped him.

"What's wrong — you can dish it out but you can't take it? You've been feeling my dick, why can't I feel your pussy?" I didn't say anything. I just stared at him for a long moment. I caught the attention of the waitress and had her bring me another drink.

"Vince, you may be well hung, but I don't think your dick knows how to handle a hot pussy like the one I have." Vince took my comment as a challenge.

"So you think that I can't handle you?"

I knew he was eager to prove me wrong. "You may be raring to go and have gusto, but I will turn your young ass out," I stated as the waitress placed another drink before me. As soon as I finished my second drink, I was feeling adventurous and daring.

"Come on, let's dance," I said, feeling the need to express myself on the dance floor.

Vince took me by the hand and we went to the center of the dance floor. He started to dance but I stopped him. I motioned for him to lean forward so that I could speak in his ear.

"Follow me," I said, and led him to a darker spot on the dance floor that was toward a back wall. I pushed his back up against the wall, placed my ass on his dick and began moving sensually to the rhythm of the Pussycat Dolls singing "Loosen Up My Buttons."

"Oh, shit," he said as he put his hands on my hips. I kept pressing myself against him because I enjoyed the feel of his erection.

"Caress my ass!" I shouted out loud over the music.

"Damn, I didn't know you could move like this." Vince laughed. I shook my ass a little faster and a little harder and I felt Vince buckle at the knees. I laughed. I then turned to face him.

"I told you that you couldn't handle this pussy." I knew I had him in the palm of my hand. Vince had a devilish look in his eyes.

"So, let's see how much of a freak you really are." He took me by the hand. We walked over to the bar and Vince said something to the bartender. The next thing I knew, the bartender wiped down the bar and Vince hoisted me up onto the bar and asked me to lie flat on my back. At first I wasn't going to do it, but I decided to go with the flow.

"Relax, okay?" He rolled up my shirt to my bra line which left my chocolate skin and belly button exposed. The bartender poured alcohol inside my navel and my skin got goose bumps. Vince then slurped up the alcohol as it ran off the sides of my abdomen and down toward my paradise. It was an erotic sensation. I arched up my back and cradled the back of his head as he continued to slurp up the alcohol off of my skin.

"You are driving me wild and I want you so damn bad!" I was half laughing and half talking.

"So what are we going to do about that?" he asked. "Because you're hot and you're driving me wild. I'm going to bust if you keep on teasing me like this. I want you."

At that moment I sat upright. Vince locked his arms around me and we began kissing. The way he kissed me made my womanhood explode. His lips were soft and tasted sweet. I placed my cheek against his and spoke purposely in his ear.

"I want to ride that long dick of yours. I've thought about your dick in ways that are sinful and wicked. My body has been craving you. I don't know why, but it is." At that moment Vince helped me get down from the bar.

"Come on, let's get out of here," he said.

When we exited the club it was about one o'clock in the morning and the streets were still jam-packed with partygoers on foot and in cars. We walked back to the car, got in, and I let the convertible top down on the Mustang. Once the convertible top was completely down Vince put his hand on my thigh.

"Look at me," he said. I complied, and read his movements. He wanted to kiss me.

"Don't be afraid," Vince whispered. He must have picked up on my uneasiness. I closed my eyes and went with the moment. When his lips touched mine, I felt an electric current shoot throughout my body. *Oh, Crystal,* I said to myself, *this young man is going to get your ass in trouble.* I knew what I was doing, but I didn't want to stop. To be honest, it felt too damn good to stop.

"Woo," I giggled. "We'd better hurry up and get back." I pulled the car out of the parking space and headed back toward the hotel. We reached a stoplight and Vince started kissing on me again. A car with two young ladies about Vince's age pulled up next to us and blew their horn. I pushed Vince away for a minute and looked at the two women who were enjoying our public display of affection.

"Work him over, girl," the driver said.

I smiled and replied, "He can't handle this."

Both of the girls laughed. The light turned green and they pulled off. I unfastened Vince's slacks and freed his manhood and was stroking it the same way I saw him do it in my kitchen.

"I want to see what he's working with," the female driver boldly asked as I pulled up to the next stoplight.

"It's out right now, come take a look." I was being very spontaneous and very wild. I was excited in a way that I'd never been before. It was as if someone else had taken over my body. I didn't have any fears or inhibitions. The driver got out of the car, walked over and peeked down at Vince's manhood, which was standing tall.

"Ooh, damn. You sure you can handle that, girl?" asked the driver.

"Oh, I got this," I responded back with a healthy laugh. "At the next stoplight I'm going to suck on it," I said, and then pulled off.

"You're going to what?" Vince asked as we sped down the road.

"You heard me. I'm going to suck on it at the next stoplight." I was feeling a sense of freedom. "You're not afraid, are you?"

"No, but —"

"But nothing — let that seat all the way back so I can get down to business at the next stoplight," I ordered him.

"You're going to let them watch?" he asked.

"Damn right I am," I answered. I couldn't wait to taste him for the first time.

"Oh my God, you're a bigger freak than I thought you were," Vince stated as he let the seat all the way back.

When we arrived at the next stoplight I put the car in Park, positioned myself on my knees above his cock, and began stroking and sucking on him. I was putting my jaw, hand and shoulders into it. I heard the car with the two girls pull up next to us.

"Damn, girl. Kill his shit," yelled out the driver and her friend. She made me laugh so I stopped. The two of them were looking at me with both envy and astonishment. I laughed because it was such a crazy thing to do.

"Girl, I have to give it to you. You're one bad bitch," yelled the driver before she took off again. I got back in the driver's seat, put the car in gear and continued on. I glanced in the rearview mirror and was thankful that no other cars or the police, for that matter, were around us.

"That is the wildest thing I've ever done," I said to Vince. "I don't believe that I just did that." I felt a sense of edginess.

"That was some next level shit there," Vince said. I had to admit it was more exciting than I thought it would be. I never knew that I would enjoy having someone watch me while I was being intimate.

"Wait until you see the levels I'm going to take you to when we get in the hotel room."

We entered my hotel room and I put the Do Not Disturb sign on the doorknob. Vince and I stripped out of our clothes and for the first time I saw how completely magnificent his body was. I positioned myself on the bed and opened my legs.

"Come murder this pussy," I said as I caressed myself and exposed my clitoris to him. He was so ready to please me. The moment his hot tongue brushed across my clit, I exploded. Vince was eager to get inside of me and I wanted to feel him, but first I reached for my purse and pulled out a condom for him. He looked disappointed, but it was either put it on or get nothing at all. Once Vince had the condom in place, I made him lie on his back. I got on top of him and rode him hard. I had several orgasms and then one explosive one that fired me up. Vince held a magnificent erection which I enjoyed feeling especially when we did it doggy style. I made him pull my hair as he pounded me. After a long, gratifying session, I finally made Vince explode inside of me by squeezing his dick really hard with my pussy muscles. I was satisfied but Vince wasn't. He wanted to taste me some more, so I got comfortable and allowed him to delight in my pussy paradise until every nerve in my body felt as if it had been struck by lightning. When I finally had enough, I snuggled up to Vince and we both fell fast asleep.

So there you have it, Joy. I'm sleeping with my stepson and I'm enjoying it. We don't fly back home for another two days and I'm going to enjoy every minute of it. I have got to go now. Vince is touching himself in his sleep and I feel like committing dick murder.

I drop the e-mail like it had caught on fire. Dayum! Macy couldn't hit those bleep buttons fast enough. I clear my throat. "There you have it, listeners. I do hope that this sister is listening. You know you can't keep this up. At some point you *are* going to have to make up your mind. This is a fatality waiting to happen. We want to hear *from* you not *about* you. Get my drift? Well, WHOT family, looks like we're out of time. We were rocking and rolling tonight. And we'll be back tomorrow for some more action-packed drama. So, until next time, remember life is what you make it. This is Joy Newhouse, Lata!"

I snatch off my headphones and drop

them on top of the console and fall back in my seat. *Oh what a night,* to borrow a line from the mighty Dells. I'm still shook up about the attempted suicide and the chick with her stepson. What is wrong with people?

Macy comes into the studio and pulls up a seat next to me. "You okay?"

I nod numbly. "Yeah. I'm good." I turn to look at her. "Some show, huh?"

"Yeah. Wanna grab some coffee?"

I shake my head. "No. I'm going to go on home."

She pats my shoulder. "See you tomorrow, then. And don't sweat Bledsoe. You know he's not ready for prime time." She forces a laugh then pushes up from the chair and leaves.

I sit there for a few minutes until I hear movement at the door and see Tommy, who heads up the gospel show until the morning drive, come through the door.

"Wild show, Joy," he says, and walks in.

"Always," I chirp, forcing cheer and nonchalance into my voice.

He grins. "Princess of the airwaves."

I get up. "Have a good show, Tommy. Maybe you can tell your holy listeners to say some prayers or sing some songs for mine."

He laughs from deep in his gut. "Your folks need more than song and prayer."

Humph. He's probably right.

I gather up my belongings and walk out. Before I leave I go to my small office and pick up my bag of mail. I figure I'll read a few letters before bed. That usually helps to relax me.

CHAPTER 7

I putter around the kitchen, waiting for the pot of water to boil for some tea, then take my cup of chamomile tea to the bedroom. On my way I notice a note under my front door. Frowning, I go to the door and pick up the folded piece of white paper and open it.

Joy,
I wanted you to know that I really dig you and hope we can see each other again. Listened to your show tonight. Glad everything turned out okay. Give me a call sometime.

Randy Temple

His number was written at the bottom. I didn't know whether to feel good or scared. Was this brother stalking me? When did he leave the note? I'd swear it wasn't there when I came in, but maybe it was. I shake my head, determined to toss off the sense of unease, and go to my bedroom.

I probably should have listened to all of Macy's warnings about letting strange men into my apartment. She had good reason to warn me.

About four years ago, just when my show was really getting hot and my ratings were on and popping, there was this guy who would be standing outside the studio at the end of my shift. At first I thought nothing of it. Living in New York, there were folks out at all times of the night. But after about the third or fourth night, it started to give me the creeps. Then he turned up in the coffee shop that I went to one morning after work. He offered to buy me a cup of coffee and I said no thanks. That's when things started getting really weird.

Letters started arriving at the studio, addressed to me, telling me how much he admired me. Then they escalated to how much he thought of me — all the time — and if I gave him a chance, he knew he could make me happy. I suppose the final straw was the package that was delivered to the front desk of my building. Inside was a diamond ring and a note asking me to marry him!

I freaked and started having security

escort me to my car, and the doorman of my building inform me of anyone coming to see me. Then the flowers started arriving — every day at the office with a note saying that I was the love of his life and he couldn't live without me.

I got to a point where I couldn't sleep, I wasn't eating and was so jittery I could barely concentrate on the show. Macy finally convinced me to go to the police.

It was the flowers that finally nailed the nut. He used his credit card! Can you believe it? The experience rattled me for a long time and now this note brought it all rushing back. But I wasn't going to let it get to me. If things got out of hand I knew exactly what to do. I had no intention of going down that road again.

Shaking off thoughts of the past, I set my tea down, pull off my clothes and crawl under the sheets with my bag of mail. Propping myself up with pillows, I take out a random letter and spread it open on my lap.

Dear Joy,

Months ago I shared a secret with you that not even my best friend was aware of. Over the years I have listened to your show and felt as if you would understand the delicate dilemma I found myself in.

Since you receive so many letters, let me refresh your memory.

I remember the words as if they were just written . . .

You are the only one who can help me. My secret is too private to tell even my best friend. I'm in love with my boss, a wonderful, studious man who has no idea of my feelings. His mind is consumed with his classes and writing a grant to study the migration of dinosaurs. He's ten years older, single and a professor of paleontology at the local university. Unfortunately, the school has a strict no dating/ fraternization of subordinates policy for fear of sexual harassment suits.

I love my job and I just purchased my first home. I'm scared that if I let Professor X know how I feel, I run the risk of embarrassing both of us, putting a strain on our wonderful working relationship or, worse, losing my job if anyone finds out.

For the last couple of weeks we've been working long hours after work to get ready for a convention in town in which he is the program chair. When he's reading something over my shoulder and I smell his woodsy cologne, I have this strange urge to grab him by the tie and pull him to me and damn the consequences.

The need to tell him is becoming stronger day by day. Matters have become even more urgent since the single sister, Miss P for pushy, of a fellow professor moved here six weeks ago and now has her eyes on him. She always finds a way to touch him when she stops by. His tie needs straightening or there's a piece of nonexistent lint on the sleeve of his jacket.

When those incidences occur, he looks a bit flustered but flattered by the attention of a beautiful woman. It galls me to admit it, but I want you to have all the facts so you can help me. My looks are only average, but I know I can love him better than any woman in the world.

In the three years that I've been Professor X's executive assistant, the only dates I know that he has had have been those of a business nature. He and Miss P have gone out three times in the past two weeks.

There's nothing to stop her from going after him. If I wait much longer I might lose him . . . if I haven't already. If I thought she really cared, I'd leave him alone. She doesn't. She's one of those women who crave the attention of men. I know for a fact she's seeing another man, and I heard her say on her cell phone that she was just having fun with the professor.

I'm torn between telling him what I know about her, and telling him how I feel about him. Both carry tremendous risks. Or would silence be better? Please tell me what to do.

Torn and tormented,
M. from Dallas

Remember me now? I hope so, because I'll never forget you. You told me to follow my heart, to risk it all, to do whatever it took to let him know how I felt. I trusted you and you know what happened? Well, let me tell you!

I knew when I woke up that fateful Saturday morning that life for me would never be the same. Throwing back the covers, I went to the bathroom to shower and go over my plan one last time.

Professor X, Carter Watkins, was coming for a working breakfast and, if things went as planned, a lot more. I shivered as the hot water ran down my body, my overactive imagination conjuring up images of Carter's lips and long-fingered hands doing the same.

Shutting off the water, I dried myself, then rubbed into my skin a moisturizing cream scented with violet, freesia and amber. Even after Carter left, I wanted him to remember the exotic fragrance and think of me, crave me.

Finished, I put on a sheer apricot thong and a floral sundress with a built-in bra, capped sleeves and a flared skirt that stopped five inches above my knees. In the office I'd always dressed conservatively, never showing off too much skin.

Even if the university hadn't been conservative, I was brought up to dress and carry myself in a professional manner, and always remain a lady and above reproach.

Until today.

I turned from side to side in front of the full-length mirror in the bedroom and smiled with approval. Carter would certainly get an eyeful. In all the years I'd been Carter's executive assistant, I'd never worn sleeveless blouses without a jacket or sweater.

Turning away, I hurried to the kitchen. Putting on a long apron, I started breakfast. Being a GRITS woman, "girl raised in the South," I could throw down with the best of them. When the doorbell rang thirty minutes later, I had just taken the biscuits out of the oven. My heart lurched, then lurched again as the chime sounded once more.

Was this too bold a move? Carter, after all, was ultraconservative. All of his clothes were black or brown or navy-blue, his shirts button-down and white. When the sound came for a third time, I finally moved. It was too late. Two days before, Joy had said to risk it all for love in an answer to my letter on her Web site.

Taking a deep breath, I opened the door. Carter blinked, his mouth gaping just the tiniest bit. His dark eyes widened, then traveled slowly from my face with a touch more makeup, to the swell of my breasts over the décolletage, down to my feet in three-inch-heeled sandals, then back up. His gaze stayed on my breasts.

It was all I could do not to squirm. I hadn't expected to feel uncomfortable. "Good morning, Professor Watkins."

His head came up. He was good-looking rather than handsome, with a trim mustache over a surprisingly sensual mouth. His skin was the tempting color of dark chocolate. This morning he wore one of his favorite navy-blue wool blazers, white shirt and no tie, which must have made him feel half-dressed.

He swallowed. "Good morning, Ms. Hill," he said, then moistened his lips as if his mouth had gone dry. "You look different. In a nice way," he hastened to add.

"Thank you. Please come in." I stepped aside. "I could say the same about you and no tie."

His hand went to his throat. I could see just the barest hint of thick, black chest hair. I

132

almost licked my lips. "I hope you don't mind," he said.

"Not at all," I assured him, taking the opportunity to touch him lightly on the arm. My reward was a timid smile.

I closed the door and took a moment to compose myself. Carter was studying the African art I collected and had incorporated into the decorating scheme of my house. As I joined him in the great room, he was standing before a fertility god.

I flushed. My mother thought the piece indecent, but it was either let me keep the family heirloom or keep it herself, since it passed from the eldest child of each generation.

"I didn't know you were interested in such things," Carter said, then he lifted his attention from the long appendage of the statue to me.

I flushed again, then stammered, "It — it belonged to my paternal grandmother."

"Did it work?"

"She had twelve children," I told him with a smile. "She lived to see all of them finish college and get married. My father is the oldest."

"And the husband?"

Their children had always maintained he'd worn himself out. "He died shortly after the last child was born."

"But with a smile on his face, no doubt."

My lips twitched. Carter had a wicked and unexpected sense of humor at times. "No doubt." I waved my arm toward the kitchen to the right. "Breakfast is ready. We can eat in there, then work on the patio by the pool."

His hand closed around my bare arm, causing my skin to heat. "Smells good, but not as good as you." He leaned closer.

My body trembled. "Th-thank you."

"Thank you." He seated me in a padded chair, which was a good thing because my knees were shaking.

"Is there anything I can get?" he asked, still standing beside me.

"Noth—" I began, then tried to rise. "I forgot. The biscuits!"

His callused hand settled gently on my bare shoulder. "You've done enough. I'll get them."

He filled the pewter bread basket with the biscuits and set it on the round glass-topped table, then took his seat.

"Is there anything I can do to help?"

Briefly he looked away. "I'll let you know."

Becoming more puzzled by the second, I simply stared at him. Then it hit me. He didn't want to leave *her*. My heart sank.

"Do you want me to say grace?" he asked.

Feeling my throat clog with tears of anger and regret, I simply nodded. *Too late. I had waited too long.*

Carter finished the blessing and forked a slice of ham, a big helping of scrambled eggs and a biscuit on his plate. He chewed with relish. "This is delicious. If I'd known you cooked this well, I would have invited myself over long ago."

I tried to take comfort in the fact that he was enjoying my food, but it was a poor substitute for him enjoying the taste of me. "Now that you do, you're always welcome."

"I might take you up on that," he said, looking straight at me. "The food is wonderful." His hand circled the glass of juice, but he didn't pick it up. He seemed lost in thought.

He's probably thinking of not having her with him all summer, I thought. By then she'd be long gone, and Carter would be nursing a broken heart. Even more reason for me not to be there to watch him daily, yearning for a woman he never had a chance with.

The doorbell rang, startling me. I swung around.

"I'll clean up while you see to your guest." Carter began clearing the table, something my male cousins would never have done in a million years.

The doorbell came again, prompting me to move. "Thank you. I'll be back in a minute."

Crossing the great room, I couldn't shake

135

the feeling that someone had interrupted something important. I reached for the door-knob, planning to get rid of whoever as quickly as possible.

I gasped. My eyes widened in surprise. Hilary Simms, the beautiful "other" woman, stood on my doorstep, dressed in a brown tulle lace camisole and brown pin-striped pants with a slim belt that cinched her tiny waist.

Hanging from her slim shoulder was a multicolored print cotton and brown leather handbag with bamboo trim. I'd seen the shoulder bag in a catalog I loved to dream over, but could never afford anything inside. The ensemble shouted couture, style, elegance. I felt dowdy in my off-the-rack dress from a department store.

"I need to see Carter."

No "Good morning," not even a smile. Her nose so far up in the air that if it rained she'd drown. The thought almost made me smile.

"Did you hear me?"

Hilary had never been friendly to me, but at least she had been cordial. How could any man fall for such a rude woman?

She sneered when I didn't move. "Don't think I don't know you're after Carter." I gasped and she smiled nastily. "Just look at you in that awful dress, flaunting yourself. It won't do you any good. You have nothing to offer him. Nothing. He's mine for the taking."

"Hilary." Carter's voice came from behind us. I cringed. Just before I shut my eyes in misery I saw Hilary's face light up. She quickly brushed past me.

I stood there, feeling exposed, wanting to run to my room and hide. Had he heard? I didn't want to turn and see the look of pity — or worse, revulsion — on his face.

"Carter, I'm so sorry to disturb you, but a group of us are flying to New York on a friend's jet," she exclaimed. "You could see Professor Sampson in person and I could help you persuade him to accept your invitation to the association meeting."

Dr. P. Sampson, the leading authority on dinosaurs, was the one guest Carter desperately wanted but hadn't been able to confirm. I made myself close the door. Perhaps she was right. I didn't have the connections to help Carter in the ways she could. All I had was my love.

"Sampson knows I want him, I don't think my bothering him while he's trying to finish an important research project is going to help my cause," Carter said.

"The man has to take a break sometime to eat or just stretch," Hilary went on. "We'll leave it open. We could drop by your parents' and take them to dinner tonight."

"They're out of town," he told her, his gaze going over her shoulder to meet mine. "Marissa and I were about to start work."

"Marissa." Hilary spit my name out as if it fouled her mouth to do so. She faced me, her hard gaze flicking over me with obvious disapproval, then she turned back to Carter. "Carter, you must see what she's trying to do."

"Hilary, don't!" I blurted. "Please."

She laughed. "Lost your nerve?"

Carter frowned. My hands clenched. I jerked my eyes away. I thought, if I could get my hands on Joy at this moment, there's no telling what I would do to her. She's the cause of all this.

"I appreciate what you're trying to do, Hilary, but Sampson has my number and Marissa and I have a lot of work to do today." Carter took her arm and started toward the front door.

"Work isn't what she has in mind unless it's the two of you in bed."

My head snapped up. My face heated with embarrassment and anger.

"You can't be falling for her pitiful attempt at seduction," Hilary said. "She looks —"

"That's enough, Hilary," Carter interrupted, his voice tight.

"You're too kind to see what she's trying to do," Hilary declared, placing her hand on his arm. "She's overplayed her hand. When I tell my brother, she'll be looking for a job and out of your life for good."

"You're that scared of competition?" I asked her. I had nothing to lose. I wouldn't go out like a wimp.

"Ha!" she harrumphed. "What competition? I look better, dress a damn sight better, and have connections, culture and money. What do you have?"

"Me, if she'll have me," Carter said softly.

I had to grab the table in the entryway to keep upright. I began to tremble. Carter stared straight at me with a look of such tender devotion that tears crested in my eyes.

"Wh-what?" Hilary said.

Carter, his hot gaze never leaving mine, came to me, then circled his arm around my waist. "Besides me, Marissa has compassion, strength, courage, and a sweetness that can't be faked." Reaching over, he opened the door. "Goodbye, Hilary. Don't miss your plane."

"But —" She stood there as if she couldn't comprehend what was happening. "You — you can't be serious."

"Hilary, contrary to the circulating myth, professors aren't stupid. I knew what you were doing from day one. I respect your brother and didn't want to create a problem. Your uncalled-for attack on Marissa changed that."

His arm tightened around my waist, and his

expression hardened. "No one talks to her that way. No one." There was sharpness in his voice that I had never heard before.

Humiliated, Hillary rushed from the house. Carter closed the door after her.

"I'm sorry you had to go through that." His fingers beneath my chin lifted my head, then grazed across my lower lip, causing me to shiver. "Sweet Marissa. Forget what she said. She couldn't hold a candle to you. No woman could."

I could barely take it all in. Was I dreaming?

"Please say something." His hands palmed my face. "I think you care about me just a little bit. Am I wrong?"

A little bit? I kissed him, my arms going around his neck, my body pressing against his as I'd dreamed of and wanted for so very long.

"Marissa . . . Marissa." He chanted my name between bold, hot kisses that took my breath away.

Staring up at him, I felt powerful and so very blessed. "Carter, I don't like you a little bit. I love you with all my heart."

I felt his hands tremble around my waist. "I've loved you for so long, but was afraid to say anything for fear I'd offend you and you'd leave. Loving you and not being able to tell you was the most difficult thing I have ever done."

I grinned up at him. "You won't have to worry about that now."

His hand palmed my cheek. "There's still the policy on dating subordinates at the university."

My smile died. "I love working with you."

"I love having you and I think I have the perfect solution." He reached into his pocket and pulled out a diamond solitaire.

My heart thudded. My eyes went from the sparkling ring to him.

"I've carried this for the past six months. It was a sort of talisman that one day I've have the courage to risk it all for love." He tenderly picked up my left hand. "Marissa, my heart, my love, will you marry me?"

Through tears, and with a heart overflowing with love and happiness, I managed to say, "Yes."

He slipped the ring on my finger and fitted his lips to mine.

Joy, during winter break we visited his parents and mine. The end of May we were married in a beautiful ceremony at the chapel at the university. That summer I went with Carter as his assistant, with wonderful results.

Our first child, Carter Jr., the most beautiful,

happiest baby in the world, was born exactly nine months from our first night there. I owe it all to you for advising me to risk it all for love.
Glowing with happiness,
M. in Dallas

I lean back against my pile of pillows and grin. I remembered the letter and the sound of desperation that came through in "M.'s" words. I *was* good for something. Every now and again I get it right. I put the letter aside then get up for another cup of tea. Instead of feeling sleepy I'm oddly rejuvenated.

With a fresh cup of piping hot tea, I hop back in bed and hunt around in the mail-bag for another letter. If my luck holds up I'll get another goodie to help soothe me to sleep. I open the letter that's titled My Brother's Keeper. Uh-oh . . .

CHAPTER 8

Dear Joy,

We never know what life has in store for us. Only one thing is guaranteed as far as I'm concerned, and that is death. I learned that lesson when I was twenty-one years old, away at college, with a "great" future ahead of me. Then the unthinkable happened: a terrorist attack claimed the life of both my parents. As fate would have it, I had to raise my pain-in-the-butt, sixteen-year-old brother, Curtis.

I admit I was angry — at the attacks, at my parents, at my brother and at God. I had plans. It wasn't fair. I was bitter for having to leave college in my last year. But I loved my brother, so I took on the responsibility of raising him the way Mom and Dad would have wanted.

That was five years ago. We made it through the worst of it. I finished my last year at Fordham University and worked hard to gain a position as an anti-money-laundering specialist at a large community bank. Curtis was a journalism major at NYU, with a promising career ahead of him. Living in New York after the attacks was still tough but, for the most part, life was good again. That was until three days ago when I got the call that had me sitting in an emergency room at two a.m., waiting for the doctors to tell me the fate of my brother's life.

Every part of my body felt numb. I feared I was losing Curtis, too. Riddled with shock I sat and stared at a blurred figure that stormed across the emergency room in my direction. Within seconds, Rachel came into focus.

"Are you happy now? Is this what you wanted? If he dies, he'll be out of both of our lives!"

I couldn't respond. Rachel's words slashed me. I was dying inside as my brother slipped away. I bowed my head down and squeezed my hands together. I hadn't prayed since my parents died. I hoped He was listening to me now, because I was praying fiercely for my brother's life. If Curtis died, it was my fault. I couldn't help myself. I didn't want anything to happen to him. I just wanted that hussy, Rachel, out of our lives.

I should start from the beginning. Two weeks ago to be exact . . .

■ ■ ■ ■

It was eleven-thirty on Friday night, and I could barely keep my eyes open. I'd been trying to reach Curtis since eight-thirty and his dinner was way past cold. It wasn't like him to stay out late without calling. He must have been deep into a story. I'd decided to wait ten more minutes before putting the food away. It wasn't long before Curt came traipsing through the door.

I automatically slipped into mother mode. "Boy, where have you been? Do you think that because you're almost twenty-one you can do as you please?"

He placed his laptop bag on the sofa and walked toward me with his arms wide open. "Sorry, Maya. I got caught up in some festivities at school."

I slapped his arms away, avoiding his attempt at a hug. "Well, I forgive you this time. Let me warm up your dinner."

"That's okay, Maya. I already ate. I'll have it for lunch tomorrow."

Something was different about my brother. Managing to get his hug in, he squeezed me tighter than usual to say good-night. The sweet, flowery scent that tickled my nose wasn't the cologne I'd given him for his birthday. I could only imagine the festivities he was wrapped up in. And whoever she was had my brother's nose wide open, 'cause he couldn't stop smiling. I felt a bit concerned at the thought of a girl in Curtis's arms.

I shrugged it off. If she was anything special, Curtis would have mentioned her. I was blowing the situation out of proportion. I watched Curt make his way to his room. What woman wouldn't want to be near his six-foot-four chiseled body? My brother could be a model looking like Shemar Moore, with his fine self. Well, at least one of us was having fun.

"Have a good night, Curt."

"Thanks, sis." He cleared his throat before he continued. "By the way, can you make your special lasagna tomorrow night? I'd like to bring a friend over for dinner after work."

"Sure. It'll be fun to have one of your friends over. Who's coming? Junior?"

"Um, not exactly. I mean, no. Her name is Rachel."

The already tight curls on my head seemed to get tighter at the sound of her name. Alarm rang in my ears and my head began to pound.

"Does she wear Beautiful?"

"Huh?" I'm sure he was playing stupid.

"Never mind. Don't be late tomorrow." I couldn't wait to meet this woman in person.

"I love you." Curt took off, and I dragged

myself to my room in his wake.

I was the only staff member crazy enough to work on Saturday. I hoped the peace and quiet would help me flow through a few investigations. What a joke. I must have stared at the same file for forty-five minutes. It was a waste of time. I packed up and headed for home.

I set the table for three and hoped the evening would go smoothly. I dropped into my favorite chair, my dad's black leather recliner. Apprehension clenched my stomach as the fear hit me. Rachel was the first girl Curtis ever asked to bring home.

A car pulled up to the front of the house. I peeked out of the window to catch a glimpse of Curt and his "friend" getting out of the cab. Only there wasn't a cab. Curtis exited from the passenger side of a white Mercedes. Just as a gentleman should, my brother opened the driver's door.

I knew she was older than my brother right away. The curly ponytail swinging from her head wasn't fooling me one bit. She appeared much more sophisticated than most girls in their early twenties. Her tall leather boots matched her buttery-brown leather jacket. Confidence sprang from her long, purposeful strides. For some unexplainable reason, I felt jealous.

I rushed to the kitchen. The quicker I fed them, the quicker she'd be out of the house. The introductions were cordial and standard; it was the conversation over dinner that did it for me.

"How did you two meet?"

Rachel reached over and caressed Curt's hand; he squeezed it gently in return. "Your brother's dedication to his work caught my attention."

He continued with a goofy smile. "If I said I didn't notice her until she treated me to a cup of coffee, I'd be lying."

"He ordered the same coffee every day — mocha nublado."

"With extra mocha," they added in unison.

Oh, brother. "So you're a waitress?"

"Not exactly. I . . ."

"She owns Grounded, a café near campus, where I've done my homework and completed some of the best stories I've written for the newspaper."

Oh Lord, they were finishing each other's sentences. I took a deep breath and slowly rubbed my palms together, which usually calmed me. Usually.

"This lasagna is delicious. Is this your own recipe?" Smart girl, that Rachel — changing

148

the subject. I retracted my claws, for the moment.

"Thank you. It's one of Curtis's favorites."

"Yeah. I have no idea what she puts in it, but no one can beat it."

One point for me.

The remainder of dinner was spent in silence. Curtis was kind enough to clear the table. An uncomfortable tension filled the air as we all struggled to be civil.

"Rachel, we better get going. You know how long the line gets at the club."

"I didn't realize you had other plans. You two get going — I'll clean up."

It was finally over. I released the breath I'd been holding most of the evening. Rachel and I exchanged civil goodbyes. Curtis blessed me with one of his bear hugs and whispered in my ear.

"Thanks, sis. I know that was hard for you." He knew me well.

That Monday, I dragged myself into work. I needed a strong cup of coffee. Curtis didn't come home the rest of the weekend. He was kind enough to leave me a message, but sleep didn't come easy. I missed his company.

My girl, Rosa, plopped her "J-Lo wannabe" ass on my desk, like she always did when she had something juicy to share.

"Ooh, girl. I was at the Copa this weekend with Hector, you know that *papi* I met at the Puerto Rican Day Parade."

I simply nodded so she could continue. She sounded just like Rosie Perez when she was super excited.

"We were groovin' to Don Omar and I saw your brother across the floor getting down with a hot *mami.*"

"Yeah. He's dating an older woman."

She crossed her legs and folded her arms. "Damn. I wish I knew he was into that, because your brother is fine."

I couldn't join her usual infectious laughter. I wasn't amused. "Are you up for a cup of coffee?"

"Maya, don't take it so seriously. Your brother is enjoying himself."

"I know, but . . ."

"But nothing. What you need to do is get your ass a man and let Curtis live his life, or you're going to end up alone one day."

I understood Rosa's point. But she had a different boyfriend every six months. I didn't have time for that. I promised my parents I'd take care of Curtis, and that included monitoring his choices for a partner.

For the remainder of the week, things appeared to be back to normal for Curt and me. He was home for dinner every night. He never brought up Rachel and neither did I. In a way, I felt bad. He was probably hurting, but I felt it was best to leave things alone. When the time was right, he'd find someone else.

It was Saturday, and when Curtis came home from work, I had his favorite devil's food cake with my special cream-cheese frosting prepared. I couldn't wait to surprise him.

Rachel's voice, coupled with my brother's laughter, paralyzed me. Shame on me for assuming they broke up. I couldn't believe she dared to step back in my house again.

"Hello, Rachel." There was no need for small talk. I wasn't going to pretend I liked her.

Curtis lifted his face and sniffed the air. "Mmm. Damn, it smells good in here."

"I baked your favorite cake. The bowl's in the kitchen. I know you love to lick it clean."

Rachel giggled.

"That's what I'm talking about." He looked at his girlfriend with his Kool-Aid smile, not the least bit embarrassed. "I don't usually share, but I'll make an exception this one time."

Rachel's giggle rolled into a full-bodied laugh. "Enjoy, honey. I'll wait for a slice of the finished product."

"Curt, why don't you bring out the cake. I'll get the coffee."

Rachel raved over my cake. I didn't need her compliment. I knew my confections were tasty. She found my sweet spot. Maybe she wasn't so bad. My brother seemed happy. I owed it to him to give her a chance.

"So, Rachel, tell me a little more about yourself."

She took a noticeably deep breath. Curtis whispered, "It's okay," before she started.

"I'm divorced. I was married at twenty-one. I was young and pregnant. My son is seven now and barely sees his father."

My heart stopped. What was this woman trying to tell me? "Are you looking for a new father?" I put my right hand up into the air, silently asking the Lord for strength and turned the question to my brother. "Are you ready to be a daddy? I didn't give up my future for you to turn around and do this to me."

Curtis jumped up from the sofa, and the cake platter went flying. "Damn it, Maya. Everything isn't about you. Rachel was just . . . Never mind. Why am I wasting my time trying to explain things to you. You've already made up your mind about her."

"Curtis, I better get going. Maya, I'm sorry our evening ended on a bad note. Good night."

Oh, *hell* no, she wasn't leaving my house with the last word. My pride wouldn't allow it. "Don't let the door hit you on the way out." I knew it was stupid, but I couldn't think of anything better at the time.

She ignored my comment and kissed Curtis.

He whispered into her ear, but I heard every word. "Baby, I'm sorry about my sister. I'll call you later." They walked to the door and hugged good-night. Then my brother turned his pent-up anger on me.

"What's your problem? That's why I never brought any of my girlfriends home to meet you."

I didn't care that he had other girlfriends. I just felt Rachel was wrong for him. "She's using you."

Curtis was bursting with laughter. I didn't see what was so funny about the situation. "Let me get this straight. A woman who owns her own business, drives a Mercedes and lives in a slammin' house, is using me. Me — a college senior, living at home with his sister."

He was right — it sounded ridiculous. But something didn't sit right with me. I'd have to sleep on it. "Clean up the kitchen. I'm tired."

"Good night, sis. I still love you."

I loved him, too. I hope he realized that.

Work followed another sleepless weekend. To clear my mind, I jumped right into work. Curtis called to meet me for lunch between his classes. I had a huge caseload stacked before me, which already guaranteed me an all-nighter. Curtis was worth it, so I squeezed him into my schedule.

At lunch Curtis didn't waste any time getting to the point.

"Maya, I'm in love with Rachel."

"That's ridiculous. You just met her."

"Actually, we've been dating for a year."

"Excuse you?"

"No offense, Maya, but I knew you wouldn't be able to handle me dating anyone, especially a woman older than you."

Damn right.

"I'm thinking about moving in with her."

What the hell was he thinking? The conversation was worse than anything I could have anticipated.

I breathed slow and deep. It was imperative I gain control before I lost him. "You have a home."

"It's Mom and Dad's home, Maya. I need to move on."

"You're being ungrateful."

"I'm being real."

I couldn't believe the crap that was falling out of my brother's mouth. I needed some time to digest his bullshit.

"Curt, let's talk about this over dinner. At home."

"I have plans tonight. Don't wait up." He dropped two twenties on the table. "Maybe I'll catch up with you tomorrow."

I pushed my platter away from me. My appetite was shot. I needed to get my own life together. It was sad, but I couldn't remember the last time I had been on a date.

That night, I must have watched the shadows dancing across my living room walls for hours before I finally went to my room to change. I threw on my favorite black dress with the plunging neckline. I hoped it didn't make me look as desperate as I was.

I took a cab to the Village, where I'd have a selection of bars to choose from. The city was alive for a Monday night, but I managed to find a quiet spot. Eighties music filled the air. It was just what the doctor ordered. There were a ton of sexy brothers in the place. Maybe I'd finally meet someone, unless I'd stumbled into a gay bar.

I ordered a chocolate martini. It was delicious, but I wished I'd ordered something stronger.

I pulled out a pack of cigarettes. I hadn't smoked since college. After the stress I'd faced over the last few days, a cigarette was in order.

"Excuse me, miss, but you can't smoke in here," the bartender barked, his arms folded across his massive chest.

I'd completely forgotten about the No Smoking law. I swallowed my drink and stepped out for my smoke. There were at least five other people engrossed in conversation amidst a light cloud of smoke. I placed my cigarette between my lips when a brother, more delicious than my martini, lit it for me.

I closed my eyes and inhaled deeply, allowing the nicotine to course through me. I opened my eyes and the sexy dream still stood before me. The glow of the street-lamp and the light mist of smoke surrounded his aura. He appeared as a sort of god.

He extended his hand toward me as he introduced himself. "My name's Ken."

I held his hard, callused hand and smiled. A hard-workin' man. I wondered how hard he worked in the bedroom.

"Thanks for the light." My cheeks warmed.

"Share a drink with me."

"What makes you think I'm alone?" I purred against my will.

"Then your man is a fool for leaving a beautiful woman like you alone."

"How many women have you used that line on tonight?"

His laughter was rich and hearty. "Well, if you must know, you're the first. And, if you reject me, I already have my eye set on the blonde in the white dress."

I liked him — he was a welcome distraction. "I'm Maya."

"Maya . . . Just Maya, like the singer?"

"Maya Perkins."

A look of surprise spread across his handsome face. "From Brooklyn Community Bank?"

My guard was up. I stepped back. "Do I know you?"

"I'm Ken Douglass from Secret Service."

Heat colored my caramel complexion. Ken and I had spoken over the phone many times regarding a number of investigations. I had fantasized about him on many of those occasions. His voice over the phone was titillating, a perfect match for the striking Adonis before me.

"Maya? I apologize if I've mistaken you for someone else."

No mistake. I just couldn't find my voice. I managed to push out a response. "I'm just amazed at what a small world it is. I never imagined ever running into you."

"Does that mean sharing a drink with you is out of the question?"

He had no idea how much I wanted to share with him. My body was charged up. I hoped a drink and some conversation would bring me down to earth. Just as I was about to respond, the hot reggae song, "Temperature," slipped out of the bar and I shook my hips.

"Ooh, that's my song."

Ken tossed my cigarette to the ground and pulled me back into the club. He sauntered across the dance floor, finding us the perfect spot. His husky build and bronze skin in the dim light left me breathless. I hoped he couldn't hear the beat of my heart over Sean Paul. Ken slid away from me and impressed me with his dance moves. I felt like I was on a menu as he feasted upon my ample figure, tracing every curve with his eyes, before he pulled me back into his arms.

"You look gorgeous." His lips brushed the nape of my neck. Chills rippled through my energized body. "I'm so glad we finally met."

It felt so good to be in this man's arms. Every kiss he placed lifted my fears of being alone. He was what I needed right then and there. If he didn't stop, I wasn't sure what I was capable of doing at that moment.

"I think I'll take that drink now."

We sat at the bar and Ken ordered a couple of drinks for us. I watched a special news report that flashed on the television above the bar.

I shook my head as the reporter described the scene where an unidentified young black man was shot by police. The unarmed suspect was driving a Mercedes that resembled one that was reported stolen, according to authorities. That was the third case in two months.

I tried to ignore my cell phone buzzing away in my purse, but the caller wouldn't give up.

"Maya, you need to get to the emergency room, right away. Curtis has been shot."

Rachel rattled off the name and address of the hospital. Like a zombie, I repeated the information to Ken. Without any further questions, he drove me and has been by my side ever since.

For years, I listened to your fans whine about their lives. I was always ready to blurt out some advice for your frazzled callers and talk about them at work the following day. I always said, "You'll never catch me on that show."

I was wrong. Please help me.

I'd tempted fate when I wished Rachel was out of our lives, and it backfired. I made a mistake. I gave Curtis no alternative but to pack up and move on, and that's what he was doing the night he was shot. I pray he makes it. How can I make it up to him?

The doctor's here now.

Pray for me,
Maya Perkins, My Brother's Keeper

Slowly, I fold the letter and gently place it back in the envelope. Wow. That's all I can say. Yes, sis, I will be praying for you. I could never say that out loud on the radio; it would mess up my MO, but in the privacy of my bedroom in the still of the night, I can pray for you. And I do. I actually close my eyes and say a prayer — and maybe it was just as much for Maya as it was for me.

I yawn loudly and stretch, then take a peek at the digital clock on my nightstand. It's almost four a.m. I rub my eyes. I think I have one more reading left in me before I call it a night. Taking out another letter, I open it and place it on my lap. *Black Power?* Oh, dayum. A revolutionary. Well, this one should be interesting. I perk up, no longer sleepy.

CHAPTER 9

Dear Joy,

I'm writing to you because I was listening to your show a couple of weeks ago and heard a woman call in talking about Black Power. She said that Black Power was dead, and you and some of the other callers agreed with that fact. But I'm here to tell you that just because something or someone has died don't mean it's dead.

A woman named Black Power had a room on the ground floor of 567 Stuyvesant Avenue. That was in 1964 when I was just eight years old and Mama owned the only bookstore for thirty blocks.

I remember spending my school holidays in the bookstore, which was just called The Bookstore back then. Me at my mama's hip, doll clutched in one hand and my favorite, *Where the Wild Things Are,* clutched in the other.

I didn't know it then, but plenty of famous

people came in to talk to my mama about politics and the plight of the black people. Amiri Baraka, Angela Davis and Assata, before she was accused of killing that state trooper, broke out of jail and fled to Cuba.

I remember their conversations the way small children do, the words floating above my head in a mist. The only thing clear and simple to me were the knees of the folk and the fabric of Mama's kente cloth skirt.

Nothing in that time was more amazing to me than the sunlit streets and the eerie way the streetlamps knew just when to come on.

Mama was a Black Panther sympathizer then and kept her beret in the top drawer of the desk that doubled as the counter. Next to the old cash register was a picture of my daddy in a gold-plated frame. He smiled out at me from behind the glass Mama kept dust- and streak-free with Windex.

I only knew my daddy through pictures, the letters that came once a week addressed to "my sweet baby girl," and the voice that floated to me from the other end of the phone every Wednesday night at six.

Mama would go upstate once a month to visit him. But I wasn't allowed to go. Daddy didn't want me to see him in that place.

I remember a white lady coming into the store. She was tall with thin pink lips and long blond hair and even though she wore her beret the way the rest of the Panthers did, for some reason it didn't look right on her. Something about her blond hair or the color of her skin took the meaning away from it.

She wore tight black pants, dark shades and a black T-shirt that said Power To The People.

She didn't say a word, just walked up and down the aisles, running her fingers along the spines of the books and making small noises in her throat. When Mama couldn't take it anymore, she asked, "Can I help you find something?" And even at that young age, I knew the "Miss" was missing from her question.

The woman shook her head no and then suddenly turned and walked out, but not before dropping a folded piece of paper down on the counter.

Mama picked up the piece of paper and then watched as the woman climbed into a fancy car that pulled away quickly.

I often wonder if the woman's eyes were blue or brown. I dream them blue, because that's what color Black Power said the devil's eyes were.

I never knew what was written on the paper, but I think it had something to do with my daddy being killed in prison, because Mama just kept saying "No, no, no" over and over as she dialed a million numbers and asked, "You hear anything 'bout Divine?"

It was true, true as the sky was blue. My daddy was dead. They said he committed suicide. Found him in his cell, swinging from a foot of rope.

But Mama never believed that that was true. When she talked about my daddy's death, she always said, "When they murdered my husband . . ."

The Black Panthers came to mourn my daddy, but never did bring groceries like they promised they would. They did leave a gun though, told my mama to use it on herself and me if she had to. Said, "Don't let the white man kill your man twice."

Mama put that gun next to the beret.

Black Power didn't come into the bookstore for a long time on the account she'd seen that white woman walk in there the day my daddy died. She thought that Mama had gone over to the other side. She told people that my mama was conspiring with the enemy.

Mama heard the rumors Black Power was spreading and even saw a petition that Black Power was trying to get people to sign to get Mama out of the neighborhood. But no one would sign. When Mama got wind of that, she nearly lost her mind and walked right up to Black Power and gave her the what for.

164

I didn't hear any of it — I was in the book-store staring out at them — but I knew Mama was giving her a good piece of her mind by the way her head was rolling on her neck.

Black Power screamed back at Mama and then looked sorry. After that Black Power started coming back in the store again, edifying Mama and me.

I asked her one day where her babies were at and Mama's mouth dropped wide open like I had said a cuss word.

Well, what did I know? Every woman that I had ever seen had babies or had had babies at one point. I had never seen Black Power with a baby — not even a picture of one in the man's wallet she carried in the back pocket of her fatigues.

Mama called me "fresh" and told me to hush. And I did.

Black Power just looked at me and said, "All the black people in the world are my babies."

I didn't believe that.

The most babies I had ever seen a woman have was ten and that was Ophelia Jackson on Halsey Street and she was a whore. Or so the talk went. I figured there had to be at least one million people in the world and Black Power couldn't have birthed them all and she certainly wasn't my mama.

I just called her crazy in my head 'cause

had I said it out loud Mama would have smacked the black off of me.

I heard Mama whisper to a friend of hers, after Black Power left the store, that the state had taken Black Power's babies away from her because she didn't allow them to eat no meat, cheese or drink milk.

I heard Mama say she was a vegan, and back then I imagined that meant she was a bad mother, 'cause I hadn't ever heard that word before.

I could have asked Mama exactly what it meant, 'cause she'd spent two whole semesters at Howard University, before she met my daddy and dropped out, but I didn't bother to ask because she would have got on me about eavesdropping on grown folks' business.

One day I was sitting out in front the bookstore on a chair that Mama had brought just for me, licking on my cherry ice pop. It was nearly three in the afternoon and the sun was shining real high and bright in the sky.

People had been in and out the bookstore all day long and for some reason — a reason I would understand later on in life — their Afros looked bigger than the sun to me on that day and the men wore two black-fisted Afro picks in their heads instead of the usual one.

People came in dashikis and wearing their

Black Is Beautiful T-shirts. Some came with lit candles and others came with pans of food. Their faces were mad, sad, and some even walked in and straight out began to weep. Well, curiosity got the best of me and I snuck back into the store because I wanted to know who died, 'cause it sure did look like a repast to me. And I was about to ask, when someone slammed his head down on the counter and shouted, "We gotta kill them sons of bitches!"

Mama sent me out of the store then.

So there I was, back in my little chair, licking on my cherry ice pop when a whole lot of racket started making its way down the street. Sounded to me like forty people coming, but when I looked up it was just Black Power.

She was beating on a drum, and strapped to her chest was a cassette player blaring someone yelling in a language I ain't never heard before. It was hot as sin that day and Black Power was dressed in her usual fatigues and the sweat was just pouring down her face.

Mama came running out of the store, and I saw from the corner of my eye that she had something small and silver in her hand that she hurriedly shoved behind her back when she saw me looking.

"Go on in the store, little girl," she said, and I did.

"What you doing, B?" Mama called over to

Black Power. She never called her Black Power, just B.

Black Power got to the front of the store and stopped beating her drum, but the man on the cassette player was still yelling and Black Power was saying something but Mama couldn't hear her and said, "Turn that mess down, B. I can't hear you."

Black Power turned it down and then tilted her head over her shoulder a bit. Mama walked around behind her, put her hands on her hips and nodded her head, and then she did something I ain't never seen her do before. She touched Black Power, put her hand right on her shoulder and squeezed it, and then said, "Carry on, sister, carry on."

Black Power turned her cassette player up, began banging on her drum again and started down the block. As I watched from behind the window, I saw that the back of Black Power's jacket was missing and her bare skin was exposed, and written there in red letters were the words: Free Nelson Mandela.

That was June 12, 1964.

But what I would learn years later, after Black Power was dead, was that those letters on her back weren't written on — they'd been branded on.

"You mourning someone, B?" Mama asked

her one day as she locked the store up.

Black Power looked at her and I swear there were tears in her eyes as she said, "I had a premonition."

"Oh yeah? What about?"

"I saw," Black Power said, and spread her fingers out before her face, "a great prophet standing on an altar, a halo over his head, his robes that of the common man."

Mama's chest heaved and she kind of smirked.

"And then the air around him came together and turned into a bolt of lightning that pierced his heart and he disintegrated into dust."

Mama just stared at her for moment before saying, "I'm gonna make me a red velvet cake tonight. Make sure you come by tomorrow and get yourself a piece."

Three days later, Martin Luther King was shot dead on the balcony of the Lorraine Motel in Memphis, Tennessee.

Mama cried something terrible and Black Power chained herself to the light pole, banging her drum and talking in tongues until someone finally called the cops and then the cops called Bellevue.

"Our people, our people," Mama repeated over and over again in 1974 as she stood behind the glass pane window of the bookstore, watching the white men install the roll-down metal gates. The bookstore had been broken into and vandalized three times in three months. The intruders had defecated on the books and spray painted cuss words across the pictures on the walls.

Mama said the neighborhood was under siege and all of the conscious people were fleeing, getting city jobs and moving out to the suburbs, out to Queens.

My generation was hooked on heroin and attacking the elderly on the first of the month when the postman delivered their social security checks.

All around us, black metal gates were being installed over windows, the beautiful wooden double doors with the elongated glass panels that welcomed the sunshine into an otherwise dark brownstone were being replaced with dark gray steel ones that blocked out the sunshine altogether.

"Our people, our people," Mama said, and then I thought the world stopped reading, because no one came in to buy books any-more and Mama had to finally give up the bookstore. She couldn't get a job at the post office even though she'd passed that test with flying colors. Hell, she'd taken it a few times over the years for other people, just to make a little change on the side, so when the results came in and said that she had failed, Mama balled up that paper and threw it across the room and yelled out, "Goddamn FBI file!"

Black Power had been locked away for most of the seventies. When she was finally let out, she came back to the only place she ever knew, the only place she'd ever called home — Bed-Stuy.

Her little apartment was gone. In fact, the entire house was gone and so Black Power made her home on a bench in Fulton Park.

The bookstore had gone from a numbers hole/candy store to a beauty salon to just an empty storefront.

There were still a few people left in the neighborhood who remembered the old days, the consciousness and Black Power, and they would hold on to their empty soda cans and beer bottles, saving them for the time they would see Black Power and her shopping cart shuffling down Fulton Street mumbling to herself.

"C'mon by," they'd say when they came upon her. "Got two bags for you, gotta be worth a good five dollars."

Black Power never even acknowledged them, just kept shuffling along. But she would eventually show up and collect on the offer.

Mama and I stayed, even when the neighborhood crumbled around us and people started referring to it as Bed-Stuy live and die. We stayed, found a way and made a home.

I never did go to college the way Mama dreamed I would, but I did get a job at the post office and in the mid-eighties, the city of New York practically started giving away Bed-Stuy's brownstones.

By then I was married to a good man who worked for sanitation and, together, we bought a four-story brownstone on Macon Street. Mama didn't want to, but we convinced her to take the apartment on the ground floor.

Two years after that, a For Rent sign went up in the space where the bookstore used to be and we refinanced the brownstone and took out ten thousand dollars to rent and renovate the place.

This is where I write to you from today.

The place where I grew, listened and learned is once again a place of enlightenment and consciousness.

The neighborhood is vibrant again. A little bit lighter than it was when I grew up, but that's okay. This generation has greater demons to fight than my mama did in the sixties and seventies, and it's going to take people of all colors and from all backgrounds to defeat this beast.

But what I wanted you and your listeners to know is that, yes, Black Power died some years ago — walked right into my store, sat down on the bench, smiled at my little girl, closed her eyes and fell right out of this life.

We had a service for her here at the bookstore, a going home like you wouldn't believe, with food and music and stories that no one had told in years, and before we knew it, we were walking down Lewis Avenue, beating a drum and yelling, "Power to the People!"

Because know it or not, that's what she'd been to the people in this neighborhood — power. She gave it power when we couldn't find it for ourselves; she kept us conscious even when we didn't want to be.

And so while Black Power is laid to rest in Cypress Hill Cemetery, I make a pilgrimage there every twelfth of the month, clean off her grave site and place fresh flowers on her headstone. And this reminds me Black Power may be gone, may be invisible to the eye, may not be marching up and down the sidewalk and screaming, "We shall overcome," but she no longer has to. Her job is done. She is embedded in me, in everyone who ever came in contact with her, and her memory lives on in the stories we tell and so she lives on. She lives on.

I drop the letter on my lap. I want to laugh, to make a mockery of the writer as I always do, but somehow I can't. What the writer said hits me somewhere deep inside, resurrects something inside of me that I thought was dead. Like I said before, I live well. But reading this letter makes me think of how all that has been made possible and it damned sure isn't only because of anything I've done, but the work and struggles of folks like this chick's mother.

Instead of feeling uplifted, a wave of sadness sweeps through me. She was proud of her mama. I know I can't say the same. My mother! Most days she couldn't even remember my name. Yeah, that's a part of my life that no one other than Macy knows about. This whole life I'm living now is far removed from how I grew up. I didn't only change my life, I changed my name and pulled myself up out of the depths of drugs, violence and unwanted sex.

There are some mornings when I wake up terrified that it's all a dream and that this life I'm living is simply a product of my vivid imagination. I gotta be on top, gotta stay on top, 'cause if I don't, I may just fall all the way back down into that pit of ugliness that I came from.

I fold the letter, but instead of putting it back in the bag, I put it in the drawer in my nightstand. Maybe on those mornings when

I wake up terrified I'll read it again. I reach for the light and turn it off, then flip onto my side and squeeze my eyes shut. If I try really hard I'll sleep through the night and the demons of my past will stay in the shadows. If I try really hard.

CHAPTER 10

It's about nine in the morning. When I don't get a sex workout to put me to sleep I generally only need a few hours' sleep to get through my day. Coffee, juice, a slice of toast and a cup of yogurt. That is my everyday breakfast. I don't get much of a chance to go to a gym, so I do attempt to watch what I eat. After all, I have to make sure I can get into my very expensive designer clothes. Holla!

The letters I read the night before still run around in the back of my head. Most of the time they don't get to me. It's all just a job, know what I mean. But every now and then some of them get under my skin, disturb all the dirt I've dumped over my own issues. Sometimes I think that's the reason I do what I do — make light of other folks' messes so that I don't have to deal with my own. Hey, this is too much introspecting for this time of the morning.

I walk into the living room and turn on the stereo. *The Steve Harvey Morning Show* is on. I love that show. Truth be told, I never listen to WHOT unless it's a rerun of my own show! Sipping on my cup of coffee I crack up listening to Steve and Tommy do Country News. That skit is always a howl.

I'm feeling better already. One of these days I'm gonna call in and tell them what a good job they're doing and how they get me through my mornings — anonymously, of course.

Humming to Robin Thicke's latest song, I saunter into my office to get down to work. Like I said in the beginning, I get tons of letters, more letters than I can ever read and certainly more than will ever get on the air. The ones that don't go live on the show I often post on my Web site and let my listeners post their comments. And trust me, the Web site is almost as wild and crazed as the show.

I sit down behind my desk and assume the position then take the first letter on the top out. I slit the envelope open with my gold-embossed letter opener. Funny, the opener came in the mail one day and I almost freaked. I just knew it was from some crazed listener sending me some kind of weird message. But it was only a thank-you gift for some advice I'd given that actually worked out. Oh yeah, I do get threats every now and again. Someone pissed off or a protester who thinks I should be banned, but I don't pay those folks much attention. The reason I'm so popular is because I'm wild and say the most outrageous things. So my motto is, if you don't like it, change the station! Simple, right?

Anyway, I open the letter from a woman who titles her letter, Between the Lines.

Dear Joy,

I hope you don't mind my calling you Joy. I was listening to your program day before yesterday, and that character . . . I mean the man on your show had me doing a slow burn. He's entitled to his stupidity, but he doesn't have the right to force it on innocent listeners. Imagine a man who speaks so fine and cultured like he does saying he doesn't believe there's anything a person can't control. He said there are no such things as impulses, fate, addiction, none of that. He doesn't believe anything he can't see, not much that he hears and very little that he touches. His words, Joy, not mine. You should've kicked him off the show. I wish I'd been there. If he had the burden my best friend's carrying, he wouldn't be so damned arrogant. Let me tell you about Dorothy Faye and what she told me.

Dorothy Faye Hodge lived high on the hog, thanks to her success as a voice teacher and the eagerness of black kids to get rich singing hip-hop and rap. She knew her BMW coupe looked out of place in Frederick, Maryland's lower middle-class black neighborhood, where the average person parked a five-year-old Hyundai in front of the house, but she didn't care. The girl had already seen her thirty-fourth birthday, but she told her friends she was twenty-eight and, to prove it, she was careful to wiggle when she walked . . . with the aid of her four-inch heels, that is.

That Saturday morning, Dorothy Faye wiggled out of the South Street Mall, found her way to the precious BMW that she'd parked in the underground garage, and had began to pull off the offending high-heeled shoes when she looked up and nearly fainted. She stared into the piercing blue eyes of an ash-blond woman she hadn't heard approach — and on that concrete she should have heard her.

"Who . . . who *are* you?" she asked the woman as shivers streaked through her.

"Why do you ask? You know who I am, because you're one of us, Dorothy Faye."

In that warm spring weather, perspiration

dripped from Dorothy Faye's forehead. Her teeth began to chatter, and she leaned back against her BMW for support. She glanced around for a means of escape or, at least, for the comfort of another person's presence, a stranger, anybody. Seeing no one, she turned back to the blue-eyed blonde but saw not even a shadow. Dorothy Faye stood in the vast underground garage completely alone.

Dorothy Faye had always refused to examine the strangeness about herself, blocking out her premonitions, forcing herself to forget the things she "saw" that later came to pass, as well as the things she "saw" that were so unreal she was ashamed to mention them to anyone.

"I wonder what that sister meant? I'm sure not blond, and my eyes are dark brown like my face."

She remembered that she hadn't bought stockings, put her purchases in the car's trunk, locked it and went back inside the mall to buy some panty hose. "Wonder how come I feel so light, like I just lost thirty pounds. Humph, it's like somebody took a weight off my shoulders," she said aloud. Her gaze took in a tall, slim man. From a distance, she saw that his eyes were fawn-like, his lips sensuous, his skin the color of a fine camel-hair coat. She licked her lips and began to salivate.

Revelation hit her and, when the man reached her, she stopped him. "Hello, Jonathan," she said to the complete stranger. "I'm Dorothy Faye. Come with me."

"I'm . . . I can't. I'm getting married next Saturday, and I'm on my way right now to get fitted for my tuxedo."

Dorothy showed no concern for the man's reticence. She knew now that she was one of *them* — whoever they were — and that with her piercing gaze and newfound abilities, she could get him to do whatever she wanted, and she wanted him to make love with her. With her special powers, she had discerned that he was a gifted stud, and she intended to enjoy him for as long as she wanted him.

She extended her hand and waited until, at last, he took it. "Come with me," she said.

"What do you want with me? And who are you, anyhow?" he asked, as if he recognized the hand of fate.

"You've got everything I always wanted and never had," she told him as she led him to her car. "Are you hungry? I mean, did you eat a big breakfast? No, you didn't, did you? Don't worry. I'll feed you."

She unlocked the front passenger's seat, and he got in. She'd never liked docile men, and she knew that this one wasn't, that he had no will at the moment other than her will.

She hadn't hypnotized him, but had merely robbed him of his will until such time as she decided to return it to him. She stopped at a gourmet delicatessen and bought pastrami sandwiches, a loaf of Italian bread, deviled eggs, oyster chowder, a lobster salad, a pound of baked ham and a dozen and a half buttermilk biscuits.

"Who's going to eat all that?" he asked her when she returned to the car with two bags, one of which contained three bottles of white Burgundy wine.

"I don't expect there'll be anything left when you leave me," she said, and watched his bottom lip drop. Aware of his chagrined demeanor, she patted his hand, started the BMW and headed for her apartment. "Don't worry. I'll keep you as happy as a little pig in hog heaven."

She stopped the car in front of the apartment building in which she lived, unlocked the front passenger door and got out. As if she'd programmed him to do so, he walked around to the trunk of the car and waited. She opened the trunk. He took out her purchases and went with her to her apartment.

"Why don't you take a shower while I get you something to eat," she said, smiling.

"What are you fixing for me?"

"Scrambled eggs, toast, sausage and coffee. And I'll give you a couple of martinis just the way you like them." His eye sparkled, and she let him see her rubbing her breasts.

"Can I have some of that, too?"

Her left eye closed in a slow wink. "As much as you want and for as long as you want it."

While he stared at her, his eyes took on a dreamy look. "I don't think I need any breakfast."

"Oh, yes you do. You need every bit of energy you can get."

His shower didn't take long, and he left his shirt and tie in the bathroom. "No point in putting that stuff on when you're only going to take it off me as soon as I eat," he said, without resentment or any other kind of emotion. He sat at the dining room table in the chair at the place where she'd put his food. "Do you usually say the grace?" he asked her.

"Not this morning. I don't think the Lord approves of what I'm doing."

After he ate heartily, she cleared the table, put the dishes in the dishwasher and returned to him with two dry martinis. "This is my favorite drink. I usually have a couple before dinner, but not after breakfast." He drained the glass. "May I have another?" She looked at her watch. Hmm, twenty minutes after ten. Better not.

She thought for a minute. She had that gorgeous stud all to herself, and she didn't want him drunk. She took his hand and walked with him into her living room. "You can have a tiny sip of this one, but it's mine." She held the glass while he sipped, put the drink on her coffee table and slid her hands slowly over his hard chest, taking pains to torment his pectorals. She teased and rubbed until his pupils began to dilate.

"My blouse is too hot."

"May I remove it?" he asked her, and when he got her out of it, his Adam's apple began to bob so fast that she thought he might have convulsions. She unhooked her bra and let her size 38-D breasts hang free.

"May I . . . uh . . . what do you want me to do?" The blue-eyed blonde hadn't told her how to get a man to behave naturally while doing what she willed him to do. She concentrated. "From now on, you do what comes naturally unless I tell you otherwise."

Immediately, his eyes darkened and desire flooded them with a heat that she knew could consume her if she was not in control.

A second later, she was flat on her back on her living room sofa. The feel of Jonathan's mouth sucking her right nipple while his fingers squeezed her left one brought moans and cries out of her and had her teetering near the precipice. He dragged her hips to the edge of the sofa, parted her legs and let her feel the power of his talented tongue while she begged for completion. He picked her up, carried her to her bedroom, kicked off his pants and shoes and, without waiting for an invitation, rested her ankles on his shoulders and plowed his penis into her. Within minutes, she erupted around him, shouting her triumph as she did so.

Dorothy Faye had just experienced her first orgasm, and she cradled his head to her breast as she anticipated many, many more. At 7:33 p.m., having unknowingly established a world record, Jonathan passed out. Not smelling salts, ice on his neck or slaps on his face revived him until, a few minutes after midnight, he stirred and asked where he was. Eager to resume their mind-shattering sexual exploits, Dorothy Faye tested Jonathan with her hands, lips and tongue, but he remained flaccid. Defeated, she commanded him to dress and leave, and when she figured he was sufficiently far from the building in which she lived, she restored his will and self-awareness.

"Now what?" she said to the silence that engulfed her. "I feel as if I've been celibate for a decade. I never used to feel like this. How am I going to find a man who's Jonathan's equal?" She didn't have to wait long.

Dorothy Faye went to church Sunday with

the intention of asking forgiveness for her sin against Jonathan.

"Excuse me," a man said as she was leaving the sanctuary after the sermon. "I didn't mean to step on your foot."

She looked at the man, and her heartbeat seemed to slow down until it almost stopped. Another one. A man who could make a woman climb the walls and dance on the ceiling. "Come with me," she said, forgetting the preacher's words about using people. "I want you. You come with me."

He seemed uneasy. "My wife's waiting for me. I told her I'd be home by eleven o'clock. If I'm late —"

"You don't have to tell me. She'll raise hell. But she likes the way you put it down, so she'll get over it. You're coming with me."

As she did with Jonathan, she stopped at a gourmet delicatessen and bought food, and as soon as they entered her apartment, she prepared the meal while he showered as she commanded.

After the meal, she stood behind his chair, massaging his neck and shoulders. "I'll get you a scotch and soda and you'll feel great." When he didn't respond, she sat on his lap, released her left breast, and put her left hand behind his head. "I want you to enjoy yourself. Here, have some dessert." He pulled the nipple into his mouth, released a harsh groan and sucked vigorously. She thought she'd lose her mind.

"You know what to do with a willing woman? Well, do it," she told him.

He put her on the broadloom that covered the floor of her dining room, and stood over her, breath shooting from his nostrils like a chimney belching bituminous waste. He settled himself on her belly and prepared to be selfish, but one look from her rid him of the idea and he became her willing servant. Eight hours later, when he thought she'd fallen asleep, he attempted to crawl out of her bedroom, but she stopped him, flipped the weakened man over on his back, climbed on him and rocked him mercilessly.

"Why don't you just kill me?" he asked her. "I have to go home to my wife, and she'll want two or three rounds from me. I can't stand it."

"You wouldn't be so tired if you hadn't spent half of last night cheating on your wife."

"I know, and I'm never going to have sex with anybody again. I don't want anybody to mention sex to me."

"My nipple itches. I want you to soothe it."

Dorothy Faye's latest victim folded his six-foot frame into a fetal position and cried uncontrollably.

Three hours later, she managed to get him

out of her apartment, into a taxi and to send him home to his wife. However, the upshot of that encounter was the certainty — from the looks and behavior of the doormen the next day — that she needed privacy. She needed the sex, and she intended to get it.

Boy, this is fun. Imagine, getting all I want whenever I want it, and without taking a chance that the guy will be a dud. Tomorrow, I'm going to get an agent to sell this apartment and find me a house well enough separated from other houses so that I'll have as much privacy as I need. I'm young. So why shouldn't I have all the good sex I want. Until I got my special powers, I didn't know what an orgasm was, and almost half a dozen men had gotten their kicks at my expense. But not anymore. From now on, I call the shots, and I'll get it when I want it and how I want it. Not a man can resist me. And if one tries, as poor Orin did tonight, I'll wear him out. Boy, was that guy putting it down!

After a careful search in the telephone directory, Dorothy Faye settled on the Hamilton Real Estate Agency and requested an appointment. She concentrated intensely in order to "see" whether she was making the right move, got no negative vibes and dialed Lance Hamilton's number.

"Hello. This is Lance Hamilton."

"Mr. Hamilton, I'm Dorothy Faye Hodge. I want to sell my condominium and buy a house in an upper middle-class neighborhood where houses are widely separated, and I want to move as soon as possible."

"I see." His voice, deep and sonorous, scattered her nerves so badly that she couldn't sit still, but began to pace the floor. She thought of a cat on the prowl and immediately began to feel like one. "Any special reason for the rush?" he asked her. "Or would you rather not say?"

"There's a reason, and I'd rather not say." Ever since she had discovered her other self, she'd had an almost demonic drive to tell the truth, and the urge seemed to come from somewhere beyond her. She told herself that Lance Hamilton didn't need to have personal information about her, and that she should button up her mouth.

"Can you be here in an hour, Ms. Hodge?"

"Make it an hour and fifteen minutes. I'll be there."

She hung up, canceled appointments with her afternoon students and changed her clothes. She left her apartment dressed in red, from her bikini panties to the silk-jersey wrap dress the length of which suggested a shortage of fabric. Her spike-heel shoes made her long legs look longer, and from her perfume one would guess that she was very wealthy, had a rich lover or was a clever shoplifter.

She tripped up the walk to the one-story brick building at 227 Lofton Street, eager to meet the man who would be her next victim and, in case any of Hamilton's associates walked behind her, she wiggled with all the agility she could muster. To her mind, image was everything. If Hamilton wore out, there would be another one close at hand. Shivers of delight and wild anticipation flushed through her body. Seconds before she rang the bell, she told herself to concentrate. This man was a humdinger, the kingpin of all studs, and she meant to enjoy him, to get everything he had to offer, if it took a week.

She rang the bell and waited as an eerie sensation, a feeling that she ventured toward uncharted waters, settled over her. Guessing that a full minute had passed, she glanced at her watch, noted that she was within the hour and fifteen minutes, and assumed that he hadn't left his office. Never a patient person, she shifted from one foot to the other, and as she extended her finger to ring the bell again, this time harder and persistently, the door opened and the unsettling gaze of the most handsome man she'd ever seen stared down at her.

"Come in, Ms. Hodge. I've been waiting for you."

The words *Then what took you so long to open the door?* came to her lips, but what she said was, "How do you do, Mr. Hamilton. Who works here with you?"

"Follow me, Ms. Hodge. Several people work here with me, but in case you forgot, this is Memorial Day, a holiday." He pointed to an open door that led to an office. "We'll talk in here."

But Dorothy Faye's interest in selling her condominium and buying a house was now on the back burner of her mind. "Yes," she said. "I forgot about the holiday." He pointed to a chair beside a mahogany desk, massive and masculine, and she eased into it, crossed her knees and began to swing one of her long and shapely legs.

He sat behind his desk, relaxed, composed and in command. Just the kind of man she liked, a man who knew what to do and how to do it. "What price house are you looking for?" She licked her lips in anticipation of her feast, for she meant to have him in every way a woman could have a man. She imagined herself starting with his sleepy, grayish-brown, long-lashed eyes and kissing her way down his long, six-foot-four-inch frame, toying with his navel, kissing and licking the insides of his thighs until he begged for mercy and then slipping him into her mouth and torturing him until he was hers and hers alone.

A smile engaged his mouth but didn't reach his eyes. "How much do you plan to pay for the house?"

"We can deal with that later." She leaned back in the chair. "Come here."

He raised one eyebrow and wrote something on a lined yellow writing tablet. Then, he crossed his legs and grinned, and her heart took off in a wild gallop. If that weren't enough, every muscle in her body seemed to pulsate with anticipation. She told herself that he'd be hard to handle, but she meant to have him if it took a week. She closed her eyes and concentrated in an effort to take his willpower from him, and when she opened her eyes, his mesmerizing face, his entire bearing seemed to her the epitome of seduction.

"No," he said. "You come over here to me." She didn't move, unable to believe that she hadn't captured his energy and self-control. "I said, come here!" It was a command.

Suddenly she had the sensation of him moving inside her, giving her all the thrill of a genuine orgasm. She gripped the arm of the chair, closed her eyes and gave in to it.

"Now, come here to me," he commanded when the sensation died away. She walked over to him and stood in front of him.

"Sit in my lap."

"I won't do it. Who are you that you should tell me what to do?"

"If you think you can twist me around your finger and make me your lackey, babe, you're way off. You want me, and you want me badly enough to fight for me, but if I get inside of you, it will be on my terms. What will it be? Wouldn't you love to know what it's like to have a man who knows his business take you around the work, giving it to you until you think you've died and gone to heaven? Huh?"

"Who do you think you are? You can't make me do a thing I don't want to do," she said, although she hardly believed her own words. Try to concentrate, she told herself and, although she tried, she knew she'd failed when he grinned at her and winked.

"I told you to sit on my lap and if you don't, I'm not going to touch you."

Where was the blue-eyed blonde who had alerted her to her powers? She wanted Lance Hamilton, and she wanted him not on his terms but on hers. She stared at him for a second. Then, her gaze slowly drifted to his thighs and, as if propelled on a Ouija board, she slowly lowered herself to his lap.

"Nice, isn't it?" He eased one of his big hands into her blouse, released her left breast, lowered his head and pulled her nipple into his mouth. She thought she'd die from the thrill of his sucking and biting, but when he parted her legs and began to massage her, she went limp in his arms.

"What do you want now?" he asked her, but she didn't fool herself. She knew that it was he who controlled the game.

"Why do you ask me?" she managed to whisper. "I want everything you can give me. Everything. I want you to make me feel every way that a woman can feel."

"Wait a minute. You don't mean that, Dorothy Faye. You want me to make you feel *good.* Right?"

"You know what I mean," she said, and began to twist her body, anxious for sexual fulfillment. "Stop playing with me. Get into me. Now." She began to unbutton her blouse. He finished the job, unhooked her bra and bared her breasts. She offered herself, and he obliged, sucking and twirling his tongue, heating her to boiling point.

"Come on," she panted. "Finish it. I need it."

He released her breast, fastened her bra and buttoned her blouse, stood and lowered her feet to the floor. "I don't think so, Dorothy Faye. My self-pride won't allow me to use my body as if I'm a rutting deer. If you really want to sell your apartment and buy a house, call this number tomorrow morning. Matt will be glad to have your business."

Still in sexual overdrive, and frustrated as she'd never been before, she found her way out of the building and walked down Lofton Street not thinking or caring where it would lead. What had happened? She knew that she still had her special powers, but he had overpowered her, and then the man had mercilessly reduced her to putty and heated her until she'd responded with an orgasm that felt as if he'd been storming inside of her.

She walked until she reached the Monocacy River, stopped and took a deep breath, relieved, of what she didn't know.

Sitting on a boulder facing the river, she picked up small stones and threw them into the stream.

"What have you been doing?"

At the sound of that voice, Dorothy Faye whipped around. "Who are you? I've asked you twice already, and all you tell me is that I'm one of you. And then this thing grips me, and I see a man I know is a stud and become a nymphomaniac. I don't understand this psychic behavior or this craving for sex. I never liked sex because my few experiences with it left me unsatisfied. Why have you done this to me?"

The blonde stood behind her, but when she

turned back toward the river, the blonde then stood before her. Wherever she turned, she saw the woman. "Please leave me alone."

"Why are you irritated? As long as you could victimize any man you wanted, you showed no mercy. You met one who denied you, and you're beside yourself. Don't you recognize justice when you see it?"

"I don't know. I've never done an immoral thing when I've been my normal self."

"I know that," the blonde said. "That's why I stopped you."

Dorothy Faye didn't like to beg, and she'd never been flush with respect for beggars who were not in dire need, but she prepared to get on her knees, if necessary, and beg the blonde.

"May I please be my old self again?" she asked. "I don't want any special powers, and I don't want to control men. I just want to be my old self again. Please!"

The blonde shook her head so sadly that fear raced through Dorothy Faye. "I'm sorry, Dorothy Faye, but that isn't possible. You can't return to your former self any more than Superman can return to Krypton."

"But —"

The blonde looked into the distance. "None of us can. I am sentenced to counsel all of us, and so I roam the world. You, at least, can lead a normal life. We belong to the ancient Celtic tribe of Wufferts, who have walked this earth since before the Druids, four thousand years before the birth of Christ. Every two or three hundred years, some of us appear somewhere on the earth. We begin life as normal people, but eventually we find our heritage. We are scattered all over the world. You will encounter us in every race and culture."

"But if you're here to counsel us, why can't you help me get rid of this, this —"

The blonde seemed to lose patience and interrupted Dorothy Faye. "Have you not heard a word I said? You are a sister of the occult, a Wuffert. You need sex, as all we Wufferts do. But you must learn to keep it between the lines. You are out of control."

"I couldn't help it."

"Oh, yes, you could have. Now, you're hot after Lance Hamilton. I wish you luck."

"I couldn't control him. He refused to let me bend his will, and he left me hot and hungry."

"Because you deserved it."

"But —"

The blonde bunched her shoulders in a careless shrug. "If you want him, go back to him and get it straightened out."

"He won't want to . . ." She released a loud gasp. The blonde was nowhere to be seen.

Maybe it was all an apparition.

"Don't even think it," the familiar voice said.

Dorothy Faye went home and telephoned Lance Hamilton. "This is Dorothy Faye Hodge. I need to talk with you, and I promise not to get out of line."

"All right. Be at my office tomorrow morning at ten. See you then."

Dorothy Faye dressed with care that morning. She wore the only dress she owned whose skirt reached her kneecaps, brushed her hair into a conservative style, put on a pair of two-inch heels, as much perfume as she dared, got into her car and headed for the Hamilton Real Estate Agency.

Lance Hamilton answered the door on the first ring, causing a sharp rise in both her temperature and her expectations. "Hi," he said, so casually that she wondered if he was ready to acquiesce. "You're punctual. That has always appealed to me. Have a seat. What did you want to talk about?"

Her eyes widened. The man didn't give an inch. Well, she had a lot to gain by leveling with him. "Have you ever heard of the Wufferts?"

He leaned back in his chair and eyed her with such intensity that she felt as if she were transported out of herself. "Yes, I have."

She took a deep breath. "I'm one of them."

198

His lack of a reaction added to her growing discomfort. "I said I'm one of them."

"I know that," he countered, and she nearly jumped from her chair. He continued. "So am I. Didn't you wonder why you couldn't master my will? A Wuffert can control a Wuffert, though no one else can. It's been that way for over six thousand years." She was standing now. He said, "Don't let yourself become irritated."

"But you toyed with me. You —"

"I taught you a good lesson. Treat others the way you want to be treated. You're not entitled to have every man you desire just because you want him. A man has a right to the privacy of his person, just as you have."

"You were far more merciless with me. At least I satisfied the men I seduced. What about me? What about us? I'm still on fire for you."

"So far you have used your talent only to bring men to heel, to make them your sex slave. That is not acceptable. You must learn self-discipline. And you must learn to use your powers for good, as I was once forced to do. Perhaps then, you and I can get together."

That's the absolute truth, Joy. Dorothy Faye's too arrogant to lie. Besides, she's given me proof of her abilities. I don't know whether she'll get her act together enough to impress Lance Hamilton, but the poor sister sure wants him badly enough to mend her ways. At least, that's the way it seems to me. But, Joy, the whole story scared the willies out of me. I don't want anybody telling me I'm a Wuffert. I'm crazy enough about sex as it is. You keep up the good work, Joy.

Sincerely yours,
Grace L.

A Wuffert! WTF. For those of you who don't know, WTF stands for What the fuck! I toss the letter to the side and shake off a sudden chill that's shimmying along my spine. Quickly I take a look around like something might have slipped in while I wasn't looking. I dare to steal a glance at the letter that stares back at me accusingly from the corner.

See what I mean, crazy shit and crazier people day in and day out. I shudder and dart to the kitchen for another cup of coffee just as my phone rings and scares the crap out of me.

It's Macy. Thank God. I lean against the wall.

"Whatsup, girl?"

"Calling to check on you. Any more word about the attempted suicide?"

"Naw. And I hope not. I'm sure we'll be getting a ton of e-mails about it. But hey, we did what we could, the asshole didn't get a chance to off herself." I laugh even though we both know it's not funny.

"I was wondering if you wanted to do lunch," Macy asks in a bad upper-crust accent.

I laugh. "Yeah, I think getting out of the house would do me a world of good."

"Why, did something happen?"

Macy could always read me even way the hell on the other end of the phone line. I tell her about the letter I just read.

"Dayum. You think that mess is true?"

"Who the hell knows?" I rub my hands up and down my arms and look around again. I knew I loved sex — a lot. But jeez, I almost felt like going to church or something. "Listen, you wanna come by here and pick me up? I want to get through a couple more letters, see if there is anything I want to use for tonight's show."

"Cool. I'll come by about two. We can hang out and then go straight to the station. I need to do some shopping anyway."

Shopping! Now that was something to take my mind off things. "Perfect. I saw a pair of Jimmy Choos that I must have."

Macy chuckles. "Girl, you and your shoes."

"Don't hate," I tease. "I need a new pair for the awards banquet tomorrow night. See you at two."

"Bring a couple of letters. We can go over them at lunch."

"No problem. See ya." I hang up, feeling better already.

Promptly at two my front doorbell rings, and me and Macy head off for our day of frivolity.

As we walk along Fifth Avenue, the Rodeo Drive of the East Coast, I ask Macy, "Did you ever think me and you would get this far?"

"Hell no. You kiddin' me." She shakes her head and hooks her arm through mine. "We had it rough, girl." She sighs softly. "Sometimes I still think it's all a dream."

"Me, too."

"But you did it, Joy. You made up your mind you were getting up and getting out."

A flash of our life in the projects rushes through my head: the pissy hallways, the broken elevators, crack vials littering the concrete lawns, drive-bys and, oh yeah, the rapes. Can't forget those — in my house and out.

"You took me with you, though." She

tightens her arm around mine and pushes all the ugly away, even the ugly that Macy knew nothing about. I drape my arm around her shoulder and plant a kiss on the top of her head, and no I don't give a fuck if somebody thinks we're gay. Macy is my girl, remember. My one and only friend.

"Sisters till the end," I say.

"Holla."

We both laugh. Life actually ain't half-bad if you have a friend.

With our bellies full, loaded down with shopping bags and our spirits lifted, we head off to the studio for another night of fun and games.

CHAPTER 11

When we arrive at the station folks are still buzzing about the antics from the night before and giving me everything from high fives and thumbs-ups to disgusted shakes of the head (those are the haters). But all I want to see are the ratings, which my trusty intern hands to me on my way to my tiny-ass office. I toss my jacket and purse on what pretends to be a couch while I scan Arbitron. Hot damn! Still number uno. I do a little victory dance around my desk just as Macy pokes her head in.

"Still at the top, I take it." She's grinning.

"You got that right, my sister," I reply with a shake of my hips from side to side. "Highest ratings this season so far. The wilder the ride the higher the ratings." I follow her out of the office and into the booth.

Me and Macy prepare for the show, getting all of our cues in sync. I have my letters lined up and I wait for my countdown.

Like I said earlier, in order to make it onto my show the letters have to read like a soap opera and the letter I've chosen to kick the show off is called Torn.

Five, four, three, two . . .

"Hey out there, radio-land. I'm Joy Newhouse all up in *your* house and you're listening to the number-one late-night show *On the Line.* As always, we have an action-packed night in store for you, so put up your feet and get all those underaged crumb snatchers away from the sound of my voice! Holla.

"Our first letter tonight is from a sister who, for lack of a better word, is screwed up — and I mean that in the kindest sense. Anyhow, her letter is titled Torn and by the time I'm finished you'll understand why.

Dear Joy,

Let me start off by saying I'm a bit spoiled. A woman's value is often weighed by how she looks. People have told me that I'm fly for as long as I can remember. I can't deny my looks have made my life easy, at least as far as men are concerned. I'm a high-dollar girl in a high-dollar world and I always get paid.

I'm naturally petite, with smooth, light, honey-colored skin, small, regular features, big, long-lashed eyes and pouty lips. My hair is long, almost to my waist with a non-kinky, wavy grade, thanks to my unknown Mexican father.

Women have never liked me much, and I can't say I blame them. The Lord has blessed me in unfair quantities and quality.

Black men particularly dig me. They can't believe my hair isn't a weave. They always ask me what I'm mixed with. I've always had any brotha I wanted. My tastes in men are very specific.

Obviously, it's most important that they have money to spend on me. But other than that, I like dark-skinned, muscular men with big, hard bodies and big hard dicks. My men have to be hung. I don't have time for less than eight inches. I like them hot, wild and a little danger-ous. I used to keep a thug with money by my side, but I've been burned in the cross fire.

I decided I needed to play it safe and went to the state college. A professor paid my tuition, including dorm room and board for the entire year. Yeah, I attended Cal State on a pussy scholarship.

The ballplayers were right up my alley. I got on the cheerleading squad. School was bor-ing, so when senior Bobby Benson got the NFL draft, I decided that was my ticket. He was dark, big, bad and packed a full nine inches, plus the two-mil salary didn't hurt a bit.

We married the June after my freshman year. I never went back to school. We relocated to the Midwest. We bought a big-ass house, one of those Colonial-looking things in the suburbs. I drove the Mercedes convertible and Bobby drove the Ferrari.

Bobby got a good contract, but he's just starting out in the NFL. We were in hock, but I picked a star, and I knew the money was gonna be all uphill from there.

All these bitches were shaking their asses at my man, but I made sure he was hooked. See, most bitches don't understand that looking good is just part of the equation. A man wants a challenge. He doesn't want a bitch that is just going to roll over and stick her legs in the air, eternally in heat. He wants a woman all the other dogs are sniffing at, a woman he never quite knows, a woman he has to work to hold.

I know I'm fine, but I have an edge over all the other fine bitches that spread their legs without getting paid the way I've always been paid. Maintaining my mystery and self-confidence has always been crucial. It's a lot tougher than any game with a ball. But to play the game with a man and win, I can't afford weakness. I never let down my guard, never

confide, and never expose myself without cal-
culation.

I play Bobby like a testosterone-laden pup-
pet. I give it to him good, freaky-deak if he
wanted it that way, but never on his demand. I
left him wanting and kept him begging for my
pussy like those mice that press the lever
incessantly when randomly awarded.

Bobby could almost come in his pants just
looking at me, no mean feat after two years of
marriage. The money got better, the debt got
paid, and Bobby was on the road most of the
time.

Life was good, but I was lonely out here in
white suburbia. Bobby tells me my job is to
stay beautiful for him. I pass the time shopping and in the spas and working out a couple
hours a day. The white bitches bore the fuck
out of me, and they want to put the drop on
my man as much as any other bitch. I've
always depended on men for companionship.
For some reason women have never liked me
much. Go figure.

Bobby also tells me I'll be busy enough
when I start this huge family he wants. Six
kids! He has to be kidding. He definitely married the wrong bitch, but as long as he doesn't
realize that, it's cool. I took my birth control
pills like they were my new religion.

Bobby was on the road when I met Yolanda

in the gym. She was a personal trainer, not mine, but I'd been watching her small, trim, muscular body with admiration.

I was in the shower when she came in, buck naked. I watched her soap her cream-almond skin out of the corner of my eye. She looked even better without clothes, smooth white skin, and not a ripple on her that wasn't firm. Her breasts were full and high. Perfect. She wore her blond hair short and, according to what was in between her thighs, it was natural.

Her face had a fey, delicate look, belied by the strength of the muscles in her back when they flexed. She let the water sluice through her hair and over her face. Her eyes opened and she caught me staring. They were blue, clear, ice-blue.

"My name is Yolanda," she said.

I stepped out from under the spray and grabbed a towel from the hook. "Stephanie."

A flush heated my cheeks as she took her time assessing my body. "Pretty Stephanie," she said, a slash of a dimple creasing her left cheek.

"You're not too bad yourself." I felt the need for banter to alleviate the strange tension growing between us. "Have you been training here long?"

"Around six months."

I knew. I'd been watching her ever since

she'd arrived. "I've been in the neighborhood for about two years."

She turned off the shower and approached, making no move to grab a towel or cover her body. Drops of water ran down her breasts, glistening on her pink-brown nipples for a moment before dropping to the floor.

"Nice to meet you, Stephanie. Do you have plans for lunch? I'm starving." Her voice was husky, inviting.

My brows shot up. "We hardly know each other," I said, only partly kidding.

"We don't know each other at all. But since we are going to get to know each other very well, why not do it comfortably over a good meal?" She smiled at me slow and lazy as she finally reached for a towel and rubbed it over her taut abdomen. Water trickled down her lower belly and disappeared into the hidden golden-bronze brush between her legs, only slightly trimmed.

My stomach tightened. "Lunch sounds great."

She took me to one of the best restaurants in the area. I felt a little uncomfortable dressed as casually as I was, in warm-ups, even though they were designer duds. But the maître d' seemed to know her and led us to a good table.

Yolanda didn't glance at the menu, but told the waiter she wanted water with lemon, and the grilled-vegetable salad. I said I wanted the same and she smiled at me. "Vegetarian is the way to go. I used to be fifty pounds heavier than I am now."

"I can't believe it. You look really great."

"Thanks. This body is a product of sweat, tears and probably more than a little blood."

The waiter set our lemon-scented water in front of us. Yolanda took a sip and settled back, her ice-blue gaze meeting mine. "So what's your story?"

"My story?"

"Yes. Tell me all about you."

"I don't know if we have time for that."

"We'll make the time."

I chuckled, uncomfortable. I hadn't spent a lot of time with girlfriends, but this banter was feeling too familiar, like what happened between me and a man.

"I'm married to Bobby Benson."

"Congratulations." Her teeth gleamed white. "I figured you weren't a working girl, given the amount of time you spend at the gym."

"No. We've been married almost two years. He's on the road now."

"Do you ever travel with him?"

I shifted. I used to travel with Bobby, right after we got married. But then he didn't really

211

want me to and, to be frank, it was boring and inconvenient. I wasn't worried about the bitches he did on the road, because he was well aware of what he had waiting at home. We spend a lot of time apart, and I liked it like that.

Bobby came home to check up on me frequently. He didn't quite trust me and that was the way it should be. If a man completely trusts a beautiful woman, something is wrong. Bobby wanted me at home, sitting on the imaginary pedestal he had me on in his mind, tending to his pussy, keeping it on ice and ready whenever he wanted it. He was getting tiresome with the notion I was to start churning out babies like he didn't have skanks all across the country trying to get pregnant by him to get a shot at some paternity money.

At least without children, I could fool myself I was free.

"Stephanie?"

The waiter had slipped our dishes of grilled vegetables on the table with a variety of dips and sauces on the plate. It smelled delicious.

"I'm sorry, I was thinking about something," I said.

Yolanda picked up a broccoli floret and dipped it into sauce. A drop of pink sauce fell from the broccoli and her tongue flicked out and caught it. I was mesmerized. My heart was pounding. I'd never felt this sort of excitement about a woman before.

"What is your story?" I asked her.

"But you haven't told me yours yet."

"I'm boring."

Her dimple flashed at me again. "I doubt that. I'm a personal trainer," she said. "I have a lot of clients and do all right. I'm not married and I have no children. I live in the moment and at this moment my story is all about you."

She was enchanting.

I ended up at her place. We talked about the stuff I imagine girls talk about — clothes, hair, everything but men. She poured us wine and put on a Jill Scott album. She danced. Her moves were slow and sensuous. I wasn't surprised when she kissed me, 'cause I knew that dance very well and where it leads.

I'd never been kissed by a woman before, but it wasn't unpleasant; it was soft, wet and sexy. Her body was clean and beautiful, both soft and hard. Her skin gleamed like a pearl in the stripes of afternoon sun through the blind slats.

I was curious, okay?

When I let her take me to bed, I thought it would just be another experience, no big deal. But, damn. She took me there, she really did. I'd never come like that in my life, nowhere near. Her tongue, her fingers, her fabulous body against mine worked a special magic I didn't quite recognize, but the taste was sweet. Too sweet. Soft and quaking, full of sighs and whispered screams. And I didn't mind touching her, either. In fact . . . I wanted to.

"I canceled three appointments for you," she whispered in my ear afterwards.

"Was it worth it?"

"Oh, yes."

We reached for each other. Oh yes, it was worth it.

Being with Yolanda was like having the girl-friend I never had, but talk about friends with benefits. I could trust her, tell her anything, and she also played my body with the skill of a virtuoso and I learned to play hers, too.

Something I thought I could only experience reliably alone with my vibrator became com-monplace with her — shaking, quivering orgasms crashing through my body. I was becoming addicted to them, and worse, I was becoming addicted to her.

I'd spent my life alone, despite the men who always wanted inside me. But nobody really wanted to know the real me the way Yolanda did. Nobody ever wanted to see the warts, or any imperfection or weakness that's part of being a real woman. Yolanda and I were real with each other, best friends, sisters, lovers.

I understood my role with men: they wanted Barbie. Sure they said they wanted to know all about me during the initial infatuation, but nothing would burn that infatuation off quicker than if I complied and ruined their illusions. With Yolanda, my guard came down, my defenses breached. There was vulnerability, but there was also a rare feeling. Was it happiness? I didn't know because I wasn't sure how it felt.

It was a couple of months later and Yolanda and I were in bed together, naked. She was on top of me, just starting to roll when Bobby walked in.

I started to scream, but the excited grin stopped me. "This is the best homecoming present any guy could want." He almost choked himself getting out of his shirt.

Yolanda started to open her mouth, but I pleaded silently with her. "Just this once," I whispered.

She snapped her mouth shut, and her eyes narrowed, glinting blue.

"For me?" I added.

When Bobby slipped into the bed, she moved aside to let him in. She allowed him to touch her, fondle her, his hands chocolate-

215

brown against her creamy French-vanilla skin. He licked her like she was made of sugar. I didn't resent, but sat back and watched, a too-familiar fatigue oozing from my bones.

When he tried to enter her, she wouldn't let him. I reached out and guided him to me instead. "Oh yeah, baby," he said, panting and pumping. "I want to see your fingers in your pussy, girl," he said to Yolanda. "Show me that pink pussy."

She hesitated, complied.

I watched Yolanda's eyes as he pounded away on me. She didn't look happy. But she had to understand that Bobby was my meal ticket and a damned generous one. Bobby would be gone soon. I'd take her shopping, buy her some pretty things and things would be all right.

But they weren't.

Bobby came home again, sooner than expected. "Where's your friend?" he asked.

"Which one?"

"You only got one friend, as far as I've ever seen."

I pouted, making sure it was pretty. "Are you saying I'm unlikable?"

"It was one of your best traits, baby. I have you all to myself. But this is even better. It's the best present you've ever given me. Tell her to come by tonight." His hand drifted to

216

the big bulge in his pants. "You know what I want."

"What if she doesn't want the same thing?"

"C'mon. You not going to let me have a taste of the goodies and then pull them away, are you? Seemed like you two had a good time last week. Tell her I'll make it worth her while."

"Bobby, I think she likes women."

His hand caressed the bulge between his legs. It was getting harder. "I like women, too. I'll watch. Bring her over."

"Bobby . . ."

"I'm not asking you," he said, frowning.

The fatigue washed over me again. Bobby wasn't as sweet as he used to be. He was a lot more irritable. I wondered if it was stress or worse, possibly steroids or some crap like that. I knew he was under a lot of stress to succeed. A player is only as good as he plays.

It was something I tried never to forget, but I was getting tired of the game. Whatever. I didn't feel like fighting with him. A happy Bobby is a generous Bobby. I want him on the road again with my credit lines open and my woman alone with me in my bed.

"Mrs. Benson, I want to ask you something," Rosa said.

Rosa is our housekeeper. She's paid well, and since it's just me at home most of the time, her work is light.

I love having a housekeeper. I don't have to put a glass in the dishwasher or a load of laundry into the dryer. Having a full-time housekeeper is better than shopping and using credit cards with unlimited spending limits. It's the one perk I'd have a really hard time doing without. So I only frowned slightly at Rosa interrupting me while I was watching television. It wasn't like I was watching a show or anything. I turned CNN down. "What do you want, Rosa?"

"I want a raise."

"Oh?" Our accountant pays the bills, so I had no clue how Rosa was paid or how much she actually made. "Has it been a long time since you've had a raise?"

"No, Mr. Benson just approved one three months ago."

My eyebrows shot up. "And you want another one?"

"I do," she said, crossing her arms and raising her chin.

"Why is that?"

"Considering what I put up with around here, I think I deserve one."

I blinked at her. The woman must have lost her mind. "Do tell me what you put up with."

"Changing the sheets so much. The fish

smell around here is getting rather overpower-
ing."

Oh no, she didn't. My lips tightened as I
contemplated kicking this Mexican bitch's ass.

"I'm sure now Mr. Benson is home, he would
hate to hear about the increased laundry,"
Rosa said.

The bitch was blackmailing me.

"Don't worry your tiny mind," I replied, my
voice saccharine sweet. "Mr. Benson is well
aware of the amount of laundry we all soil
together."

"I need my raise."

"I don't think so. Since laundry's such a
hardship for you, you best gather your things
and leave my house. I'll have Marty, the accountant, mail your last check."

Rosa flushed red, her fists clenching. I
moved toward the phone and picked up the
receiver. "Or do I need to call the police to
escort you out?"

"Sinful, adulterous, faggot whore! May you
burn in hell!"

Rosa's time with us was clearly over.

I clicked on the dial tone and a second later
I heard the satisfying slam of the front door.

Shit. Now I had to call an agency and
replace her. Fish, indeed. She must be thinking about her own nasty pussy.

My cell rang. It was a text message from Bobby.

I'm warming it up for you and that fine bitch, baby.

It was going to be a long night. I had just clicked my cell closed when the doorbell rang. It was Yolanda.

"No frickin' way," she said, when I asked her about what I needed her to do tonight.

I took her hand. "Please. It keeps him off my back, it keeps him happy."

She pulled her hand away. "I don't give a damn if Bobby Benson's happy or not."

"He's been real testy lately. He closed my account at Bergdorf's. He said I was wasting too much money."

"Maybe you were."

"Don't joke with me. I work hard for every cent I get from that man."

She cocked her head. "No doubt you do work hard, but answer me this. Have you ever had a job?"

"A job? Please. I married Bobby after my first year of college."

"Why didn't you finish?"

"For what? I have everything I want."

"But you're dependent on a man."

"Humph. I say Bobby's dependent on me."

"Don't lie to yourself. You had it right when you said you work hard for your money." She caressed the curve of my breast and my eyes closed as a wash of pleasure started through me. "Don't you ever want to be free?"

"I need you to do this for me."

She leaned into my kiss. Then she pulled back, looking into my eyes. "I can't."

"Do you realize how hard this is going to make it for us?" I pulled away from her. "If you don't want to work with me, maybe I can't be there for you, either."

"Are you threatening me?"

"No, it's not like that. I'm asking you to do something for me. This relationship needs to go both ways. You don't have to fuck him. He just wants to see us make love." I caressed her face. "We can do that." I leaned to her ear. "We can do that now."

"Okay," she said, a long sigh at the end.

I thought I could have all the goodies I wanted and eat them, too.

After we made love, we relaxed in the Jacuzzi. I leaned my head back, feeling happy for . . . the first time in a while, I think.

"This is the last time I'm doing this, Stephanie. You have to come clean with Bobby. You don't love him. I know you don't. You only love his money."

"How do you know I don't love my husband?"

"Please." She chuckled. "He's nothing but a meal ticket to you. I know who you love."

I blinked at her. She was right. I loved her perfect body, the way she made me feel. I

221

loved the orgasms that a man could only give me occasionally, but crashed through me with excruciating sweetness every time I made love with her. I loved when we talked; she actually listened to what I said. I loved the way it felt that she cared about who I was, even my flaws. I loved how she saw all of me, my selfishness, my laziness, everything, and still she cared. I knew she'd still be there if I got fat, ugly, hurt. And I'd be there for her, too. This was real.

"I love you, too," she said. "But you gotta let him go, Steph. You gotta stand on your own two feet."

The water was getting cold. "There's more to it, more than you think."

"What more than your addiction to credit cards with high spending limits and household help?"

I had it all worked out in my mind, the way I wanted to tell her. This wasn't the way it was supposed to play out. "I need you," I whispered.

"I need you, too."

"You don't understand."

"Understand what, baby?"

"I wanted you to help me, to keep everything going, to keep him happy."

"We don't need him, baby. We only need each other. We'll be fine." She waved her

222

hand. "All this never made you happy. I know it doesn't. Only I make you happy."

"We do need him. It's more complicated than you think. Way more complicated." I bowed my head and my tears dropped into the fading bubbles.

I felt her warm, wet, silk skin against mine, her lips on my cheek, tasting my tears. "Love is never that complicated," she said. "We only make it that way. We need to get out of here." I know she meant more than the tub.

"I'm pregnant."

She sucked in a breath. "Are you sure?"

I nodded. "I can't do this by myself."

"You can —"

"I can't! Don't you understand? I don't want to be like my mother and her mother before her, scrabbling and scrapping and raising my babies all alone. I want better. I worked for better — I deserve better!"

"I thought you were on the Pill?"

"I am."

"Where do you keep them?"

I pointed to the medicine cabinet.

"Are you sure you're pregnant?" she asked.

"I just saw the doctor. It's a month."

"Then you can get rid of it."

I shot her a glance. "No, I can't."

"It would be the easy thing to do. Then you would be free."

"This is my baby. I'm not getting rid of it. Besides, Bobby would probably fight me for custody."

She stood, water cascading off her glorious body. "Okay. That's cool." She wrapped a towel around her. "Maybe you should consider getting rid of him then."

I drew in a breath. It was crystal clear in front of me, as ice-blue as her eyes. With Bobby gone, so was his earning potential, but his money would be mine, including the generous insurance settlements I'd get.

I shook my head. I was considering the unthinkable. "How could I?"

"Does he have any allergies?"

"No."

"Take any drugs?"

"I suspect he takes steroids. But I never see him do it. We need to stop talking about this. I'm not allowing my baby to be raised by somebody else while I spend the rest of my life in prison."

"I'll take care of everything. It'll be on me, and it's fool-proof."

I stared at Yolanda, opened my mouth and then closed it.

She laid a finger across my lips. "Shh. No details, no knowledge and you'll be fine. Nobody knows about us."

I thought about Rosa. Somebody knew.

"He's going to be home soon," I said, desperate to change the subject. "Are you staying? He only wants to watch."

A smile curved her lips. "I wouldn't miss it for the world."

I was frightened by the look on her face. I didn't love Bobby, but he was the father of my child-to-be. I didn't know the Yolanda who talked casually about getting rid of people. I wasn't sure I wanted to know her.

Three hours later, a thundering orgasm from Yolanda's tongue and fingers crashed through my body. The tremors caused my insides to quake and squeeze in painful pleasure. Bobby had his big, rock-hard dick out and was stroking it frantically, up and down with his fist. He grabbed Yolanda. I heard her protest, but I could hardly move, I was so drained.

He flipped her on her back and drove long, deep strokes into her pussy, his ass moving like a well-oiled piston. She screamed and fought him, her nails leaving red gouges on his shoulder. I don't think he heard her or felt anything but the feel of her pussy against his dick.

I lifted myself up on my knees and tried to pull him off Yolanda, but there was no stopping him. He was like a freight train, bent on his one destination.

He was doing her good and hard, and most women could have got into it, but not her. It was as if she deflated, and she looked at me, fury mixed with resignation in her eyes.

He started to pound even harder, grinding against her clit, yelling deep-throated, "I'm fucking you good, bitch, tell me I'm fucking you good."

There was hatred in Yolanda's eyes as she stared at him, tight-lipped.

Then he gave a final roar and collapsed on her body. "Damn, that was good," he muttered.

She pushed him off her and scrambled away. I reached for her, but she backed away.

She pulled on her clothes. "Never again," she said, as she headed for the door. "Never again." She looked at him with such venomous hatred, I felt I didn't know her, couldn't know her.

I stared at Bobby, lying on the bed, contented as a baby. He was a man, just a man. He lived up to my expectations of him, which had never been much. I had no idea of what he was capable of as far as love. I'd never loved him, or allowed his love to touch me. It was always a game, a front.

How would Bobby be as a father? Would he rise to the challenge? Would he love and take pride in his child, or would he be absent and neglectful, on the road, screwing other women, spending his time anywhere and everywhere but with his family?

Was a man capable of loving me like Yolanda did? Was it possible? I couldn't imagine a man accepting me as is, unconditionally. Would I be able to live without the love I'd only just discovered with Yolanda?

I looked at Bobby and remembered the hatred on Yolanda's face. I was scared.

What was I going to do? I knew she was going to kill him if I didn't stop her. And for Yolanda, the one who hated as passionately as she loved, I knew there was no stopping with mere words and pleas.

Never again.

The only way to save Bobby without sacrificing Yolanda would be to leave him. But would that be sacrificing my baby and my hopes and dreams to be with a woman capable of . . . ? I shuddered, remembering what I saw in Yolanda's face.

Bobby was asleep. What if I told him and became vulnerable with him for the first time? *Could he, would he* protect himself from Yolanda without hurting her? *Could he, would he* love me?

Could I stay away from Yolanda? Would I?

I buried my face in my arms and sobbed. When I finally pulled myself together enough,

I sat down and wrote this letter. So, Joy, so fly yourself, so together, so know-it-all, what's a girl to do?

I blow out a breath. "There you have it, listeners. A sister playing both sides of the fence — for real. Like the old saying goes — hell hath no fury like a woman scorned. My advice is get away from the crazy bitch posthaste. Take your little savings, what's left of your dignity and your life and get to stepping. All your good looks and good hair won't mean jack if we have to look at you in a box. Like I tell all my listeners we want to hear *from* you not read *about* you. You get my drift? We'll be taking calls right after this commercial break."

The balance of the night was tame in comparison to some. We were flooded with e-mails and phone calls offering advice to our bisexual honeypot, everything from keep the man to stay with the woman and anything in between. The consensus was that she was in over her head and that Ms. Yolanda would never mean her any good. Nobody needed that kind of loving, I don't give a hoot how great the sex is. She could smack it, flip it, rub it down, but killing somebody over some booty — that's where I draw the line.

"Going straight home?" Macy asks as we meet in the corridor.

I yawn. "Yeah. I thought about hanging out for a while, but I want to actually sleep tonight."

We walk to the elevator, waving good-night to the graveyard shift.

"You decide what you're going to wear to the banquet?" Macy asks me once we are down in the parking garage.

"I'm pretty much decided on the red number. I've been dieting my ass off to make sure I can fit in that bad boy."

Macy laughs. "Girl, you need to diet like I need a bigger behind."

I had nightmares and daymares about one day looking like the other women in my dysfunctional family — unable to wear anything other than a flowered shift and open-toed, rubber-soled shoes. I shiver at the image.

Since we took Macy's car earlier, she drops me off in front of my building. I lean over the gears to share our usual parting hug then, out of the blue, I ask her, "Hey, Mac, you ever think about being with a woman?"

She cocks a brow at me. "Uh, no. I'm strictly dickley as the saying goes. You?"

"Naw. But I'm just thinking about that

woman's letter tonight. Could it be that good?"

"Ain't nothing that good, and if it is I don't want to know about it."

We high-five and I get out. "See you tomorrow."

"Lata!" She jets off as if the judge just fired the starter pistol. I shake my head, walk inside. Another day bites the dust.

When I reach the front desk, the night watchman stops me.

"Ms. Newhouse, there was a delivery for you earlier."

I frown. I wasn't expecting anything. I'd sworn off of shopping online for a while, so I couldn't imagine what it would be.

He goes behind the desk and comes up with an enormous arrangement of the most exquisite roses in a rainbow of colors. I actually gasp like they do in those romance novels. I can't even see the watchman's face as he brings them to me.

"Would you like me to take these up for you?" he huffs.

"Uh, yes. Please." I try to see if there's a card but can't through all the flora.

We get up to my place and I instruct him to set them down on the long table in the foyer. I dig in my bag for a five and hand it to him. "Thanks." I want to call him Jeeves, but don't. The minute he's out the door, I rifle through the blooms and locate a tiny white card.

Dear Joy, These in no way compare to your beauty but do enjoy them. Randy.

I drop the card on the floor as if it had caught fire. Frantically I look around. No sign that anyone has been there. WTF. Randy was beginning to give me the willies. Shit, that word made me think about Wufferts. Jeez. I rub my brow. Suppose he was some crazy loon like Yolanda? Maybe Macy was right about me letting strange men up in my apartment.

I pick up an umbrella from the rack and tiptoe to the back of my apartment — just in case. Between the nutty listeners and now Randy . . . I needed a vacation.

Needless to say, I'm sleeping with the light on.

CHAPTER 12

The previous night left me so rattled that I didn't even bother going over any letters for the evening's show. Let the intern earn her non-salary. I'm grumpy and irritable when I arrive at the station and in no mood for chitchat. On the entire ride over I kept checking my rearview mirror, thinking that at any moment a strange black van was going to pull over, snatch me out of my ride and I would disappear forever. I don't even bother with pleasantries for Macy, who could tell right off that I was not in the mood. That's the good thing about having someone who knows you like the corns on their feet.

I settle myself down, adjust my headset and wait for my cue. Whoever had the balls to call in tonight was going to get an earful, that's for sure.

The track "On and On" from Erykah Badu fades as I bob my head. We're off commercial break and on to our show. I prepare my oh-so-pleasant on-air voice for another go at it.

The broadcasting banquet is tomorrow and yours truly is nominated for the fourth consecutive year. I keep that on my mind and push the other crazy mess "to the left, to the left."

"Today's topic is . . ." I look at Macy as my mind comes back to business. She shrugs and glares at the intern, who puts down her bag from Mickey D's where I know she forgot my salad dressing. I need some flavor with my rabbit food. On a Mc-Napkin, she hastily scribbles . . .

"I have it. How could I forget? People in relationships where they've discovered a secret . . ." I pause.

She didn't forget the dressing. I grin at her. She smirks.

"Something unknown about their significant other that has just come to light. So, let's hear it, people. What's on your mind? What do you have to say? All lines are open. You've got the number, so use it."

The board lights up. Our intern has been screening. Macy and I know the regulars by heart. We give the intern that list to compare. We want someone new to break in on the show. Virgins are fun. She finds them and gives me a thumbs-up.

That's what I'm talkin' 'bout.

The first ones are the usual assortment of the unusual — brothers on the DL (Thank you, Oprah), a pregnancy not attributed to the spouse (Thank you, Maury), a woman in the dark about her boyfriend's bad credit (Thank you, Judge Mathis. And thank you, broke brothers, too). Daytime television, I tell you.

At the top of the next hour, the intern hits pay dirt. This caller is different.

Nervous. Pensive.

Scared?

Scared equals fun.

"Hello? Joy?"

"Please. Call me 'Miss Newhouse.' I hate it when first-timers try to get all cozy. Don't you?" Macy nods and cues the sound effect of screeching brakes.

"Well . . . I apologize."

"I forgive you this time." I sigh, looking at my nails. The tips need some filler. "Now. What is your big revelation for the listeners? I'm sure they are on pins and needles."

"It's not so much a revelation as it is a concern."

"And you called here? *On the Line,* the numero uno radio show in the country? I am so honored."

"Really?"

Is she *really* this dumb?

"No. Now speak . . . um . . . what is your name?"

"Margot."

Margot. Okay. Fake name. "Can I call you Maggie? I just feel in a *Maggie* mood today. Do you ever have those moods? Know what I mean?"

"No. I can't say that I do."

"You don't listen to this station on the regular, do you? I can tell."

"That is correct. I was changing stations and heard you."

"And you were drawn in by my voice," I assert. "You can admit it. I hear it often."

"Yes, but more by what you were asking. I know of you, Miss Newhouse."

"Don't believe everything you hear, but please call me 'Joy.' You're so slow to get to the point that I feel we've known each other forever."

"Thank you, Joy. And I'm sorry about stumbling along. This is unusual for me to call in to these kinds of shows. I have something I just discovered about my husband."

I sigh heavily into my mic; a rumble reverberates through the studio. "Is he gay? 'Cause that is so . . ."

"No," she chuckles. "He's not gay. As far as I know."

"Then what, dearie?"

Her voice lowers. "He's black."

"Come again?"

"I think he's black . . . um African-American."

"Whoa." Macy gives me that shit-eating grin. I run with it. "And by your statement, I assume you are not."

"Correct."

"Are you white?"

"Yes."

"Well, well, well. Someone was 'passing'? Is that what was going on, Maggie? Did your hubby fool ya? Did he pull that 'I got Sicilian in my family' card?"

"I wouldn't say that. I just don't see color when I deal with people."

"Oh lawd. Here it comes. *I don't see color,*" I mock. "Kumbaya, Kumbaya! Uh-huh. We are truly in an enlightened age. But now that you've suddenly *noticed,* you decide to call Miss Joy. Well, you know what . . ."

The intern waves her hands frantically. I'm about to end it, but callers are swarming to get in. Rather than wrapping this one up, I let it ride for a second. Ratings are ratings.

"Listeners, we are in the middle of a bona

fide therapy session. I'm about to get all Dr. Phil with Maggie. Let's help her come to grips with the fact that her husband's black, y'all."

"I don't know for certain. I said that I thought he was."

"Whatever," I reply. "What's his name?"

She pauses. "Kendall."

"Is that his real name? Or did you just make that one up, too?"

"That's his real name . . . but he rarely uses it."

"Oh hell naw! The name didn't tell you, girl?"

"No, it didn't. Like I said, he rarely uses it, Joy."

"That's 'Dr. Newhouse' now. Our friendship ended abruptly when I began billing you for this therapy." Yeah, I'm in a funky mood.

"Sorry."

"It's okay. Continue. How long have you known Kendall?"

"Since college."

"How did the two of you meet? College Republicans? Rib joint across the tracks?"

"That's not funny. He bumped into me outside a library and helped me with my books. You don't have to be so insulting."

"So you *have* listened to my program

before," I squeal. "No, let me tell you what's insulting. That you expect me to believe you didn't realize that your husband was black when you met him."

"It's the truth."

"Who does he look like? That guy from *Prison Break*? Maybe Vin Diesel? I know! I know! Mike Bibby from the Sacramento Kings. That'll make you scratch your head. Matter of fact, I'm scratching mine as we speak."

Macy laughs as she hits another sound effect.

"I don't know what those people look like."

"Damn. You really are isolated. He must've been on the hunt for someone like you."

"His color doesn't matter to me. I'm in love with the man inside."

"Okay," I whistle, going along with the second verse same as the first. "So can I refer to you as Miss Colorblind?"

"Do I have a choice, Dr. Newhouse?"

I'm under her skin. Love it.

"You're learning. It is my show, after all."

"And I don't know why I called your stupid show in the first place."

She hangs up.

I'm astonished.

How dare she? I do the hanging up around

here. I shake it off and continue with the show, but that doesn't stop me from being pissed. Some of the other callers make a couple of cracks about Margot. Everyone knows I am the queen of hang-ups. I can't believe I let that woman beat me to it.

"Margot, if you're dusting and happen to have the radio on, I want you to listen. As a doctor, I hate leaving the patient on the operating table. I know you're a virgin to my graces, so I can be a little hard to handle. But I forgive you. Please call me back, so we can finish your story."

I go on with the show, centering on a new topic. The calls are wild and entertaining, putting me back on my game.

Then the intern stands up, waving at me from behind the glass. I motion for her to put them on.

Someone's breathing.

"Margot, is that you?"

"I'm here."

"Good! Good!" I squeal. "Confession time, dear. I'll admit it. The doctor messed up. A lot of our listeners want to know more about your and Kendall's history, so I want to give you that chance now."

"I don't know if I should be talking to you. Not only were you rude and offensive to me, you were downright obnoxious."

I grimace, wanting to shoot her. I promised, so I bite my tongue a while longer. Macy motions me to remain calm.

"It's just us girls, Margot. I get that way sometimes, but only because I thought you were BSing. But you weren't, were you? You really didn't know your husband was black."

"No."

"Hmm. How long have the two of you been married?"

"A year."

"Okay. And the two of you never discussed race? What about at the wedding? You had to have looked at his side of the church and said, 'Hey, maybe Kendall's got some Dominican branches on that family tree or sumthin'.'"

"No. We were married in a courthouse ceremony. He never discussed his family."

"What about yours?"

"I don't discuss mine, either. As a child, I had some difficulties and they . . ."

"Kicked you to the curb?"

"If you want to phrase it that way, yes."

"That is totally messed up, Margot. But back to hubby . . . What did it for you? What were the signs? Copies of *Jet* magazine on the coffee table? The TV channel always on BET? You called Affirmative Action a quota system and he slapped the hell out of you?"

The intern motions that I'm crazy. I shrug my shoulders. I don't know how to be any other way. And the ratings prove it.

"I thought you weren't going to belittle me."

She wants to run again.

"Relax, Margot. I'm just joking. That's what I do."

Cue the circus music.

"But to make you more comfortable, I'll ask it more professionally. Were there any hints that your man might be something other than what you originally thought?"

"There were a few hints, but I ignored them. I was more focused on the man than his ethnicity. One day I mentioned visiting the South. That's when he told me he was from a small town in rural Alabama."

"Honey, I've been there. All of Alabama's rural. Trust me on that."

Macy scowls. I forgot she attended Tuskegee. Still true. I stick my tongue out at her. She probably won't buy me salads for a week.

"May I finish?"

"Sorry."

"When I said I'd like to meet his family one day, he became agitated. He said he had no plans on returning there under any circumstances. Then he added that we might get some funny looks from some of his less sensitive kin."

"Big clue. Big."

"I didn't take it like that. You see, I —"

"Then you are a dumb one. But don't be offended, Margot. I'm not calling you dumb. It's an acronym for Doesn't Understand Most Basics. Any other hammers upside your head?"

"Excuse me?"

"Anything else that clued you in to this big revelation you're dazzling us with?"

"Last week. He found out he was nominated for an award at his job. He called his grandmother. Something I've never known him to do. He was on the phone with her in the bedroom when I came in. I wasn't eavesdropping, but I overheard him mentioning how much it meant to him to be nominated as a black man in his industry."

"Did you tell him what you'd heard?"

"No. I was afraid that maybe I misunderstood. And it shouldn't matter to me anyway."

"Please. I'm getting sick of this game. I thought I could handle it, but I can't. I just can't, dear. And I'm sure my listeners are rolling their eyes and sucking their teeth," I admonish. "This is ridiculous no matter how you put it. You proclaim you don't care,

242

but it bothers you when you 'find out' that Kendall is a black man. Maggie, you'd have to be blind not to have noticed these things about your husband all these years, no matter how pale he may be."

"That's just it. I —"

". . . am saying goodbye!"

Cue the toilet flush.

Nobody hangs up on me.

"Uh-huh," I say to my listeners. The ones who stuck around for this foolishness. "I'll bet you were yukking it up. Thought I let old Maggie get me, huh? If so, then you really don't know Lady Joy Newhouse. Recognize. I ain't the one to play with."

Macy smiles.

"Well, folks, another night of reality radio at its best. For those who don't know tomorrow, all I can offer you is the best of *On The Line* as me and the crew will be attending the broadcasting banquet. I'm up for another award, so keep your fingers crossed. And on that note, fam, until next time, always remember life is what you make it. This is Joy Newhouse, lata!"

I leave my show on an emotional high, my swagger returned. Just in time to claim my award tomorrow night.

The ballroom is packed, the gents in their

penguin suits and the ladies sparkling from head to toe. As usual I'm doing the solo thing, better to sample the pickings. I spot Macy at the table reserved for our station and I wind my way around the adulation and adoration, the red dress I'd sprung for showcasing the negative fifteen pounds. All the whispers and the surreptitious looks in my direction assure me that I will be taking home the plaque once again.

Well, me and the show's production staff. Couldn't do it without them. And if I keep repeating it, I won't forget when I'm accepting my award.

I'm rehearsing when I bump into a man I've never met at these gatherings of our parent company. He turns around, interrupted from his conversation with other dark suits. Tall, confident and younger than me by about ten years.

Scratch that.

Five years.

I ain't that old.

"Pardon me," he says. Soft-spoken and articulate. Must be one of the front-office types milling about for attention. Aquiline nose accentuated by his deep brown skin. Black curly hair and uncharacteristically thin lips. Maybe some Indian or Caribbean roots in his family by the look of things.

Negative fifteen pounds is a positive in this situation.

"No harm, no foul," I throw out. "I think it was my fault anyway."

"That's rather surprising coming from you, Miss Newhouse." He smiles, relishing my surprise. I shouldn't be. Everybody knows me.

"Don't confuse the on-air persona with the real woman. I'm really quite nice once you get to know me."

"I can see that," he remarks. Noncommittal. I'm unsure if he's interested or simply making small talk. "K.C. Armstrong."

I see his wedding ring on the other hand. Small talk, indeed.

"Charmed," I reply, sparing the wit. I'll save that energy (and this dress) for someone else.

"Good luck with your nomination. My wife's a big fan."

"Thanks, sweetie."

He returns to conversing with his circle of executive losers. I saunter off in search of another flute of Krug.

They are honoring performance within the entire company. Most of my station is in attendance as well as sister stations/affiliates from around the Tri-State area. This is the time when the pecking order is established.

The evening crawls horribly slowly. Empire Broadcasting recaps their corporate history and philosophy as I smile, feigning interest. Just get on with it.

I'm almost in tears when I see someone familiar accept an award.

"Hey," I mutter aloud as recognition overtakes me. No more drinks for me tonight.

The presenter speaks as the recipient approaches the podium. "K.C. Armstrong, you have exemplified a strong work ethic and outstanding sales results during your short time with WIDD . . ."

WIDD? Wait. Isn't that the . . .

". . . the Country Giant. So on behalf of the station manager and the Empire Broadcasting board of directors, we'd like to honor you with the award for sales executive of the year."

Well, surprise and aw shucks on me.

Everyone stands. Apparently he is known by many in the room. And held in high regard. As I'm already on my feet, I continue. I even bother applauding. Go 'head on, brother.

He wipes his hand on his pant leg before shaking with the presenter. His lip quivers, genuinely touched by this moment — a rarity at these sorts of things. It reminds me to step up my game when my name's called.

K.C. clears his throat then adjusts the microphone. Feedback then a final adjustment before he speaks. Curiously, I'm listening like the rest.

"Well. Um . . ." He smiles as he admires the plaque. Then he shakes his head. "I apologize for being at a loss for words, but . . ."

Go on, boy. It's for sales, for a country music station at that. They're not going to give you the whole night.

"There have just been a lot of positive things happening lately in my life. My beautiful wife . . ."

He motions toward a table out of view. I'm curious for a look-see, but rein it in.

". . . as well as the rest of my family that I haven't been very close with as of late. You know, it's funny. This . . . this tonight, I'm taking as a sign. A sign that things are looking up in all aspects. My grandmother, who took me in as a kid and raised me on love and grits, is here with me. I'm just glad she's able to meet the woman I've pledged my devotion to."

His grandmother stands at her table. The silver-haired matron poses and waves as if waiting for someone to snap her picture.

"In addition to being photogenic, she's

also a big country music fan."

A chorus — part applause, part laughter, part yee-haw — reverberates.

"I know I need to wrap this up. Well. What I'm trying to say is this award means more than an individual accomplishment. It represents reconciliation and healing as I bring two sides of my life together. I thank you and my family thanks you."

Toward night's end, Macy and I get what we came here for when *On the Line* is called out by the presenter. After a mini-celebration and quick prayer at our table, we wind our way through the applause. Just another year. Upon the stage, I let Macy speak first. The whole world gets to hear me on the regular. She eloquently expresses our appreciation while I ponder what I'm going to say.

When she's finished, she steps aside, passing the plaque. I begin by giving them the Joy Newhouse they've come to love . . . and hate.

"Another award? How many years has it been anyway? Oh. That's right. My show won last year. How do you like the dress this time?" I tease. "You know me. I joke around and say wild, crazy things. But watching a young man earlier tonight accept his award with some humility and a quiet pride made me rethink how I was going to handle this. This . . . this is something that I took for granted. I'm just thinking that maybe I shouldn't."

I wink at K.C.

"Sincerely, I'm grateful for my fans, Macy, and my station that allows my antics. All I can promise is that I will continue to deliver the unpredictable. Thank you, all."

As we leave the stage, Macy mumbles under her breath, "Girl, what has gotten into you? You had me thinking I need my eyeglass prescription updated."

"I'm all about shock. And didn't I do just that?"

"Yes," she admits. "But did you mean what you were saying?"

"Maybe," I reply coyly for her to think about. "But I'll never tell."

As we pose for more pictures before the trade industry, K.C. comes over. I grin while reminding myself he's married.

"Would you mind if we took a picture together . . . with our awards?" he asks sheepishly.

"Why would I mind? I may as well get the most out of this dress," I gush.

The photographer directs us to get closer. I feel his arm as he brings me into him. "You're very photogenic, Miss Newhouse."

"Please, sweetie. Call me 'Joy.' " No, I am not flirting with this man. No more Krug.

As the final flash fades, he turns to me. "Wow. Thank you, Joy." He's aw-shucks like a true Southern gentleman. No wonder he's king of sales over there. "Um . . . since we're more cordial now, may I make a request of you?"

"The evening's almost over, so you better make it quick."

"Okay. Come with me."

"What?"

He takes me by the hand, jerking me along. I've never done anything like this before. Well . . . at least not at an awards banquet.

"Where are we going?" I'm ready to break out the schoolgirl outfit.

"I want you to meet my wife."

Scratch the outfit. No. Burn it.

"What?" I say, putting on the brakes. I almost snap a heel as I dig into the carpet.

He doesn't relent. My heels do as I continue behind him.

"She claims she just began listening to your show, but I think she's fibbing some."

Having no choice, I accept the swap of lust for adulation. It will suffice tonight. "I have a bunch of closet fans," I reply. "She won't be the first to lie."

There are six seated at the covered table. I notice granny first, snapping her fingers to the music. He introduces me to her. I react favorably to the wet kiss deposited upon my cheek and the blessings bestowed upon my soul. Those mother types.

Seated beside her is a thin woman with large eyes. She ogles me as if beset by royalty. Her hair is brushed back into a ponytail. The dress is straight off the mark-down rack, I swear. More homey than homely. K.C. will be seeing some raises soon and will take care of that.

"Is this your gorgeous wife?" I ask. "Joy Newhouse. Charmed," I purr.

He taps me on the shoulder then prods me toward a different warm body at the table. When he keeps nudging, I become annoyed. He's lucky I'm indulging him.

"That's not my wife. That's my cousin."

Oops.

He takes my hand and deposits it in the hand of another.

Another color.

"This is my wife. Marjorie," he states as the hand gently encases mine. Nice nails on her. Red. Like the hair atop the woman's head.

I'm situated just over her right shoulder. Rather than lean in, I wait for her to swivel to see me. She doesn't. Stuck-up bitch. I refuse to acquiesce though. Make her get up.

As her face turns slightly, K.C. urges me to move closer. I'm about to tell him what's on my mind for real.

"Is this *the* Joy Newhouse?" she asks.

"It sure is, honey," he gushes. "She's right there."

Stupid, I think. *Can't you see it's me?*

"Nice hands. Nails, too."

Oh no, she didn't.

"Thanks," I reply facetiously, thinking I know her but can't recall how.

She turns to the sound of my voice.

Oh my God.

She's . . .

"Hello, Dr. Newhouse. I apologize for not getting up."

K.C. tries to correct her. Inform her that I'm not a doctor. But I get it.

I get it.

"Oh," is all I can say. I'm stunned. Totally stunned and embarrassed. I turn enough shades of red to match my Dolce & Gabbana.

"Maggie . . ."

She giggles. From behind the dark sunglasses, she giggles.

"I really wish I could see the look on your

face right now. Of course, I can't. . . . this whole 'blindness' thing and all. No matter though. I don't judge people on looks anyway . . . although from the trembling of your hand, it might be pretty funny to witness."

"Is something wrong?" K.C. asks his wife.

"Not at all, Kendall. Things are totally fine. I'm just letting Miss Newhouse know that I'm her biggest fan."

If we were on the air . . . at this point in the show, I would say, *We'll be right back after this word from our sponsor.*

After mumbling something unintelligible, I know I need to get some air quick before I lose my very expensive dinner all over my hot red dress. I dart toward the terrace and run smack into . . .

Randy!

CHAPTER 13

He grabs me by the shoulders to keep me from tumbling backward both from shock and from the chest-to-breasts impact.

"You okay?" He looks into my eyes and something funny starts happening in my stomach.

"Uh, yes. Fine. Should have been watching where I was going." I'm sure my expression is a mass of squishy lines of confusion.

"Congratulations on your award."

"Thank you." Now we're back on familiar turf. "Speaking of awards, what are you doing here?"

He grins all sexy, and my stomach does that thing again. "We didn't get to talk much when we were last together. I'm the editorial director over at Universal Books. I get tickets to all these things."

My eyes widen of their own accord. "Get out."

"Yep."

"I had no idea."

"Would it have made a difference?"

"A difference about what?"

"About the morning after."

I'm sure if I were about two shades lighter, I would be blushing crimson. I clear my throat. "Sorry about that. I can be a little bitchy in the morning. Oh, and thanks for the flowers. You really didn't have to do that."

"I wanted to."

"Why?"

"I wanted you to know that the night meant something to me and so did you."

Did I mention that Babe aka Randy has one of those midnight voices that you love to hear after hours? I try to look away from him, but it's like I'm hypnotized. All of a sudden I'm not freaked out by his interest in me anymore. I'm kinda interested myself. All dressed up and smelling good, he was more edible than before.

"Where were you rushing off to, by the way?"

I snap out of my trance. "Just to get some air, but I really need to go home. It's been a long day."

"I'll walk you out if you're ready."

"Thanks."

We head for the exit and I stop at my table

to retrieve my award but not without taking a quick look around for Maggie, the reason that sent me flying into Randy's arms in the first place. Hmm, ironic that something that rattled my chains could actually turn into something special. I look up at Randy and smile as we head out.

Once outside, the night air is what they call balmy. Late spring edging into summer. The streets of Manhattan are teeming with folks as if it were still rush hour and not nearly midnight.

"Did you drive, were you driven, or can I give you a lift?"

I laugh. "Actually, I took a cab over. I figured if I had one too many, I wouldn't have the worry about driving while under the influence."

"Good move. I drove. Come on, I'll take you home."

Just as we make a move, I hear Macy yelling for me like we're on the football field back at Boys and Girls High School.

She hustles up to us, totally ignoring me. Her focus is locked on Randy. She's all grins and I'd swear she pushed up those 38 Ds a little closer to his face. I would smack her for being rude, but she is my girl.

"I was just leaving. I should have let you know."

"I wondered where you went. I asked around and someone said they saw you walk out."

Mind you, Macy has yet to make eye contact with me. "Uh, Macy, I'm sure you're wondering who this is."

Her grin grows wider.

"Macy, this is Randy Temple." It takes her a New York minute, but it sinks in and just as quickly that damned "I'm available" grin disappears. "Randy, Macy is my dear friend and producer for my show."

He sticks out his hand. "Pleasure to meet you. You do a fabulous job."

"Thanks." She blows out a breath of disappointment then finally turns to me. "See you tomorrow."

"Do you need a lift?" Randy asks.

Macy shakes her head no and I send up a silent prayer of thanks. "I'll call you around midday," I tell her, giving her the finger wave and a smile.

"If you're up." She gives me that "I know you" look and sashays away. "Nice to meet you, Randy," she tosses over her shoulder.

"My car is in the garage on the next block."

I walk beside him. My hip bumps against his. Hmm, nice.

"I've been coming to this shindig for at

least ten years. I don't ever remember seeing you here before."

"That's because I never saw a reason to
use my ticket until today."

"Why is that?"

"To see you." He turns and looks at me
and damn it if I don't trip and nearly fall
on my face.

This time Randy grabs me around the
waist. When I look up, his face is so close to
mine I can smell the peppermint on his
breath, just like in the movies.

"We *must* keep meeting like this." He
helps me to my feet.

Now mind you, I've never been considered
clumsy. I can't remember the last time I accidentally knocked something over or ran
into someone, or fell down. Yet, twice, in
less than a half hour, I've lost all sense of
balance and find myself falling into and all
over this man. Hey, folks, something ain't
quite right.

"Maybe I should hold your hand."

Now waaaait a minute! But the words
don't come out and the next thing I know
my hand is tucked snugly in his. Damn it, it
feels good.

We get to his car and Randy helps me
inside. I press myself as close as possible to
the passenger door.

"Contrary to anything you may have heard, I don't bite." He throws a look in my direction.

I giggle stupidly and peel my shoulder off the door. "So . . ." And I can't think of what is supposed to come next. Strange as this may sound, this is all new terrain for me. I'm usually the one who goes after the guy. I'm the one who sends them packing. I'm the one who doesn't let feelings enter into the game. I have my reasons and they've served me well over the years. But for reasons that escape me, I don't want to play the game with Randy and I don't like it one damned bit.

"Mind if I turn on the radio?" he asks.

"It's your ride," I say, trying to sound indifferent. "Help yourself."

He reaches over and his arm brushes mine, accidentally on purpose . . . who the hell knows, but it sends a shockwave right up my arm to the left side of my head and when it snap, crackle and pops, I jump like I've been struck with a stun gun.

"You okay?"

"Yeah." I snap and wiggle around in the seat, then adjust my purse on my lap. Jeez, is it hot in here or is it just me?

Robin Thicke's new CD fills the space between us. I bob my head to the music, thankful for the distraction. Gotta admit, Robin is a baaad white boy.

"So besides doing your show and winning awards, what do you do for fun?" Randy asks.

"Oh, you mean besides picking up strange men in clubs and bringing them home?" I turn to him and cock a perfectly arched brow.

He chuckles. "Oh, so now I'm strange."

"You know what I mean," I respond half apologetically.

"No offense taken. But yes, besides all that."

Hmm, I really have to think about that for a minute. Truthfully speaking, that *is* my life: work and faceless sex. Living that way keeps me safe. I can hide behind other people's problems and relieve myself with someone I have no feelings for and who doesn't give a damn about me, either. The only one who understands that is Macy. And I'm not about to try to explain it to Randy.

"Work keeps me pretty busy."

"Do you like plays, movies, comedy clubs?"

I shrug. "I suppose. Why?"

"Exploring the options."

I choose not to respond.

"Ever been married?"

I snap my head in his direction. "Trust me, I'm not the one."

"Why?"

"What's with the interrogation?"

"I want get to know you, Joy. Is that so awful?"

I fold my arms and poke out my polished lips. "Why?"

"Because you remind me of an unread manuscript. The opening page is so well put together that it entreats you to read more, delve deeper. The more you read the more you want to know. Right now I want to know if the intriguing opening pages are all that they present themselves to be."

Now I've been called a lot of things in my day, but a freaking manuscript tops the list! Though I must admit that I'm blushing. "Oh," is all I can manage. I clear my throat. "Uh, what about you? What do you do besides work and go home with strange women?"

He tosses his head back and laughs from deep in his gut and the sound makes me feel warm inside.

"Touché," he says, then grows serious. "When I'm not reading rather lousy manuscript submissions, praying to find a diamond in the rough, I mentor a young men's group on Saturday mornings, go to the gym a couple of times a week, clubs every now and then, hang out with friends . . . pick up strange women in my spare time."

It's my turn to laugh. "You're a very busy man. Tell me about the kids you work with."

Randy begins to tell me about the Future Foundation, an organization that visits urban high schools and, through guidance counselor recommendations, partners with young men at risk for failing in school or worse.

"Most of them have no male figures in their lives and the ones who do would probably be better off without them. So we go in there, talk with them, take them on trips, college tours, places out of the city, make sure they keep their grades up and just be there when they need someone to talk to."

I'm impressed. I stare at him the whole time he's speaking, and the more I look at him the more he seems to change right in front of my eyes. There really is something to that saying about seeing someone differently. Randy Temple is more than a fine brotha who knows his way around a bedroom — he's intelligent and caring, and he has a purpose in life.

"Next year we want to start working in the lower grades and hopefully get to some of these young brothers before too much damage is done."

I nod my head. Listening to Randy makes me question myself. Sure, I provide entertainment, but what else do I contribute to the world? *Nada.* Hmm, oh well, everyone can't be a Randy Temple.

"Well, here we are."

He pulls the car to a stop in front of my building. Oh, did I mention that he has a Benz, black on black and smelling like he just drove it off the showroom floor.

"That was quick." All of a sudden I'm nervous. But at least I can't fall down since I'm still sitting.

He turns in his seat to face me and drapes his arm across the back of my seat. Uh-oh.

"I'd like to see you again."

Gulp.

"Really?"

"Yeah, really. How about dinner next Saturday?"

This is where I'm supposed to say, *Thanks but I'm busy.* "Saturday? What time?"

"How's eight?"

Gulp. "Sure."

He grins and my stomach does that funny thing again.

"Can I call you?"

"Uh . . . sure." I give him my number,

which he promptly programs into his cell phone.

"I'll give you a call Friday to confirm."

I bob my head like one of those dumb toys that sit on car dashboards. And then all of a sudden he's so close to me that his image becomes blurred and his lips are on mine and mine are on his . . . dayum! Then, just as quick, he's back in his rightful place behind the wheel and my heart is racing like I'd been running from a potential mugger.

"See you Saturday," he says. And his voice has that Barry White thing going on.

My panties are wet and I know I gotta go. Now. I clutch my purse and my award and just about leap out of the car. By the time I set my Ferragamos on the ground, Randy has his hand out helping me to my feet. He was so fast it was damn near supernatural. He pulls me right up to him. I hold my breath. He kisses the top of my head.

"Have a good night."

"Thanks. You, too."

We stand there facing each other until I finally break eye contact. "Good night," I mutter. "Thanks for the ride." I want to run inside my building, but instead I give him my best side and saunter away.

Once upstairs, rattling around in my

lonely apartment, I wish that I would have asked him to come up. Instead, I look for a place to put my award, take a shower and spend the rest of the night staring up at the ceiling and wondering what it was like to actually be in a relationship with someone. Hey, if Margot could find someone, maybe I could, too.

CHAPTER 14

"A date? You?"

I glance at Macy and bug my eyes. "Yeah, me, a date. Why in hell is that so unbelievable?"

"Uh, 'cause you don't date."

I roll my eyes. "Things can change."

"Yeah, but you don't."

I finish washing the dishes in the sink and Macy puts them away. She's right, you know. I don't date, I don't have relationships, and I stay uninvolved. It was my own personal credo. Over the years it had served me well. Maybe I was getting old.

"Hey, I thought I'd give it a try," I offer, and shrug like it's no big deal.

Macy puts her arm around my shoulder. "Look, sis, you know there's no one out there who wants you to find some kind of happiness more than I do. Right?"

I nod my head.

"Maybe this Randy is the one for you."

"Kinda scary."

She grins. "It always is." She put the last dish in the cupboard. "You want to go over the outline for tonight's show?"

"Naw, not in the mood. Let's just wing it tonight."

"Fine with me."

We walk into the living room and turn on *Judge Judy* and spend the next hour laughing our asses off at the stupid people on the show.

"It never ceases to amaze me how folks can get on TV and expose all their business — and dumb business at that." I take a sip from my glass of iced tea.

"Humph, the same way those dummies write and call in to your show. Fifteen minutes of fame, honey."

"You got that right. But at least the nuts on our show can remain relatively anonymous."

"True."

"Except the other night at the awards . . ."

"What do you mean?"

I go on to tell her about meeting Margot.

"Get the hell outta here!"

"Yep, in the flesh. I almost peed on myself."

Macy starts laughing. "I bet you did."

I laugh myself. "But you know what? As

much as it was shocking and embarrassing, it really got me thinking . . ."

She frowns. "About what?"

I blow out a long breath as I try to put words to my thoughts. "A lot of these people write in really wanting help and I make fun of them, tear them apart."

"Girl, your show is about shock and entertainment. You never claimed to be an expert or psychologist. What do they expect for free?"

I chuckle, but for the first time it isn't really funny.

"Word on the street is that management is going to be making more changes."

"Yeah, so I hear. I kinda thought they were done."

"Me, too. We don't have anything to worry about, especially after you just landed yet another statue."

"And still kicking butt in the ratings." I take a bow.

"Holla!"

We high-five and laugh the rest of our way through *Judge Judy.*

When me and Macy arrive at the station, everything is at its usual high-pitched intensity. Folks are buzzing around, music is playing and it's all good. I'm glad Macy and I decided to go freestyle tonight. That's what keeps my juices flowing — the unexpected.

Just as I turn the corner to head to my tiny, tiny office, I get waylaid by Mr. Bigshot himself.

"Good. Here you are."

I force myself to smile. "Evening, Mr. Bledsoe." I try to move past his rotund frame without success.

"Please come to my office."

"Can't this wait until after the show? I need to prepare."

"Ms. Newhouse, if it could wait, I would have said, *Come after the show.*"

Condescending doesn't adequately describe his tone. For someone of his size, he practically pirouettes around and continues down the corridor. I make a face behind his back and dutifully follow.

"Please close the door."

I do and take two baby steps inside the inner sanctum.

"Ms. Newhouse, I'll get right to the point. There was a meeting with the board of directors following that . . . episode with the near suicide."

I definitely don't like where this was going. I fold my arms and brace my weight on my right side.

"Uh-huh."

He clears his throat. "It was decided . . . unanimously, that tonight will be your last show. After this evening, your contract will be terminated. We will, of course, give you due compensation."

The room shifts to the left and gets hot as hell. My head started to pound. "Say what?"

"You're being let go, Ms. Newhouse."

I rock my neck. "Let go? I have the highest ratings of anyone in this place. I just got another award."

"That notwithstanding. We feel that the reputation of this station is more important than ratings and . . . awards."

Well, I'll be dammed. "So let me get this straight. You're firing me."

"I'd rather phrase it . . . releasing you from your contractual obligations."

I sure as shit wish he would say, *Sit down*, 'cause I feel like I'm going to pass out.

"Your paperwork has been drawn up and you can pick it up from my secretary after your show."

I felt like telling him to meet me in the parking lot after work, but that would have been going too far back to my roots. I lift my chin. "Fine. On my behalf, I just want to say . . ."

"Yes, Ms. Newhouse?"

"Kiss my ass." I spin around and walk out of the room before I burst into tears and really make a fool of myself. I think I might have knocked someone against the wall as I fly down the hallway, but I don't care. I feel as if every eye in the place is on me and they know that I've been canned.

I storm into the control room, where Macy is getting set up.

"What the hell is wrong with you?"

I huff and puff, pace a few times before I can get the words out.

"Joy, you're scaring me."

"I just got fired."

"What!"

I collapse into the nearest seat. "He fired me."

"Why?"

I recount what Fatso told me.

"I can't believe it. Tonight is the last show, just like that?" She snaps her fingers.

"Looks that way."

"Shit!" she sputters and sits next to me. "What are we going to do?"

I love that Macy says "we."

I turn to look at her and then an idea forms. "Sis, if we're going to go down, we're going down in flames, and I'm taking WHOT with me. Forget the bleep button tonight. We're going all the way live! You

271

hear me. Pass me that bag of letters."

Lightning fast, we tear through the letters and find just the right ones.

"You sure you want to do this?"

"You damned right I'm sure. Lock your door. Don't let anyone in. Understood?"

Macy nods her head and I dart out to get ready. I get settled behind the mic after locking the door and turn toward Macy on the other side of the glass to give her a thumbs-up. She gives me the ten-second count. Okay, folks, it's showtime.

CHAPTER 15

My theme music winds down. I take a deep breath. And I'm live.

"Hey out there in radio heaven. You're just in time. This is Joy Newhouse all up in your house with tonight's edition of *On the Line.* I have some real treats for you tonight so hold on to your seats, grab that glass of wine and get ready. But before I get into our first letter of the night, I want to let you all know that tonight is my last night on the air. Yeah, you heard me. I'm out. You'll probably get something like easy-listening music or one of those brothers with the deep voice playing love songs all night." I laugh. "But it's all good. It's been a blast. And so without further ado, let's get tonight on and popping." Before I can even launch into my first letter, the phone lines are lit up. No calls tonight. I had thangs to do. I spread the letter entitled Chocolate Cho Cha out in front of me. I can barely contain myself.

Dear Joy,

I've been listening to your show regularly for quite a while now, and there's something about you that turns me off. No need to get hostile, because there's also something about you that fascinates me at the same time. You know how it is with us women. We see something in another sister that we're lacking, and we want some of it for ourselves. Usually it's something we'd be better off living without like jewelry or some expensive-ass shoes we can't afford. For some it's long hair, for others it's perky breasts and a big ass or a pricey new car.

Well, I've got all that. The half-white woman looks, the tantalizing black-woman curves, the bling and the bank accounts. Now, Joy, I've seen what you look like, and I'm not saying you're hard on the eyes or anything, but you're definitely not me. I mean, you would probably be considered attractive in some circles, and I happen to love my sisters in all shades and sizes, but unlike you, I've got the kind of face you see plastered on magazine covers. Most times people get so awestruck by my looks that they go out of their way to accommodate me based on my physical appearance alone. So what could a woman like you have that I might need? Why in the world would I need to write to you?

It's your confidence.

Okay, by now you're probably thinking I have some fuckin' nerve talking about you like I'm all that and you're below average. Isn't it a trip how we can just up and insult folks and then turn right around and need them for something? But I said I was beautiful, not prideful. I'm ashamed, damn it, not arrogant. I come to you humbly, and submit my situation before your personal counsel because God knows this thing I've been wrestling with is big. Big, goddammit. I'm talking BIG. Big.

You see, I'm what you would call a freak of nature, although you'd never know it by looking at me. Like my mother and grandmother, the eyes are green and the cheekbones are high. I stand a sweet five feet, ten inches tall with one of those onion asses that can bring water to the eye. My skin is light and clear, and I have that long, jet-black hair that some black people call "good" but has never been anything other than just hair to me.

My darkness started when I was almost twelve. I was spending two weeks at a summer camp for privileged girls. It was the first swim day at camp and the lake water was cold as hell for late June. About a dozen of us were laughing and shivering as we crowded into a wooden changing area and began stripping out of our wet bathing suits and changing into dry clothes.

We were in various stages of undress when it happened. I wasn't one who had *bloomed* early — I'd exploded. Some of those little white girls had arms and legs like sticks, while I had a plump bottom, some nicely rounded breasts, and more than a few strands of sleek black pubic hair. I'd taken off my bikini top and shaken my firm breasts free, and had just wriggled out of my wet shorts when a loud shriek split the air.

I looked up along with the other little girls, puzzled. A tall, blond-haired girl from the Pocono Mountains was hopping up and down and pointing her crooked white finger, and to my horror, she was pointing it straight at me.

"Oh my GOD!" she shrieked, shaking her head and grimacing around a mouth filled with shiny silver braces. "Gross! What *is* that?"

Every eye, including mine, followed the line of her pointing finger, which ended at the triangle between my curvy thighs.

"What?" I whispered, lowering my gaze and looking down between my own naked legs. One of my cousins had gotten her period a few months earlier, and I was just about to be overjoyed that perhaps my first period had come on while swimming. But it hadn't. I glanced down. As usual, my vaginal lips were long and protruding. Fleshy. Floppy. Hanging low. My eyes traveled to the two thin, neat vaginal slices between the blond girl's legs. Firm. Tight. Pretty. Quickly, my eyes scanned the room for verification. My pussy was right! Hers had to be wrong! I looked from naked triangle to naked triangle, and what I saw completely demolished every bit of self-esteem that my eleven-year-old self had ever possessed.

"Now *that's* disgusting," said Fiona, backing away. She and I were the only two black girls in our cabin, and we'd formed an early friendship and alliance. "You oughta stop touching yourself down there," she said, wrinkling her big brown nose. "You've stretched your coochie out like taffy."

I was floored. Sure, my meaty skin sweated and got chafed down there a lot, and once in gymnastics class somebody jokingly asked me if I had a dick stuck in my tights, but I'd never seen another girl completely naked before so my body had seemed perfectly normal to me.

But the eyes don't lie, and Fiona was right. None of the other girls had such thick folds of flesh wadded between their legs. No one else had so much meat hanging down there that they had to spread themselves wide open just to pee. As I looked between my legs at what had, in an instant, become the ugliest thing I'd ever seen, my entire childhood fell away and my spirit suffered a shameful death. I hated myself.

Now, Joy, please don't ask me all the obvious questions. I've seen you in action and you're smart enough to fill in some of the blanks. Yes, my mother should have taken time to see a doctor, but she was terrified about exposing my problem.

"The world will *shame* you," Mama moaned through tears. "Anybody who so much as hears about this is gonna shame you, darling." She hugged me close to her breast. "Listen to me, sweetie. You have to keep this to yourself." She pulled up my panties and smoothed down my skirt. Then she sat my big old self on her lap and rocked me as we cried together softly. "You have to keep this to yourself. Unless you want what happened at that camp to keep right on happening forever. It won't be just little girls who point and laugh and look at you all nasty, either. Men. Boys. They'll all make you cry. I heard about a lady who lived with something like this in France a long time ago. They put her naked in a cage and sold tickets so folks could poke fun at her night and day. No. Your mama won't have nobody treating her baby like a monster and laughing at you like some freak on a stage. You just keep this thing to yourself, you hear me? Not another soul must ever know about this except me and you."

I believed Mama. I really did. But I liked boys, and boys loved me. I was pretty. I had a big ass. I dressed well and I was outgoing. Still, my teenage years were just full of frustration. I stayed hot all the time. Just burning up. I kissed a lot of boys and I'd grab their crotches and let them rub my ass and my nipples, too, but my legs stayed closed and my pants stayed up. I was dying to be penetrated. I thought about it all the time, and fantasized about how it would feel the first time something big and hard slid into me and filled me up . . . I learned how to masturbate myself to an orgasm, and the hotter I got the fuller my lower lips would get. I'd be lying there gripping a soggy handful of my own loose flesh. I'd squirm and moan, and those lips would be hot and swollen and sagging along either side of my probing fingers.

Well, the years passed and I finished college. There was this boy I'd been liking, and he really liked me, too. He doted on me. Did anything I asked. He had pretty eyes and rough hands. "Let's move to a big city together," he said. "You're just the kind of girl I

279

want to build a future with. We're educated and young. We can get jobs and share an apartment. The world is ours, baby. Let's explore it together."

I packed.

Mama frowned, but she didn't try to stop me. What the hell did Mama know anyway? Daddy had died in my junior year of college, and there'd been no shortage of gentlemen comforting her at night.

The boy with the pretty eyes and I planned to head east. We became very close. He said a lot of love words to me. He kissed me and licked my nipples in the cold air. I stroked him, first through his pants, and then with my bare hand. I tasted him and he held on to my hair and pumped hard as he declared his undying love. He touched the wet spot in my pants and begged me to trust him. Joy, I needed to trust him, do you understand? I needed to trust him!

And I did.

My zipper whispered and my clothes fell away. I felt his hands and his kisses on my hot skin, and I climaxed under his touch. He parted my leg with a knee and told me not to worry. He promised not to hurt me. "If it's too much for you, just tell me, baby, and I'll stop."

Stop hell. Stopping was the last thing on my mind. I arched my back and moaned, and prepared for bliss as he guided his hardness toward my ugly affliction. I was wet there and swollen with need. His manhood rubbed against me and I smiled inside and waited for the rapture of penetration.

But it never came.

Instead, he cursed.

"What?" I asked, hoping I didn't know. He'd risen up off me and was now kneeling on the bed beside me. He reached for the light switch and threw on his glasses. I held my breath as he peered at my naked self. I waited for the love words. To hear plans for our move out east.

But instead I heard the shriek of an eleven-year-old white girl with braces on her teeth and a picture-perfect pussy.

"What is that?" he demanded. His dark finger pointed and his lip curled in disgust. He loomed above me. Anger distorted his face. His eyes were clouded as he grabbed me and flung me off the bed. "What the fuck are you trying to pull on me, niggah?" His fist landed in the pit of my stomach and he grabbed my legs and dragged me into the middle of the floor. "Oh, I know! You one of them sex-change faggots, ain't you? What? You used to be a man or something?" The boy with the pretty eyes kicked me in the face. He bent over me naked, his fist flying and disgust in his eyes. "You nasty motherfucker! What they do? Cut off your dick and left you with all this?"

I balled up and accepted my ass whipping in silence. When I got back home to Mama, she took one look at my black eye and swollen nose and turned away without a word. She busied herself cleaning me up, wiping away the dried blood and putting ice on my busted lip. She didn't chastise me and she didn't admonish me either. She didn't have to. Because both of us knew that the world would do enough of that for her.

The years passed and God was good enough to answer a few of my prayers. My sexual urges seemed to fall off some, and I resigned myself to a life without intimacy. Things were going well for years until Mama got sick and I had to call an ambulance to come for her. One of the paramedics took a liking to me, and truth be told, I had noticed him, too.

He took good care of Mama and came back by to visit us a few times, and before I knew it we were keeping each other company and hanging out like old friends. His name was Avery, and he was a few years older than me. He'd been married years ago, but had lost his wife and had been by himself ever since.

Mama liked him, but she tried to act like she didn't. She'd be frowning out warnings whenever me and Avery came in from dinner, or from roller-skating or from one of the picnics we liked to share in the park. Avery worked shifts and I had a tight schedule, too, but we made time for each other and I liked the way his pretty eyes crinkled up when he laughed, and the way his rough hands practically swallowed mine yet were so tender and gentle when he gave Mama her insulin shots or changed the dressings on her sores.

We were both grown-ass people so you know we kissed and flirted and talked a little sexy to each other, but Avery was a real man who wasn't ashamed of how he lived his life, and when he told me that the last woman he had made love to was his wife, I knew right then that here was a man I could really get used to.

Now, I didn't tell Avery I was a virgin. And I sure as hell didn't tell him about my ugly, unnatural affliction, either. But I told him almost everything else about me, and he opened himself up wide to me, too. Avery told me I could trust him. He said I was the kind of woman he could see himself having a future with. He talked about moving east and going to medical school, but said he didn't want to leave me behind and he sure wouldn't move me nowhere and leave my mama.

Still . . . a year flew past and it was only

right that he would begin to want something more. We ate dinner together most nights, and I joined his bowling league and he joined my church. I spent time with his mother and he helped me care for mine in her final months. Life was right with Avery, and if it wasn't for my special problem our love thing would have been perfect.

But a month before Mama died Avery messed around and asked me to marry him. Girl, that big old strong black man actually got down on his knees and pulled out a ring, and when he looked up at me there were tears in his eyes.

"Baby," he said, giving me the most beautiful grin I'd ever seen in my life. "I'm already all yours. And I want you to be all mine. We're right for each other, sugar, and I promise to do whatever it takes in this world to keep you happy and satisfied. This is a fit, Silky. I don't wanna live my life without you, and I'm asking you to be my wife."

Oh, how I cried. The tears, Joy. The tears. I cried outta my soul, you hear me? Here I had the most beautiful man in the world bowed down in front of me, and I was gonna have to let him go! I took the ring, but I was already mourning him. See, love had done gotten so good to me that I'd almost forgot I wasn't right! I'd been laughing and dreaming and trolloping around town like I was a regular somebody who could have a regular life. I had been pretending that my lower ugliness didn't exist. Like this man wouldn't one day expect to get a little bit of what I was hiding between my legs. All that damn baggage down there! All that mess!

I hadn't forgotten what happened the last time I tried to get intimate with a man. And when I called Avery over and gave him his ring back and told him that I couldn't marry him, it was all I could do not to remember.

"Look at me, Silky," Avery had said, holding on to me as he lifted my chin. I couldn't. My guilt was too strong, my love way too deep. "Woman! You look at me and tell me you don't love me! Look at me and tell me I don't make you happy, baby. Tell me you don't want me!"

I felt like dying. Joy, there was no way in all hell that I could look at my man and say those words to him. Those would have been lies falling out of my mouth, you hear me? Damned lies!

The weeks passed by slowly and I lost my mama.

I was all alone in the world, and that thought hurt me so bad I didn't think I would survive it. Avery came by the house to offer me his condolences. He was a good man and a good friend, and he said no matter what had happened between us, there was no way he was gonna let me bury my mama all by myself.

So I leaned on him. On that big rock of a shoulder he had extended for me. Avery got me through the days, and he comforted me through the nights, too. For a whole week we lay together in my bed with all our clothes on. Holding each other and crying together until I didn't know if I was crying over Mama, or crying over me.

During that time Avery didn't press me for anything, and he didn't talk about marriage or having anything other than a friendship with me.

"I'm here to help you through this, Silky," he told me. "Just hold tight to old Avery, and let me see you through."

I was grieving, Lord. Oh, was I grieving! But even with Mama in the cold ground, a part of me still hoped for a little happiness. A tiny part of my spirit refused to be quiet. It wanted love. It wanted a man. It wanted joy! It wanted Avery.

I asked him late one night just as he was leaving, "Do . . . you think we might . . . you know . . . try to have something again?"

He was quiet for so long that my hands started sweating in embarrassment. Maybe he already had somebody else! Maybe he was already planning to move her out east!

But then he spoke.

"Silky, me and you . . ." His voice trailed off as he touched my hair and grinned. "We gone always have us something, baby. I'm yours, and you mine. No matter what. Even if I never see you again, nothing can change that."

So there, Joy. You got it out of me. I told you my secret, now I'm asking for your help. I need somebody to tell me that my love is okay. That it's possible. Say it to me loud on the radio, Joy. Just give me a yes or a no. Tell me it's okay to put my trust in a man like Avery, and to maybe see a doctor somewhere about my ugly affliction. I can't be the only woman in the world with such a big cho-cha. Maybe there's help out there for me. I would never trick Avery into marrying me knowing I'm a freak, but maybe I wouldn't have to trick him. Maybe I could just tell him.

I loved my mama, Joy, and may God bless her precious soul . . . but she wasn't always right about everything! Maybe she was wrong about Avery. I promise you he's nothing like that boy with the pretty eyes. My Avery's a real man. He's all man. Avery says he's *my* man. Maybe.

Just . . . maybe.

By this time the station manager is banging on my door, frantically trying to get in. I'm

287

sure the FCC is on one of the phone lines. And quite frankly, my dear, I don't give a damn.

"Hey, sista Silky. I say go for it, girl. Take that man and all that he has to offer. Who says your oversized pussy lips are a freak of nature? Show 'em what you got!" Ha-ha, no bleeping tonight.

The lights on the phones are flashing so fast and furious it's like being in a disco.

"I told ya'll it was going to be hot up in here tonight, and we ain't stopping till . . . well, till I say so." I laugh long and hard. "I'm going to give ya'll thirty seconds to refill your glass and then we'll be back."

My adrenaline is pumping. I know there will be hell to pay, but what else could they do to me? They sure as sugar couldn't fire me twice! I glance behind me and Mr. Bledsoe has his big, fat red face pressed to the small glass window of my booth. I give him the finger then my back. Macy gives me the five-second countdown.

"So as I was saying before we were rudely interrupted with a station break . . . we are on and popping tonight. And for those of you tardy listeners who didn't catch the beginning of the show, tonight is my last night on the airwaves. Yeah, yeah, I was surprised, too, but hey, ya'll ain't heard the last of Joy Newhouse. So let's keep it moving. I have a caller on the line. . . ."

CHAPTER 16

"You said you want to call your story *A Player's Anthem*?" I ask the caller.

"Yes."

"You have a name to go with that?"

"I'd rather not."

"Okay, 'Rather Not.' " I crack up laughing. "You're on the line and we're listening." I hear her take a deep breath and it whistles as she blows it out through the phone lines . . .

Have you ever wanted to taste a man so badly that your mouth watered?

Oh damn. Maybe this was going to be good.

Craved his hardness to stir your sweetness so intensely that the minute his touch graced your skin you damn near ran down the street because you thought you were going to catch fire? Have you ever felt heat that extreme?

Ever met a man that was so good for you that he became bad for you because you wanted him too much? Hungered for him too often? Would trade your last breath so he could know a minute more of happiness? Did you ever love a man so completely that without him you'd be incomplete?

My best friend Harmony did. Moved from Chicago to L.A. and fell hard for a *player-player* from the east side of South Central. Forty-eighth Street between Central and McKinley — an area of the gangster grid. Avalon territory.

His handle was Riz. No bona fide first name. No government last. Just Riz. *Her* Riz. Harmony's.

And that's the reason I'm calling in. I don't know if I should reopen an old wound or not. My best friend has a problem, and I want to help her but don't know how to go about it. Her problem is Riz. A brotha she fell hard for a while ago and *believed* she couldn't have, but never stuck around long enough to find out if her belief was right. She ran three thousand miles away but still can't shake him because there was never an ending to their relationship. And now some other man has fallen for her the same way she fell for Riz. Now she's considering this other man's marriage proposal, and I don't want her commit to the wrong person. I also don't want her to get hurt again but, at the same time, I can't sit back and watch her settle — not without real closure. Not when I know for a fact that her heart is still in L.A. with Riz and that she still belongs to him in a soulmate sort of way.

Before Harmony ever wrapped her legs around Riz, she was his. The minute she met him in her apartment on 76th and Western, she had to know him. Was overcome by his swagger that was the male equivalent of hers. His bold declaration of *God damn! I gotta have you!* as soon as her cousin Alicia introduced them. And once Harmony'd gotten inside his world, something in her caved. The most important part of her that she'd kept protected, walled up in cement. A thing she was sure was untouchable. Her heart.

Riz had given her life, and she lost it as soon as she left him. For her, death would've been easier because the hardest thing I've known her to do is walk away from him. But she had to because Riz was risky. Dangerous. In the most delicious way. He was the type of player who could turn a woman inside out and make love to her soul until she became weak enough for him to remold. And weakness didn't flow through Harmony's blue veins. Her life, stomping ground — everything she'd known to be real — dictated she be otherwise.

She'd come from dry-cleaned folks. Family who had the ability to appear clean under the pressure of heat but deep down in their fibers they were dirty. And that was all she'd known. Invisible dirt. Serious money. Men who could make anything happen or disappear. Women who did the same. Harmony owned identical power but with an added splash of untouchableness, a slice of coolness that had separated her from the rest. But Riz kicked down her impenetrable door and rocked her known world off its axis. He was The One. That one man who'd change her life forever. Not because she loved him. But because she couldn't have him. Wouldn't allow him to have her — knowingly. But he did have her. I know he still does.

Her feelings for him flowed so naturally they seemed unnatural — especially that evening. The night they'd played the wall. Harmony sat propped up on pillows, watching Riz from where she lay on the bed. Craving him from the depths of her soul. They hadn't had sex. Hadn't reached that part of their relationship. Yet. He'd just lain next to her, eyes closed, tangling himself in her essence like always while she wrote things in the journal she'd never invite him to read. What would he think if he knew he'd brought out the little girl in her, exposed a softer side that she'd never shown? Couldn't reveal. She feared she'd push him away if he knew how badly she'd wanted him — for life — and hadn't yet had a taste of him. They were folks. Just friends, she'd tried to convince herself. Talk herself down from the high that'd suddenly invaded her when his hand mistakenly brushed her thigh as he moved to the edge of the mattress. Her desiring *forever* was crazy, she knew that. But she couldn't help it. Lacked control of her heart, just as she wasn't able to cool the heat that blazed within her whenever he was near. Or overcome the emptiness she felt when he left.

"Getting ready to go?" she asked, watching her upside-down explanation point brightly reflect in his rich brown eyes.

"Yeah," he answered.

Harmony followed him to the doorway. Stared at his back under heavy lids as his footfalls carried him down a few stairs. Silently, she moved into the hall, willed him to look back at her.

Riz had disappeared, and his absence killed her. Without him, Harmony's waking hours were empty and her nights were cold. There were no phone calls. No "What's goin' on, baby?" No Riz stopping by to rest his head on her pillow while she wrote. Not one trace of the confusion she'd complained about but now longed for. No Riz anywhere.

Harmony stripped herself out her blues and changed into all black clothes. She wanted to slip into the night. Blend in with the darkness while she caught her breath and measured her future. Riz may have possessed her heart but the last time she'd checked, she still owned her life. Not him. And she decided to do just that. Own her future — with or without him. She'd been born by herself, would die by herself. And no one could live her life for her but herself.

Labor Day in Palm Springs was hot. And so was Harmony. Standing by the pool, fitted snugly into the red Playboy bunny costume that'd been tailored to ride her curves, she received a lot of attention. Too much for someone in particular — the host whose party she was unknowingly crashing. Against her better judgment, and because she was moving, she'd agreed to attend the masquerade party with Alicia at the vacation home. In two days, New York City would be her new home and Los Angeles would be behind her, and she wanted one last Cali outing with her family no matter how twisted Alicia was.

Bikinis. Swimming trunks. Costumes. Braids and fades whizzed by her as the other party attendees celebrated the holiday. But not

Harmony. She was at the function but wasn't a part of it. She'd gone with hopes of enjoying herself but didn't know anyone there except Alicia, and she'd disappeared. And Harmony wasn't exactly harmonious about dealing with people she didn't know. On tiptoe, she snaked her neck trying to make out Alicia through the crowd. She was ready to go back to their hotel but Alicia had the car keys.

"*What's up,* baby?" Riz stood, greeted her like they'd never separated.

Harmony grinned. "You."

Riz gripped her in a hug, spun her around. Admired her openly. "Is *that* right? Like that? Damn you look good —" he whirled her again "— damn near naked, Harmony? I can't let you get outta my sight. Not like this." He sat, patted his leg and pulled her down onto his lap.

Harmony sat sideways on him like he was her throne. She knew his pulling her onto his lap was as big a move for him as it was for her. And a loud warning to any man watching. Riz was private. He didn't do public displays. Neither did she.

She was just as happy to see him. Tracing her finger on his collar, she looked intently into his eyes, then shifted her weight until she was leaning on his shoulder. Harmony was getting comfortable with him again. "What're you doing here?"

Riz winked. Patted her thighs. "Come on, now. You're at my party."

Harmony reared back her head. "*Your* party?"

Riz nodded. "How you think I knew you were here? And what're you doing going to parties anyway — without me? You don't go out."

Harmony winked. Caught women in her peripheral staring at Riz. "Things change."

Riz ran his fingers up the back of her neck, tangled them in her hair. Gripped familiarly. "But the game remains the same."

A few mai tais later and Harmony latched on to Riz. Let go of her insecurities, her wanting him to want her first. All resistance flew. Her soft touch turned strong as she grabbed his collar, held on to him. Owned him. Became possessive and competitive when some other women didn't take the hint or their eyes off him.

He patted her leg again. "I'll be right back, baby," he said, gently removing her from his lap.

Harmony watched him disappear into the vacation home, slipped out of her stilettos. Decided she'd be right back, too, while she followed him.

He went into the bathroom.

So did she. "You forgot to lock the door,"

she said, locking it behind her.

Riz looked at her.

She gazed at him, eyes glazed but not because of the alcohol. From the heat. Her hotness. "Now," was all she uttered, grabbing Riz again. Yanking him by his shirt until his body met hers. His lips. Hardness. Hands in her hair. On her face. Covering her breasts and massaging between her legs set her ablaze. Melted her sweet spot until he'd honeyed her.

Her Playboy bunny costume was now a puddle on the floor. Naked, Harmony followed it, dropped to her knees. Took Riz's swimming shorts down with her. She paused, stared at his package. Riz was very gifted, and she couldn't wait to wrap his large present with her heat. She kissed what she'd been yearning for. Her tongue flickered, tasted his molasses. "*Look* at me," she demanded, then savored his warm chocolate in her mouth until he was ready to melt, too.

"Wait," he warned, then got down on his knees. Laid her on the floor. Grabbed her ankles. Positioned one to the east shoulder, the other he pointed west, then moved his mouth toward her equator.

"No." Harmony stopped him. "I want you inside me. Please let me feel you."

"You sure?" he asked from between her legs.

Harmony grabbed his shoulders, guided him up. "Yes."

"But I want to taste you."

"You can taste me later. After the party. I promise. Just please gift me."

Riz positioned himself on his knees and shouldered her legs. His finger parted her gently, and she closed her eyes, gave in to the succulent rush that pulsated.

But nothing happened.

Harmony opened her eyes. Saw him staring at her sweetness. "What's wrong?"

Riz shook his head. "Nothing. Everything is perfect. It's so wonderful. So pretty. Let me taste it."

Harmony pulled him down over her. Bucked her hips. Grabbed his bigness. Slid it between her slit. "Fuck me! Now!"

And then it happened. And she thought she was going to die. Right then. Right there. On a Palm Springs bathroom floor. Because never in her life had she imagined that something could feel so pleasurable and painful at once. Riz had spread her. Opened her. Touched her so deep she could feel him making love to her heart.

And she cried.

Harmony woke up in the master bedroom and looked next to her. She stared at Riz. Couldn't believe that he was there, live and in the flesh. Couldn't believe that their night had been real. It seemed so magical that she was afraid to take her eyes off him for fear that he'd disappear and she would realize it'd all been a dream. But it was true. The soreness and stickiness between her legs told her so. They had danced in the bathroom, tangled again minutes after the party was over. "I love you," she whispered, knowing his sleeping ears couldn't hear her. Gently, she traced her finger on the side of his face. She hated to wake him, but had to. She'd told him she was moving out of town, but now she didn't want to go. Not after what they'd shared. She rubbed his back, not wanting to startle him. He had to get up. She had to know what he wanted before she boarded the plane in two days. There would be no games this time. No hidden feelings. Riz would be her deciding factor as to whether she'd leave or not.

Riz opened his eyes and sat up. "I don't want you to go. I want you here at home with me in L.A."

"In the *same* house?"

Riz smiled. Gave her a knowing look. "You know I've never lived with a woman. Don't know if I could. But we can work on it," he said, steepling his hands and shaking his head as if he were already apologizing for taking her stolen dream. "But I do want you here with me, I just don't wanna put you in harm's way."

Harmony leaned forward, kissed him on the cheek. His answer had hurt like hell. "Riz, you know I'm not the type of woman you can just buy a house for. I'm not a deck of cards you play with and then stash away until you're ready to play again. I'm the kind of woman you'd have to come home to. Every night. I'm the type of woman you'd have to marry."

Riz's head bounced, and Harmony knew that he understood. He opened his mouth to speak, and she silenced him with a finger.

"Shh. We both have our limits and principles. We know what we want and can't handle. Let's just keep it like it is."

"You still my Harmony?" he asked sincerely.

Harmony masked her pain behind a laugh. "I'll always be your Harmony. Your personal anthem who'll be with you wherever you go. We're a part of each other, so we can't lose one another."

Harmony gathered her things after Riz went back to sleep. With tears in her eyes, she tiptoed out the door, knowing he'd never find her. She was good at disappearing.

I'm waiting for the punch line, but all I get is silence. "Hello? Caller, are you still there?"

"I'm still here."

Macy is waving at me frantically, signaling me to pick up line nine. "We're going to take a ten-second break," I say into the mic. "We have some major drama unfolding right here *On the Line.* Hold on to your shorts." I pick up the phone line and my mouth drops open. This is too good. I tell each of my callers to hang on and they will be live on the air in three, two, one . . .

"Go ahead, caller. You want to tell us your name."

"My name's not important, my reason for calling in is."

"Riz? Oh my God! Is that you? I didn't know you were on the line."

I sit back and grin. Ms. Girl had been playing possum all along. She wasn't *anonymous,* she was Harmony. It wasn't a story about some friend, it was her. And damn if Mr. Riz wasn't listening in the whole time.

"Why don't I let you two work it all out? And big ups to you, Riz. You sure rocked Harmony's world. You go, boy! See, folks, this show is good for something."

A loud crash shakes me out of my seat. Security breaks in the door and comes storming in like I have weapons of mass destruction. Mr. Bledsoe comes in safely behind them then snatches off my headset and tosses it onto the console.

"Get her out of here!"

The two guards grab me by my arms as I struggle against them. I can't go down without a fight, so I start kicking and screaming like a wild woman. They are so startled that they release me. Guess they think they might catch a case of the crazies. Plus I know these two — we've partied together.

Everyone is out in the hallway watching my unceremonious dismissal. Once I get them off of me I tug on my clothes to get them right, snatch my purse from off the desk and march out like the martyr that I am. I swear I hear applause.

The two guards are so close to me I can tell what they had for breakfast. I suppose they want to make sure I don't pull a fast one and bitch slap Bledsoe before I leave. I get halfway down the hall and one of the overnight interns runs up to me.

"This came in right after your last call," she says, a bit breathless. She hands me a piece of paper. It was an e-mail that had come into the station. It was from Harmony.

Joy,

I can never thank you enough for connecting Riz and I. Because of you and your show,

I'll be walking down the aisle in two months, directly into the arms of my soul mate.

I'll officially be Riz's sacred song for life. His only anthem because I've pulled his player's card!

Blessings,
Harmony

I smile triumphantly to myself and tuck the note in my jacket pocket. How ironic that my last act of treason actually brought two people together. Life. Go figure.

The guards escort me all the way to the front door.

"Sorry about all this, just doing my job," says Lenny, one of the guards, before gallantly opening the front door. Me and Lenny have tossed back a few beers over the years.

"I think they're making a big mistake," Burt adds.

" 'Preciate it, fellas." I put on my best sheepish expression. "Sorry about kicking you in the shins. A little ice will help." I tug in a breath and take my first steps toward unemployment, where Macy is waiting.

"You go, I go," she says.

We link arms and walk out to the parking lot. What the hell we were going to do with our lives and livelihoods now was the

million-dollar question. But in the mean-
time, I need a drink.

CHAPTER 17

After an hour of cussing, drinking and damning the board of directors of WHOT and all of their progeny to hell, I drag myself home with promises to call Macy later in the day.

When I push through the door of my building I do a double take. Randy is chatting it up with Vinny the doorman as if they were best friends.

Vinny jumps up. "Ms. Newhouse, Mr. Temple insisted on waiting," he says.

I shoot him a look then turn my attention on Randy and quickly realize that I'm really glad to see him. And for no reason that I can think of, tears start to burn my eyes. He walks toward me and, without a word, puts his arm around me and leads me to the elevator.

"How did you know?" I finally ask him once we get upstairs.

Randy closes and locks the apartment

door. "I worked late tonight and was listening to the show in the car." He started to chuckle. "I almost had an accident listening."

I grin. "Yeah it was a bit over the top."

"A bit!"

He's smiling and coming my way. My heart is beating like crazy. He looks into my eyes.

"I'm sorry this happened to you. Your management are a bunch of assholes. But this is a blip on your radar. Take some time, think about what you want to do then, like Nike says, *just do it.*"

"Yeah, I guess."

He cups my face in his hands. "I'll be here for you if you let me."

I find myself wrapped in his arms with my head pressed against his chest. A part of me wants to maintain my tough-girl attitude but the other part of me needs just what he's giving and I say something I've never said to a man in my entire life.

"Stay with me tonight."

And he does.

"He spent the night?" Macy asks me in disbelief. "On purpose?"

"Yeah."

She's silent for a minute. "You really like

307

this guy?"

"I think so." I look at her, the one person in the world who knows me better than I know myself sometimes. "I don't understand it."

"What's to understand, Joy? You're a woman who's spent all of her life running from attachments — and we both know why. You hide behind other folks' angst so that you don't have to deal with your own. Maybe it's time to finally stop running."

I know she's right. Lately I'd found myself questioning what I was doing. The letters and calls I'd gotten recently had really begun to make me think.

"Any ideas about what you are going to do to continue living in the style to which you've grown accustomed?"

"Not really. I've been in the radio game my entire working life."

Macy paces back and forth in front of me, a sure sign that she has her thinking cap on. Suddenly she stops and I swear I can see a lightbulb hanging over her head.

"Check this out. You've seen and heard just about every kind of personal drama known to man."

"Yeah, and . . . ?" I'm getting suspicious.

"And you still have tons of letters, tapes and e-mails that you haven't touched."

"Yeah . . ."

"What if you put them all together in a book!"

"What?"

"Write a book. Use some of the letters and stuff, some old shows. Call it *The Best of On the Line.*"

I stare at her in confusion, but slowly the idea begins to take shape and make sense. I plop down on the love seat. A grin moves across my face. "Yeah, I like it. I love it!"

Macy claps her hands in delight.

My bubble bursts. "But I don't know a damned thing about writing a book."

"You don't, but your new boyfriend does."

Bingo!

"I can see it now," Macy says. "Bookstores, TV, radio interviews, Oprah!"

The idea is really taking shape in my head. If I could do it on the air, why not on the page? I just up and dash into my office and call Randy at work.

"Joy! Hi, is everything okay?"

"Everything is better than okay. I have an idea I want to run past you . . ." I tell him about the idea to turn my radio show into a book.

"I love the idea."

"You do!" I start doing the happy dance. Macy appears in my doorway and I give her the thumbs-up. "So what do I have to do?"

"Well, first you need to decide what material you're going to use and you need to put a proposal together."

"Proposal?"

"I can help you with that. Once you have that done and a sampling of what the content will be, I can push it through and we can go to contract."

"Whoo-hoo! How much do you think I can get?"

"A high six figures, I'm sure. Folks love books written by celebrities. And you are definitely a celebrity." He chuckles.

"I better get busy going through these letters and tapes. I have boxes of the stuff."

"Great. When you get a few of them together, we can get started on the proposal."

"I'm going to get started right now. Macy is here and she can help."

"We're still on for tonight, right?"

My heart knocks. "Uh, sure. I'd like that."

"I get out of here around six. Is eight still good for you?"

"I'll be ready."

"See you then."

Slowly I hang up the phone. A date. Damn, can't remember the last time I was on one of those.

"Are you going to tell me what he said or keep staring into space?"

I totally forgot Macy was standing there. "I'm going on a date," I tell her, and I hear how goofy I sound.

"About damned time," she says, and I start grinning like a fool. "What did he say about the book idea?"

"High six figures!"

"That's what I'm talking about! Let's get busy."

"Grab the box on the top shelf of the closet. Those are some of the older shows."

We sit on the floor and begin going through the letters, e-mails and audio tapes of the show, separating our treasures into yes, no and maybe piles. I pull out a tape from a show I did about a year earlier. It had to be from the craziest broad I'd ever heard from.

"Remember this, *Hotline*?" I hold up the tape.

Macy's eyes widen. "Yeah, the crazy woman with the werewolves?"

I start cracking up. "Yeah, scared the hell outta me, *after* I stopped laughing." I reach for my tape recorder and put in the tape. "This was a good one." The tape begins to whir and, after a few moments, our voices fill the room. As I listen, getting both turned-on and scared witless, I let my imagination wander and fill in the visuals for all the things the caller didn't say. . . .

CHAPTER 18

"WHOT, the Joy Newhouse show," Macy said. "You're up next, hold tight and be sure your radio is turned down low so there's no feedback. Your name and age?"

"Uh . . . I'm thirty-nine, but, uhmmm . . ."

"Cool, anonymous. No problem. What's your issue?"

"I, uh, just lost my husband and have a new lover and . . . well . . . it's complicated."

"Good — a sex question," Macy said, as though talking to someone else in the studio. "Joy can work that to the bone. You've been celibate or need to know when it's cool to start doing it again — somethin' like that?"

"Yeah," Sidney said. "And, uh, I think I might have caught something from him after the first time. Although, it could be genetic."

"Oh, this is gonna be great. Hold on, baby — Joy is gonna be on the line in a few after the break."

"So, we've got Anonymous on the line, a sister about thirty-nine years old, my good studio sister says . . . and from what I understand, hon, your husband died, you got your freak on, and some rat bastard gave you something you can't shake — that's messed up, y'all. Talk to me, sis. What happened? How can Joy bring it to you real?"

Sidney took a deep breath. "It didn't happen like that. My husband was the rat bastard."

"Oh, okay, so my bad — my producer got it wrong," Joy said, her voice soothing. "Macy, next time —"

"I know, I know." Macy fussed in the background, causing the typical studio banter that boosted ratings.

"All right, now let me get this straight, your husband gave you a —"

"No," Sidney interrupted. "He's dead. And I may have been the cause, sort of. We had a fight, after he pulled a nine on me. It wasn't the first time he did something like that — the first time he sent some guys to beat me up. So, isn't that self-defense?"

"Whoooooo!" Joy exclaimed with a practiced whistle. "So you were the one carrying the plague, huh?"

"Yeah," Sidney said, with a tinge of reluctance. "Sort of, but not really."

"Is that why he pulled a nine? I mean, I'm just saying, sis — not that it makes it right but —"

"No, no, no. He never caught anything from me, and it's hard to explain. My ex and I hadn't been together in two years. Separate bedrooms, the marriage was a sham."

"Okay, now we're getting somewhere. This so-called husband leaves you high and dry, no booty, no intimacy for two years. Then you met a man . . ." Joy said, allowing her words to trail off with emphasis.

"He's the most fantastic, sexy, incredibly wonderful man . . ."

"Ain't they all, girl — but he ain't worth your life!" Joy shouted, and the smack of a high five echoed through the studio along with her producer's background comments.

"Yes he is, Joy," Sidney said. "This one was worth it. But that's not why I called."

"This sister is straight crazy if she has what I think she does," Joy Newhouse exclaimed. "I have *got* to keep your insane ass on the line to hear this one. You are gonna have to break it all the way down to the nub for me, girl. How do you let some man give you the plague and — just help me understand? You sound like a fairly educated woman, make me understand this."

"Okay . . . here's the deal," Sidney said with a surge of confidence, evading the question about the virus. "My husband was an ass. He died and I want to know if, by some chance, if a person got mauled by a wolf — an animal that was clearly provoked into attack mode by threatening behavior — do you personally feel that —"

"Hold it, stop playing on my phone!" Joy said, hollering and laughing. "Oh my gawd. No, she did not say wolf, like a werewolf! A pit bull, all right, messed up as that may be. A Rot, I can deal with — but are you saying you sicced a wolf dog on the man, or are you leaning to some supernatural conspiracy theory thing tonight?"

"No, I didn't sic the animal — it attacked because he attacked me." Sidney hesitated. "That's the . . ."

The studio was in an uproar, and laughter echoed from the speakers into the house as the show crew argued what constituted a werewolf and made references to several rap artists that could pass as one.

"I just needed to know from a disinterested party . . . if I was going crazy," Sidney murmured.

"You're asking us about werewolves and

you need me to tell you if you're crazy?" Joy said, laughing. "Don't be shy. Caller, you're awfully quiet — are you still on the line?" Joy continued to laugh with Macy and her engineer. "It takes all kinds to make a world. What happened, girl?"

"Okay, here's what happened," Sidney said. "He tried to attack me, my wolf came out and went for him — which evened out the strength differential — then got himself beat up so badly by both of us that it looked like he'd been mauled, is what I was saying."

"That's craaaazy," Joy said. "Dayum! I call it self-defense if some deranged man attacks you and your dog rescues you, girl. Shoulda mauled his sorry ass — brothers need to keep their hands off women."

"That's what I'm saying. Sho' you right," Macy agreed, gaining a rumble of agreement from the engineer.

"He got his ass beat down," Brick said.

"Is that the boyfriend? Who's the bass in the background?" Joy shouted. "This is too wild. Yo, boyfriend," she teased. "So, you got in the mix, too, and kicked the husband's ass? What'd y'all do, roll up on him like a Nia Long type of thing? That sounds too ghetto, you know that, right?"

"No. Wasn't me, would love to take the

credit. The sick bastard was messing with my lady, didn't know she could go straight gulley on him, and, hey . . . he got his ass kicked. I was just the referee."

"Whooo!" Joy said, making the studio erupt again with comments from the peanut gallery as she and Macy verbally sparred and even got the engineer involved.

"Gangsta, daaaayum," Macy hollered. "Right, Tyrone?"

"You know it," the engineer said, laughing. "I like a sister who can hold her own, but she can't be looking like no knife-fighter."

"Oh, yeah, oh, yeah, no doubt — she gotta be fine," the producer agreed.

"Naw, man, *fionne,*" Tyrone corrected.

"This one, my lady," Brick said with pride in his voice, "is fine as — *bleep* —"

"We feel you, man," the engineer said.

"Anonymous, we said we feel you," Joy repeated. "But how did you feel when you were kicking your husband's ass with your lover standing there?"

"I really hadn't thought about it that way. He'd dogged me for a l-long time," she managed to stammer. "Tried to take everything I'd worked hard for all my life, and had affair after affair, did everything you could imagine. Set me up. Even tried to kill me."

"So, this was pent-up, had been brewing?" Joy said, her voice filled with empathy. "That's enough to drive somebody over the edge, to seriously try to hurt the person who was doing all of this — not that I advocate violence, but you can see how it could get. ridiculous."

"Yeah," Sidney said.

"Wait, we gotta hear this," Joy said. "I want you to hold on while we break for commercial and come back.

"All right," Joy said, "now that we've handled our business to keep the lights on in here, we're back with an anonymous, fine — from her own lover's description — thirty-nine-year-old female caller, who says she kicked her husband's ass, he subsequently died . . . I don't know, that's murder, right? Unless he died from something else, or was it self-defense?"

"It was self-defense," Brick rumbled.

"That's what they all say," Joy scoffed.

"The sister didn't go to jail, and was obviously vindicated," Brick said calmly. "So, hey."

"All right," Joy said, sounding unconvinced but willing to move forward. "I'm not po po or a lawyer, so we're not going there for the sake of time. But the boyfriend says he didn't do the husband, we know your dog got in it . . . still, the part I wanna get back to is this STD y'all was passing between you. Tell me about that."

"Told you purebred humans were judgmental," Brick crooned to Sidney.

"It's not an STD," Sidney said.

"What, like a nervous tic? A blood condition? C'mon, we need to be honest and address issues that are wrecking havoc in the community."

"Oh, God, it's something that only one in several million people contract — like West Nile, or Bird Flu . . . or . . . Joy, I can't really think what it's like, but it's . . . oh, *just like that.*"

"Oh, okay, now we're getting somewhere," Joy replied, after a round of comments from her crew. "But how did *you* get it?"

"It's something so rare that . . ." Sidney's voice trailed off as she choked back a gasp. "If you were already a carrier — I had it in my system already as a child. Like a recessive gene that's dormant."

"So this would sort of be like one of those crazy, never-heard-of type of diseases, is what you're telling us? What's it called?"

"Tell her," Sidney breathed.

"I'm . . . I'm not sure what the true

technical name is," Brick said, desire bottoming out his voice.

"This is some deep mess you all are trying to get me to buy into," Joy said. "We need to get a doctor on the line or something to verify some of these wild-ass allegations. I've never heard of something that can just make you flip, that's a blood disease — have you, Ty? Macy, what about you?"

"It's like schizophrenia, makes you act bipolar," Brick said quickly.

"So, this mental, blood thing that you don't know the technical name for, this made your woman flip on her ex after years of abuse, who subsequently died in some way we have yet to fully hear about — anybody go to jail?"

"Uh-uh," Brick said through his teeth.

"All right, in the interest of responsibility here, tell me you didn't kill the man? I'm just being real."

"Naw, that didn't happen," Brick said fast, then paused to take a deep breath. "Not like that."

"Oh, all right, glad to hear that," Joy said, relief washing through her voice. "Dude died later?"

The sound of heavy breathing could be heard on the other end before the line dropped.

"You're not big on details, I see," Joy teased. "Strong silent type? Man! I am so sorry that call dropped off the hotline, though, y'all. I really wanted to ask that wild couple a bazillion more questions on the werewolf comment. Like, how do you train a wolf and where the hell do you keep it in the city? Isn't that illegal, against all kinds of codes, and whatnot? I know a man had a tiger in a New York apartment, and you hear about these huge snakes crazy people keep, so who knows? I still think they did her husband and there's more to the story, but I don't know. That wolf comment seemed like it came out of nowhere. But they sounded real sexy together, the two of them . . . Like her voice and his, they just sounded in tune — both crazy, mind you, but synced. What do y'all say?"

"I say it was getting real quiet on the phone, ya mean?" the engineer said.

"Oh, get out — your mind is in the gutter. They *were not* getting busy while they were on the phone on *the radio!*" Joy laughed.

"I don't know," Macy said. "It sounded like the convo on their side was drifting. I'm not a phone-sex expert — but, hey, I'm just saying."

"You two are incorrigible. You see what I

have to deal with on the air, late night's folks, and the crew I have to work with in here? I just hope our callers were satisfied with what they got from the call."

I hit the stop button. "Now that was some wild shit." I shake my head and look across at Macy, who's hugging herself as if she's freezing.

"What's wrong?"

"What if that Sidney chick was telling the truth?"

"Say what?"

"What if she is some kind of werewolf and she was getting it on with him during that call?"

I make a face at Macy. "Chile, please." A chill suddenly runs through me. "No way." But to tell you the truth, I remember that call like it was yesterday. It scared the hell outta me then just like it did now. Who am I to say what's real and what's not? All I know is, if some hairy-looking man runs up on me, he's getting shot! I blow out a breath. "Let's keep digging."

"You want that in the yes, no or maybe pile?" Macy asks.

"Definitely yes. It's classic."

We spend the next couple of hours on the floor tossing and laughing, the years of our time together at WHOT piling up at our feet. Finally I get up to stretch my legs. "Hungry?"

"Starved."

"I'll fix us something to eat."

"Cool, I'll keep digging."

I leave Macy to the task at hand and head out to the kitchen. While I'm grilling some turkey burgers and fixing a salad, a letter that I'd dubbed Desperate Housewife, from about a year ago, pops into my head. I smile at the memory. Naughty girl. . . .

CHAPTER 19

Twenty-one meals a week. Twenty-one damn meals a week. That's what I'm responsible for. Twenty-one times that I stand in front of that mammoth refrigerator and wonder what the hell I'm going to make. I wonder how the hell I got into this, when the hell the refrigerator began to feel like Goliath to me, why the hell my whole life revolves around food. I have a graduate degree, damn it. I'm smart, talented, and obviously beautiful enough to have gotten trapped in this marriage. And now, here I stand, looking at the empty space between the soy milk and the bottles of lime-flavored Perrier on the top shelf.

"Mommy, I want to eat," a tiny voice said, breaking into my lamentations. It was my daughter, Tatiana. At two and a half, she spoke more clearly than most of the three- and four-year-olds in her playgroups. She was the reason I took a step away from my job, a very lucrative job, mind you, in advertising. I hadn't regretted my decision. But then one year at home, away from my career, turned into two, which unfortunately, despite the politically correct reports flooding the media, is professional suicide in corporate America. I hunkered down, preparing myself to reenter the game years later, once Tat was old enough to enter school full-time.

But being solely responsible for a child twenty-four hours a day was taking its toll. I needed adult conversation and companionship, and I thought that if I had some help with her, I could have some free time to reconnect with old friends and reclaim me. So I broached the subject one night when Clay, my husband, got home early at nine o'clock.

"Honey, I was thinking about looking for some help," I began gently. I was holding his drink in my hand, a tumbler containing two fingers of Scotch.

With his cigar clinched between his teeth and his gaze turned upward at the stars as we stood on the deck of our Bucks County, Pennsylvania, home, he looked like he was in a decent mood. Removing his cigar from his mouth and taking the drink from me with a nod of acknowledgment, he said, "We already have a housekeeper. You can't have her every day while you're sitting at home playing with Tat."

I took a deep breath. Conversations with Clay were more like cross-examinations than exchanges of ideas. I often wondered why I was ever drawn to him in the first place. But then I remembered that his drive and ambition were key in my initial attraction to him. His status came in second, and placing in third were the numerous zeros in his financial portfolio. He was twenty-five years my senior and bad habits had settled into him, working their way into the grooves so now they were cemented into unsightly stains. It was no wonder his first and second wives left him, the latter refusing alimony, saying she just wanted to get away from him with no ties at all.

"Chelsea, you sound lazy and selfish. What do you want to do? Be her mother or abandon her? Take your pick, dear," he said, quaffing down the Scotch before turning to look at me.

I stared at him, wishing that I'd poisoned his drink. Truthfully, as little as he was at home, I could have hired someone without consulting him, but as he was my husband and Tatiana's father, I wanted to include him in any decisions that I made concerning her. I wouldn't be so considerate, polite, or partner-like next time.

"Good night, Clay," I'd said, walking away from the interrogation. I'd blown out a defeated sigh as I'd headed back into the house, through the foyer and up the staircase to my bedroom. Clay, a creature of habit, would finish his drink and cigar, retire to his room and be out of the house by eight in the morning.

That had been a year ago. To ease some of the loneliness I'd felt, I'd joined a few moms' clubs and signed up for a few playdates. If needed, one of the other members would babysit Tatiana while I ran a few quick errands or desperately needed a couple of hours of hands-free time. For longer periods like doctor's visits or hair appointments, I leaned on my mother for support.

Selecting the day-care center behind Clay's back had been relatively easy. Some members of the moms' club had given me suggestions, and I had called three of them right away, scheduling tours for the next day. Tatiana had accompanied me to all three, and I'd gone through a checklist that I'd found online of things to look for in a day-care center. I'd added my own criteria, and from there, the choice had been simple. I took a few more days for observation and transition for Tat, and by the second week in October, Tatiana was officially enrolled in school.

Tatiana had been in school for four days, and for the fourth day in a row, I found myself sitting in the library enjoying the quiet while I reread one of the old classics I had enjoyed as an undergrad. The librarian smiled with recognition at me, and I waved in response. I read nonstop for three hours, finishing the book and setting back with a sigh and a smile as I reflected on it.

"I guess you enjoyed it," the librarian whispered as she walked past me.

"Not nearly as much as I enjoyed having the opportunity to read."

Her face wore a smile, but her eyebrows wore a question mark. "My daughter just started day care, so now I have a little free time."

"Well, you've been spending it in a great place."

"Yeah," I replied. "I've always loved the library."

"Really?"

"Mmm-hmm. Ever since I was a little girl."

"We are a little understaffed and could use some help a few times a week," she hinted.

"I'd love to," I piped up, needing no other prompting.

"When could you —"

"Tomorrow," I interrupted, happy to reenter the land of adults once again.

The next day, after dropping Tatiana off, I did a quick workout before showering at the gym and heading to the library. The head librarian gave me a tour before pointing me toward a cart that I would use for reshelving books. As she spoke I was thinking, I have an MBA, and I've won awards for some of my ads, but here I am pushing a cart of books around. The thought vanished just as quickly when I remember that this was a way for me to spend my time usefully before my brain turned to mush from watching another kids' television show.

I'd been at the counter, checking out some materials for a patron, and I went over to the front desk to answer the ringing phone. I was transferring the call to the circulation desk when I felt someone standing in front of me. When I looked up, I saw a man with skin like carob standing before me. His slanted, almond-shaped eyes were reminiscent of Tyson Beckford, and looking at his succulent lips made my own twitch. The goatee framing his mouth was etched with precision, and when he smiled at me, I felt myself flush. He wore faded jeans whose waist kissed the top of his hipbones. The neckline of his cream thermal undershirt peeked over the top of his red flannel shirt. His ears were tucked under the sides of his red-and-black baseball cap.

"I'm looking for some books on starting a business," he said, responding to my standard greeting.

"Okay. Is there any specific book that you're looking for?"

"Not one in particular, but I'm starting from the ground floor, so any books that you could recommend would help."

"So what kind of business is it?" I asked.

"Huh, oh, it's a coffee shop slash bookstore," he said with an uncertain smile.

"Okay. What are some of your marketing strategies?"

"I hadn't thought that far in advance. Hey, can I pick your brain over coffee?"

"Sure. I finish working at noon. That's a half hour."

He looked at his watch. "I'll be finished getting books by then."

I sauntered away smiling.

A half hour later I was sitting in my truck with my shades on watching him walk down the sidewalk to his car. His walk was smooth and sexy, like he had someplace to be, but he was confident that whoever he was meeting would wait. I backed out of my space when I saw that he was in his car behind me, and I exited the parking lot heading toward Panera. Inside, he sat with a small notepad open and his pen poised, ready to take notes.

"I just realized that I don't know your name," I said, then sipped my weak tea.

"It's Marcus."

"Marcus, I'm Chelsea."

"It's a real pleasure meeting you."

"Enchanté," I replied with a smile.

He laughed. "I certainly would love to have you around as a consultant. I can't afford to pay you anything now, though."

"I'd give you my services for free," I said with a wink. "In my past life I was in advertising before I got married and had a child."

Marcus smiled and rubbed his goatee.

I'd finished my tea and, after checking my watch, I saw that it was time to pick Tatiana up from school. I usually picked her up before nap time so that we could go home and sleep together, and it was nearing one, when all of the other kids were getting ready to pull their sleeping mats out.

"I have to go get my daughter," I said, gathering my purse and taking out my keys.

"Would it be out of line if I asked you if I could see you again?"

"I'm a married woman," I said with a sad smile.

"I'm sorry, I didn't . . ."

"I'm just making sure that you know what you're doing."

Marcus nodded. "I think I know."

"Okay."

I picked up his pen and leaned in close enough to write on his notepad. I scribbled my cell phone number down.

"You smell good, too. What is that?"

"It's my natural scent. *It* smells like strawberries," I ventured further.

Grinning broadly, he said, "It's my favorite fruit. I suddenly got a taste for them."

I stood up and walked away, not bothering to look over my shoulder. I could feel the heat of his eyes as he watched me walk away.

Each time that I'd seen Marcus it had been in the safety of a small crowd, in a restaurant, a coffee shop and along the exercise path called Kelly Drive in Philadelphia. I'd been saved by those other people. Rather, he'd been saved, because I had so much pent-up passion I probably would have broken him in two.

But today when he called at nine o'clock, asking simply, "Are you available?" I did something I didn't I think I'd ever do. I invited him to my house.

It was ten o'clock when he called from the entrance of our gated community, and I buzzed him in, readying myself to meet him at the front door.

I opened the door when I heard him knock, ushering him into the spacious foyer. I smiled nervously as he looked around.

"This is nice," he commented. "No wonder you stopped working."

I flinched, hearing his last comment.

"Do you want to see it?" I asked.

"Sure. It'll be a long time before I can live like this."

I walked him around the first floor, opening doors to offices, dens, sitting rooms and the other rooms that went virtually unused. I took him to the basement where he checked out Clay's weight room, home movie theater and wine cellar, gaping at them in awe. Then we toured the second floor, where I walked past Clay's room with no explanation. I paused in Tatiana's doorway, breathing in the smell of the baby lotion that I still used on her over the expensive cream that was all the rage among the moms in our circle. I didn't care what the jet set was using. I liked my baby to smell like a baby.

"This is my angel's room," I said, nodding at the black-and-white photos of her on the wall over her mini table and chairs. The table was still set from the tea party we'd had that morning before I took her to school.

I backed out of the room, nodding in the direction of the spare bedroom. It was supposed to be for another child, but I certainly wasn't about to let that happen again. I was already the married single mom of one. I wasn't going to double the fun.

The last room on the tour was my bedroom,

and as I opened the door to it, I shuddered involuntarily. Marcus stood behind me with his hand on the small of my back.

"Are you okay?" he asked.

I nodded, not wanting to verbalize a lie. The truth was, as I opened the door, I visualized myself spinning around the retractable pole that came out of the ceiling. It was one of the many tools that Clay had outfitted my room with. There was also a swing that hooked into the ceiling over the bed. It was in the closet now, but I still could see the place where the hooks went. The feather boas, diamond-studded and lacy undergarments were packed away in the closet, but as long as they were in that room, they were with me.

So when Marcus turned me around and kissed me, I couldn't respond. Instead, I collapsed in his arms and wept. He led me out of the bedroom and toward the steps to go downstairs.

Downstairs, I didn't explain anything. Wiping my tear-streaked face, I said simply, "Not in there. Clay's heading for Tokyo on Friday. He'll be gone for two weeks. Let's connect then."

"Okay," he said gently.

I called my mother and asked her to keep Tatiana for a few days. She agreed without hesitation.

Marcus lay panting, tangled in the sheets of the bed in the Ritz-Carlton hotel room where we'd been holed up for three days straight. The only break from our intense lovemaking sessions had been to eat, get massages, shower, talk and sleep.

"I don't know how you do it," he'd said over and over. "I'm, what, five years younger than you, and I can't keep up."

I smiled when he said it, unwilling to let him know that this marathon was going to have to last me because I was about to go back to the damn circus where I'd been walking on tightropes and jumping on trampolines but getting no thrills of my own.

Truthfully, it had been a little strange having Marcus in my space continuously.

But even though I wasn't accustomed to sharing so much of my space with someone else, it wasn't a bad kind of strange. It felt good.

But all good things must come to an end. Mom called me on my cell phone after day five. I had been calling there twice a day to check in on Tat, and she sounded happy. My mom had been keeping her busy, but by day five, my daughter said that she didn't want to live with Grandmom forever because she missed me.

With three more days until Clay's return, I was moody and withdrawn. I worked out and went to the library as usual, but I lost the spring in my step. I couldn't make sense of my emotions.

A few days later Clay arrived home looking like death on ice. One look at him when I picked him up from the airport, and I said, "You need to get to the hospital."

I drove to Temple University Hospital, where he was admitted after a battery of tests had been performed.

"Your husband was a walking dead man," the doctor told me as Clay lay in the bed.

My mother had come to the hospital to get Tatiana and take her back to her house, but I surely needed Mom by my side for emotional support.

"We're trying to stabilize his blood sugar now, but honestly, I don't know why he wasn't in a diabetic coma. The normal range for blood sugar is between seventy and one-twenty. His was seven hundred."

My mouth dropped open as I looked at him. His eyes were closed as if he were trying to wish himself to be anywhere but there. I reached out to touch his hand, and I was surprised when his fingers gripped mine tightly in return.

Clay was released after a weeklong stay, and when he got home, he seemed to see things for the very first time. On the first morning, when Tatiana and I went downstairs for breakfast, he was already down there in the kitchen drinking a glass of water.

"Daddy," Tat squealed excitedly, happy to see him by daylight on a weekday.

He picked her up, startled but pleased with her display of emotion.

I went into the kitchen to cut the fruit for her breakfast. I picked out a container of her yogurt and a package of cottage cheese and fruit puree for mine. After popping a couple of turkey sausages in the microwave, I poured orange juice for the two of us and began measuring Clay's oatmeal. The doctor had told him that he should eat it for breakfast every morning, and I intended to follow the doctor's orders. As nasty as Clay had been, I don't know why I wanted him around for the future, but I did.

When I returned to the table, Tat was telling Clay about school. I hadn't told him that I had enrolled her, and I certainly hadn't thought about how or when I'd tell him. But now seemed as good a time as any to clear the air.

338

"She goes part-time every day," I began. "It's good for her socialization, and frankly I just needed some hands-free time. Some time that I could be an adult again."

I wasn't sure what to expect in response, but "I understand" was the furthest thing from my mind. I blinked hard to make sure I heard him properly. He smiled in response.

"Since we're clearing the air, I have to tell you something, too. But it will have to wait until Tat's not here."

"Okay," I replied, going back to the stove to scoop up his oatmeal.

After breakfast, I went upstairs to get Tatiana and myself dressed. To my surprise, Clay got dressed, as well, and he was waiting at the bottom of the steps for us.

"I thought I'd ride with you to take her to school," he offered.

"Okay," I said. I was already holding my daughter's hand. Now I reached out to hold my husband's, too.

We drove to school, and Clay walked inside with us. We walked her to her classroom, and gave him a tour of the school, pointing out her artwork in the common gallery for all of the classes.

When we settled back into the car, Clay grabbed my hand and looked at me earnestly. We drove home in silence. Back at the house, he popped in one of the educational videos about diabetes, and he seemed antsy, like he was avoiding the confession that he'd mentioned earlier.

After the video, we left his home theater and headed up to the kitchen for a snack. With his back to me, Clay began to speak as he rummaged through the refrigerator.

"You certainly don't deserve what I'm about to say, but I've had an epiphany of sorts since my illness. I've been a rather bad husband in so many ways, but this takes the cake. I've been having an affair for the past three years, and I mean to end it today. You've put up with all of my garbage, but I intend to make a new start and be a new man. I just want to know if you can forgive me for the affair and everything else."

I looked at him, and I began to cry. It wasn't about the affair or the bull that he'd dished out with regularity over the years. It wasn't even about my guilt over Marcus. It was about making a fresh start, a new beginning. He was ready, and I was ready. That was great. But just in case he ever slipped back into jackass mode, I'd keep Marcus my little secret, that piece of joy I went to when times were hard, and I needed a sweet memory to keep me company.

■ ■ ■ ■

I shake my head at the memory of her letter. I wonder if Clay has screwed up again. Her life was better than a late-night soap opera any day. I'd have to make sure her story got in the book.

"Girl, I'm 'bout to starve to death," Macy says all gangsta-like as she appears in the kitchen doorway.

"All done. What's that?" I lift my chin to indicate the papers in her hand.

"I ran across this letter. I don't remember you ever reading it on the show. It's kind of kinky but touching."

Macy sits down at the table and I bring over our lunch and join her. "Let me see." She hands me the letter. . . .

CHAPTER 20

I tried to yell above the noise in the bar. A perky young blonde had plopped down beside me, crossing her long white legs and signaling for the barkeep to serve her one. I watched her motion at him regally, like she was entitled to be waited on hand and foot. She was dressed very simply, in a tight, short black dress, almost exposing her femininity. All of the men, all races, noticed her adjust her bottom on the leather stool, smiling innocently at me.

"Do you come here often?" the blonde said, grinning.

"No, not really." I really didn't want to be disturbed. I just wanted to get my buzz.

"Are you coming from work?" She didn't know how to quit.

"Yep," I replied.

"What do you do?"

"An electrician, and it's a boring job. And you?"

"A pawn," she said quietly.

"Like in chess, right?"

"Almost. I obey orders for a living. I act out people's fantasies without resistance or questions. You could say I answer wishes. Like a good fairy. I obey commands whether they are private or public."

My face contorted. "Do you always obey anything a person commands you to do?"

"Yes," she said, her blue eyes twinkling.

As a savvy New Yorker, I knew not to make extended eye contact with her. So I stared at my drink, Scotch on the rocks, thinking about how timely it was that she would sit right next to me. I'd had a fight, a nasty verbal one, with the woman who was living with me. She told me things that curled my hair. About our love, about us, about our future, about her and her dreams. Her expression had the intent of a cold-blooded murderer in a killing zone, near the prey, close to the target.

"Are you a nurse or a teacher in the city?" I scratched my head.

"No, I am a pawn," she answered with a firmness that started me thinking. "Putting yourself into the clutches of a male can have tragic circumstances, don't you think? Some people don't have lofty goals or intentions. Being a pawn can really lead to trouble. You have to be careful who you choose. After all, the woman chooses a man and not vice versa."

I sipped the drink. "I know."

The barkeep put the drink, a Sex on the Beach concoction, on the counter, and when she pulled some bills to pay him, she flicked her long yellow hair into his brown face. Mr. Leong. He was a young Vietnamese kid, barely in his twenties, short stubby fingers. The son of the Boat People. A village near Saigon. We could both smell the strong lavender scent worn on her slender cranelike neck. I didn't like it, but he seemed to prefer it, lurking nearby with his nostrils flared.

"Why did you pick this seat?" I asked.

"I liked you, Mister Man," she chirped. I could see she had a nice figure.

I really looked at the woman, very pale, big bust, tapered waist, flat boyish ass. All I needed was for my lady to think I was out here catting around. That would constitute an ultimate betrayal.

Before I was with my wife, Melba, I was a dog. Oh, man, I nailed anything with a hole in it. I remember the cops raided a massage parlor and arrested me for soliciting a sex worker. They sent me to a school for johns in Brooklyn. It was in a high school with about thirty guys, all of them caught with prostitutes. The cops had a former whore who read them the riot act, asking them if they liked screwing girls who no longer cared about themselves and were victimized as kids.

The guys nodded shamelessly and whispered that all they cared about was getting the orgasm. Getting that nut. But I was different. I never did anything like that again.

Maybe I want to spice up my sex life by fooling around. However, only with pure, clean-cut women and girls. Not tricks or treats. No public sex. Very decent and polite.

The blonde snapped me out of my fog. "Are you straight? I don't want any switch-hitters, you know what I mean?"

"I'm cool. I'm straight."

"Do you have a woman? A ladylove?"

I didn't answer that. Instead I drank some of my booze.

"Who did you lose your virginity to?" she asked with a smirk on her lips.

"I should ask that question of you," I replied. "You're the pawn."

"I'll answer. I lost my girlhood to my uncle. He bought my silence for a Sno-Kone. I don't mind answering questions. What about you?"

I grinned sheepishly. "My mother's best friend. She really pinned my ears back."

"Where did she do the deed?" she quizzed me.

"In her car. It was good but scary, very scary.

I could imagine how she would be as a lover, very demanding, very precise, very selfish. But she did all the right things."

She gulped her drink and swallowed it. "How many serious relationships have you had? Counting the one you're in. How many?"

"How do you know I'm in a relationship?" I watched the men leaning over to look at her breasts. They were not discreet.

"How many?" she asked. She knew the secret to a man's intimacy: just ask him about himself.

"About five," I answered.

"How many sexual partners?"

"I should ask you that. As a pawn, you must have plowed your way through the studs. I know you're not the shy and retiring type. Three more questions and then it's my turn."

"How many?" she repeated.

"I lost count," I laughed, knowing that the number of pleasure partners had evaporated in my memory.

"What's your favorite position?"

"Cowgirl . . . and maybe reverse cowgirl."

"What's your ultimate fantasy?" She sniggered and leaned across the bar, letting me view her ample breasts. It was almost if she were putting them on display.

"A willing blonde who knew the score and didn't blab."

She looked over her glass at me, making her mouth a very inviting place. "Have you ever cheated on your partner?"

"I'd probably do the nasty with you," I confessed. "I like your style."

"Have you ever been caught?" she asked me.

I squinted at her and allowed my voice to rise. "No fair. You've asked your quota of questions. No more."

She winked and smiled ear to ear. "Would you want to fuck me?"

The blonde's question was so overt, up-front, that I could see through the smoke screen right to the trap. I had read an article about these women who were called "decoys," who were paid to tempt the wayward boyfriends and husbands. The women, always lookers, would throw themselves at the victim in lust, ask him a lot of questions about himself and his tastes, and then shuffle him off to the bed and the trap.

"Don't you like pink nipples?" She giggled.

"You know I do." I laughed and she laughed, too.

"I have a room near here," she said, teeth whiter than ever. "I can drop us off."

"Did my wife hire you?" I asked her straight out.

Things became so quiet between us that

you could hear the ice being tormented by the barkeep. I knew the answer already. I knew how much my lady cared. She didn't want me to cheat, didn't want me to lie, didn't want me to betray her. And it really didn't matter if the woman was black or Asian or white. She didn't want me to put myself inside another woman's body. That made sense.

"Yes, she did," the blonde replied.

"How far did she tell you to go before you yelled foul?"

"Until the point of entry, either a finger, a tongue or the other thing." She smiled widely.

Without fanfare, I stood and waved a ten at the barkeep. Leong walked over to me and plucked it out of my hand, nodded. Leaning over to the blonde, I planted a wet kiss on her pink cheek, smiled and left the bar. It had stopped raining and the stars, bright and crisp, were coming out, peeping through the dark clouds.

Signed,
Everything to Gain

"Wow." I fold up the letter and put it aside. "Makes you think about what's important, ya know."

"Exactly."

"I want to use this one, too." As I sit here chewing on my burger, the haunting quality of the letter sticks with me. If I really thought about it, it could have been my story. How many beds have I jumped in and out of without caring, without looking back? Maybe with Randy I can gain something, too, a part of myself that had been excised so many years ago.

"Don't go there," Macy says, cutting into my thoughts. "I know that look. It was a long time ago."

I sniff. "I know. Sometimes it just feels like a minute."

Macy covers my hand with hers and squeezes it tight.

No words are needed between friends.

CHAPTER 21

It's been a little over a month since I was canned. I check the station periodically to see what's happening in my slot — *elevator music.* Word on the street is that ratings for my former time slot are in the toilet. But I really don't have too much time to dwell on that minor victory. Randy fills my days with pulling my manuscript together and my nights with loving.

Quiet as it's kept, I've never been in a real relationship before, but Randy is real patient. And I'm slowly beginning to believe that I deserve some happiness and a man who cares about me. Some nights we don't make love — we just talk, laugh and cuddle. I kinda like it.

Anyway, I've been sitting by the phone all morning waiting for the call from Randy. Today he's making the presentation of *The Best of On the Line* to the editors. I'm a nervous wreck. I check the phone one more time to make sure it's working and it rings in my hand.

"Hello?"

"You ready to be rich and extremely famous?"

My heart takes off on a wild ride. "Are you serious?"

"Absolutely. They love it and want to go to contract immediately."

"What! Oh my God." I start spinning around in a circle.

"I'll have the contract ready by the end of the week. There's going to be a full court media press, book tour, advertisements, talk shows, the whole gamut."

"This is incredible. I can't thank you enough."

"My pleasure. Look, I have a ton of stuff to get together. I'll see you tonight and we can celebrate."

"Okay." In a dream state I hang up the phone. Wow, I'm going to be an author. The prospect is suddenly terrifying. For years I'd only been a voice, a personality. According to Randy I was going to be pushed out into the spotlight for the world to see and scrutinize. I'm filled with mixed emotions. It was one thing to sit in a sound-proof room and rag people, it was another to be put front and center for your own issues to be looked at. True, the book was only a combination of stories from previous shows and letters that have been in my to-be-read file for ages, but I was still going to have to be the front woman answering the questions. I'm not really sure what I'm worried about — the book ain't about me!

I gotta call my girl Macy, who, by the way, is now a producer on WHOT's major competitor station. Ha, how ironic is that? I knew she wouldn't be down for long. The girl has skilz.

She picks up on the third ring and, before she can get a word out, I tell her the news.

"I knew it! Told you. Girl, you are in there. Just make sure you take me on tour with you."

"You know I got you, sis."

"So when are you going to sign the contract?"

"Randy said it would be ready by the end of the week."

"I guess the real question is, when are you going to get your fat check?"

"Not really sure how long that takes. I'll ask Randy."

"Well, I have to get ready for work. Keep me posted."

"I will."

"See you on the *New York Times* list."

"For real."

The rest of my day pretty much flies by. Randy told me that I needed about three or four more stories, so I spend my time looking for some really good ones. Before I know it, it's time to get ready for my celebratory date with my man. Wow, *my man.* I've never said that before. Never had one before. Most of the men who've been in my life have been in and out. It was better that way, at least it had been. But from the moment Randy stepped into my life, he decided he wanted more than a one-night stand. Right up to this moment, I'm not sure why I let him have his way, but I'm beginning to like it — a lot.

When the doorbell rings, I'm just about ready.

"Hey, baby." He walks up to me and kisses me nice and slow, just the way I like it, and I start feeling all squishy inside.

"Hi, yourself."

I take his hand and we walk into the living room. "I just have to get my purse. Did you decide on a place for dinner?"

"I thought we could go down to Tribeca, get something to eat and then check out the film festival. How's that sound?"

"Perfect. I've never been to the film festival."

"Me either. It will be a first for both of us."

Randy was wonderful about stuff like that. There were so many things that we did together for the first time, like canoeing in Central Park, or the time we went to Brooklyn to roller-skate before they closed the Empire Roller Dome, or the Saturday visit to the Botanical Gardens. He opened a new world to me and I loved every minute of it. I'd lived in New York all my life and there was so much of it that I'd never seen before.

As always our evening is wonderful. We laugh and talk and hold hands just like a real couple. Randy tells me all about how he got started in the publishing world and some of the crazy clients he's had over the years, and I swear on a stack of Bibles that I see Robert DeNiro at the festival, but Randy insists that it wasn't him.

"You feel like some company for the rest of the night?" he asks me once we get back to my place.

"Did you have someone in mind," I tease him.

He puts his arms around my waist and pulls me close. "Why don't you tell me."

"Well, there's this guy that I really like and I'd been thinking about asking him for a sleepover."

"Really? Anyone I know?"

"I think you do." I push the door closed and pull him inside.

Today is the big day. I sign my contract and, according to Randy, they will hand me a check for two hundred and fifty thousand dollars, and I'll receive the other half when I turn in the finished product. A half a million bucks for splashing the foils and phobias of other folks' angst. Can't beat it with a stick. Let's just say I'll be heading straight to the bank. There's already been buzz on the airwaves and several media blogs that I'm poised to sign a mega book deal. But the last thing I expect when I walk out of the editorial offices is to be assaulted by the press, who demand a statement. You would think that I'd just been set free on a murder rap with the number of cameras and news hogs waiting for me.

"Ms. Newhouse, Ms. Newhouse, can you confirm that you just signed a half-million-dollar book deal?"

"Ms. Newhouse, is it true that the book is based on the stories from your callers?"

"Will any of the people that you use in your book get any of the proceeds?"

"Do you feel any sense of conscience in

using your listeners' stories to benefit your-self?"

"When will the book be released? What does your old station have to say?"

The questions are flying at me so fast that my head starts spinning. I'm usually the one asking the questions and demanding answers.

Miraculously, Randy appears at my side. "A press release has been prepared that will answer all of your questions," he announces, silencing the melee. "The book is scheduled to be released this summer and we'll be sure that each of you gets an advanced copy." He grabs my arm and hustles me back inside the building and out the back way.

"What the hell was that all about?"

"I guess I should have warned you. The publicity department intentionally leaked your meeting today. It's all part of the publicity campaign to start building buzz about the book." He stops and turns to me. "It's going to get crazy."

I don't know what to say. I'm still in shock, and I'm rarely at a loss for words.

"It'll be fine," he says.

"I just want to go home. Okay?"

"Sure."

We get to the back exit, walk around the block and Randy hails me a cab. "Look, some interviews are being set up for you. We really want to get moving on this book. It's already on the fast track to publication. We know it's going to be hot. The public loves tell-all books and yours is totally original. We want to capitalize on it before some other radio jock decides to do the same thing."

I nod numbly. This is much more than I expected.

"They're going to try to get all in your business and in your head, so be prepared." He opens the cab door and I get in.

"Someone from our PR staff will be contacting you to get some information for the press release. Once that's done, all the questions and your schedule will be handled through our publicity office." He leans down and looks me in the eye. "I didn't want to tell you this before but we've already gotten inquires about film rights."

My heart slams in my chest. He kisses the top of my head. "See you later."

The cab pulls off into the mess of midtown Manhattan traffic and, for the first time since this odyssey began, I'm starting to feel very uneasy.

As promised, a chick named Tanya Steele, my assigned publicist, calls later in the day and does an impromptu interview via phone and wants to know my whole history: where I was born, my parents, where I went to school, how I got started in the business and what prompted me to write the book. We talk for more than an hour. By the time we're done, I'm pretty burned-out. It took a lot to skirt around my real life, the real Joy. For the listening public I was simply Joy Newhouse, the bigmouthed DJ who took provocative to the next level. No one knows the real me or why I turned out the way I did. I want to keep it that way, but I have an eerie feeling that my past is soon going to become my present.

CHAPTER 22

The book is almost out of production and will be on shelves in a matter of weeks. Tanya has set up a whirlwind of interviews for me. So far they have been going really well. The early reviews have been good and Randy says he's sure that with the early orders from bookstores, *The Best of On the Line* is destined to debut on the *New York Times* list. Maybe I've dodged the bullet after all.

Just as I'm about to take my first sip of coffee for the day, my phone rings. Probably Macy.

"Hello?"

"We have a problem," Randy says, instead of hello.

Slowly, I sit down. "What is it?"

"The PR department has received several letters and calls over the past week demanding that a halt be put on the release of the book."

"What? From who?"

"Apparently from some of your callers. They don't want their stories in the book without being compensated."

"What?"

"You're scheduled for your television interview today with Dallas Winters."

Dallas Winters has one of the highest rated television talk shows in the country. To land a spot on her show is major. It would guarantee that sales of the book would shoot through the roof.

"They've threatened to stage a protest during the show."

My insides turn over. I don't believe it. "What are we going to do?"

"This is as much my fault as any. We really should have determined if we were within our rights to publish the stories. I'm going into a meeting with our legal team in about an hour to see what our options are. As soon as we're done, I'll get back to you."

I can't even respond.

"Try not to worry. We'll work it out. I'm pretty sure that there really isn't anything they can do to you. There were no real names used, and once they aired their laundry on your show, it became public knowledge. This is just about greed at this point. I'll call you later."

I hang up the phone and, for a while, all I can do is sit there and stare into space. Finally, I pull myself together and get up. My thoughts are spinning in a million directions at once. One thing I've learned over the years in the media biz is damage control. No way am I getting on national television to get busted. But what to do is the question. I have about four hours to figure it out.

My publishing company has a car pick me up and take me to the station. My girl Macy is right next to me holding my hand. Once I decided what I was going to do, I ran it past her. Not so much for her approval but simply because she is my best friend.

"You're sure you want to do this?"

"I have to. It's about time."

"Did you tell Randy?"

"No. I'm pretty sure after he hears it, he won't want to deal with me anymore anyway. I may as well hold on to the illusion as long as possible."

Macy pats my hand. "If he really cares, it won't matter."

"Yeah," I say. But I'm not too sure.

When we arrive at the studio, Randy is there with Tanya.

"Sorry I didn't get a chance to call you

back. It's been crazy," he says. "As far as legalities are concerned we have nothing to worry about. You're in the clear. Tanya has already spoken with Dallas regarding the questions she's planning to ask. You'll be fine."

"Thanks."

Randy grins. "Break a leg," he says as I hear my introduction.

I walk out onto the stage, which is so much smaller in real life than on television. The audience is on their feet cheering. Dallas greets me with her renowned big smile and open arms. Finally the crowd calms down and resumes their seats.

"Thank you so much for being on the show. Everywhere I look these days there's something about you and this awesome book of yours. Tell us what made you decide to write it."

I give her the down and dirty about the change in management and my unceremonious dismissal, which has the audience in stitches.

"It was really my friend and former producer, Macy Martin, who came up with the idea to write the book. I took the idea and ran with it."

Dallas leans in as if she wants to share a secret. "Joy, I understand that there have been some rumblings from your former callers about using their stories. Is there any truth to that and how do you plan to deal with it?"

I steal a glance offstage and see Macy standing there biting her fingernails. She nods her head.

I draw in a breath, realizing that what I'm about to do will change the world's perception of me, but maybe it will finally set me free.

"When I first got into the business, I knew that if I wanted to be successful I was going to have to be out there, be different. I listened to all of the talk shows and tried to figure how I could stand out. So I went to WHOT with the idea of *On the Line.* I told them I even had a letter to kick the show off with." I clear my throat. "I'd like to read that letter now."

Dallas leans back in her seat. "We're all ears."

Shalonda squeezed her eyes shut and imagined luscious green palm trees stretching out to meet deep, relaxing ocean waves. She shivered from the cold breeze that seeped through her windowsill and wondered what it would be like to live in a place where the weather was warm all year round. Maybe someplace down South, where strangers actually smiled at you. A place where life was different.

At times like these all she could do was imagine the miracle of bright, sunny beaches connected to warm, blue water. It was the only way to survive. She would lose herself inside a hopeful fantasy until the large, sweaty body on top of her collapsed. When the pumping finally stopped, Shalonda didn't return right away. She lay still and quiet beneath him, willing herself not to look at his face. She didn't look at faces anymore.

This was the seventh appointment of the day. The first one talked too much — he was nervous, a kid not much older than she was. The second was maybe about fifty, and he came almost before he could get it inside. Who was the third one? She couldn't remember. The fourth had a slight limp and claimed he was wounded in Iraq. And the fifth and sixth, they were nothing more than body parts jumbled up together.

Number seven was almost done. A quick glance when he entered her room brought the blurred image of tall, thin and brown. She clamped her eyes tightly and held her breath to avoid the smell of tacos or nachos as he gasped for air.

"How much for a second go-round?" the

man asked between grunts.

"Another thirty," she replied, her stomach suddenly queasy.

He twisted up his face and rolled off of her. "Ain't no discount like buy one get one free, or half off the second one?"

She rolled her eyes in his direction. "Sorry."

Grabbing his pants from the floor, the man pulled out three tens from his wallet and dropped them into her slightly opened nightstand drawer. "Well, I want another ride, little girl, 'cause you nice and tight and that won't last for long." He walked over to a nearby chair, sat down, pulled the used rubber off and tossed it on the floor. "Come on over here," he ordered.

Shalonda obeyed, thanking God for her imagination. Shalonda cringed when Rianna's dead body flashed into her mind. She had tried to help Rianna develop the ability to see something else, too, be somewhere else in her mind. Too young and too naive, Rianna was no more than thirteen years old when Juice deposited her in the apartment across the hall. Within a year the drugs turned a beautiful little girl with short curly hair and big dimpled curves in her cheeks into a mangled zombie. When decent men stopped paying for her malnourished body, the sicko and weirdo clients stood in line. For fifty dollars, Juice would let them do anything, except kill her. She used a mixture of crank, heroine and alcohol to do that herself.

Guiding Shalonda onto the edge of his long, spider legs, the man barked instructions. "Just work me around like this and I'll be hard again real soon." She used her hands to massage him exactly the way he had shown her. In two years she learned to follow orders meticulously in order to avoid the consequences. She pressed harder when he told her to and faster as he demanded. Once he was ready, she carefully rolled on a new rubber and he thrust himself inside for the second time.

Rather than feel the throbbing between her legs, Shalonda drifted off again. This time she imagined it was Juice in the chair beneath her instead of a stranger. That's who she wanted to be with. When they first met, Juice would brag about her to everybody. He treated her to expensive dinners and bought her anything she wanted. But now the only time she saw him was for collection.

They met in a popular nightclub where Shalonda's fake ID and suggestive clothes changed her from a tall, awkward fifteen-year-old child into a sexy, well-endowed, eighteen-year-old woman. The steroids in the food had worked over time, so it was not difficult to make people believe what they thought they could see. Technically she didn't lie to her parents about attending a slumber party at her best friend Donetta's house that night. There was a slumber party and going to the club was one of the planned activities. With Donetta's mother working third shift, they dressed to pull. High heels accented big, shapely legs, slinky miniskirts hugged tight to their full hips, and low-cut halter tops showed all they had to offer.

When Juice entered the room, everything and everybody seemed to stop. He was perfect. A sexy bad boy sporting some serious bling. Two fingers on his left hand were circled by platinum rings, each covered with huge diamonds. A large gold chain swung dangerously from his neck, accented by the diamond-encrusted rugged cross that paid homage to his faith. His black-and-white Sean John ensemble was topped off with two large diamond post earrings that glittered from both ears.

The women in the club vied for his attention, some flirting subtly, others offering themselves more brazenly. But it was Shalonda who brought the sun up and called it dawn. She knew Juice was drawn to the way the innocence of her smile enhanced the curve of her hips, and after about an hour of teasing and taunting, he finally pulled her onto the dance floor and whispered, "Show me what you workin' with."

Shalonda moved impressively, knowing exactly what to do and how to do it. Hours in front of the television watching music videos had boosted her confidence. She twisted and shook and gyrated all around him, knowing she had made her point when she "backed that ass up," as the song suggested, and felt his hard-on.

The man inside her now was as hard as Juice had been that night. Shalonda bounced up and down on his lap while his face contorted. He held on to her hips, with both hands shifting her body forward and back or side to side as necessary.

"I'm coming, baby. This is it," he finally yelled out just before he exploded.

She waited to stand up and move away. It was another tough lesson learned. Once, when Shalonda separated from a john too fast, he slapped her across the face so hard that a tooth came loose. She still had the small scar over her left eye where her head had hit the edge of the nightstand. Telling Juice about it brought no sympathy. Instead, he scolded her and said he would have slapped her, too, if she messed up his groove by moving too soon. He went on to chastise her, explaining that when a guy pays his hard-earned money he must walk away completely satisfied.

"Damn, girl! You was even better the second time." The john whistled. Shalonda stood up and covered her body with a robe. Without thinking, she glanced at him and looked directly into a mouthful of rotten teeth. Her stomach lurched, and she rushed into the bathroom.

The man stood up, removed the condom and wiped himself off with a paper towel. He looked over to the bathroom door then at the nightstand. Strolling casually across the room, he glanced behind him one more time before reaching inside the drawer and quickly grabbing a handful of bills.

By the time Shalonda had rinsed out her mouth and emerged from the bathroom, the man was dressed and on his way out the door. "See you, sweet thing," he said, blowing her a kiss.

Shalonda checked the clock. Her next appointment was in forty-five minutes, so she made up the bed hastily and ran a tub of hot water. This was not her normal routine. She usually didn't bother cleaning up until the day was over. But this appointment was different. Rodney had been coming almost every week for the past two months and their time together was special.

Shalonda lowered herself into the warm liquid and savored how it soothed her battered body. She grimaced when she thought back to the night that she declared her independence and ran away to be with Juice. This was not what she was running to, but somehow this was where she was. This was not the freedom he promised, but it was all the freedom she had. This was not the love she thought she'd found, but it was the only love she knew.

Laughing was hard when she really wanted to cry. Shalonda had hated her parents for things that now seemed so insignificant. They were snobbish and too old-fashioned. There were too many rules. They wouldn't let her have any fun. And there was no way she was going to listen when they told her Juice was no good. How could she trust them? They despised, rejected and even feared her generation: the hip-hop generation. They didn't understand Juice the way she did. He was a black man in America who didn't have a chance to go to college, making it the best way he could. He was a black man in America who grew up in the projects, a stereotype, no father, a drug addict for a mother. He was a black man in America and the system was not designed to treat him fairly. Everyone was out to get him — especially the police.

The moment Juice first kissed her, Shalonda felt the guilt of being raised in a middle-class home, spoiled with name-brand clothes, Disney vacations and a college fund. His sad brown eyes endeared him to her and she wanted to be there for him, to support him, to love him. When the phone rang, it startled her.

"Hello," she mumbled, after picking up the receiver.

"Hey, Londa!"

Shalonda's eyes shot open when she heard her baby sister's voice.

"Mimi? Is that you?"

"It's me. How are you?"

"I'm fine, Mimi. What are you doing? Where did you get my number?"

"Donetta gave it to me at the mall. She said she didn't know if it was the right number anymore because she hadn't talked to you in a while, but I'm glad it is."

Shalonda frowned. It was Donetta who had set everything up for the fake slumber party that night. It was Donetta who had arranged for the false ID's so that they could hang out at the club. As a matter of fact, it was Donetta who had wanted to meet Juice, and when he showed an interest in Shalonda, she was obviously jealous. And somehow it was Donetta who had graduated from high school last year and was now attending college.

"I'm so glad you called me, Mimi. How is school? How're Mama and Ben?"

"I'm going to be in fourth grade next year. I can't wait. My teacher says I read real good, but I don't really like reading that much. I like math better."

"You should like reading. Reading is a good thing to do, but math is important, too." Shalonda swallowed hard. "It is so great to hear from you, Mimi. Have you grown taller?"

"Daddy said I'm taller than you were at ten. But Mama told him not to mention your name. I wish you could come home, Londa."

"I'd like to, Mimi, but I can't. Things are complicated and I don't think it's a good idea right now. But I'm glad you're doing good in school. And I miss you very much."

"Mama won't let me watch the videos on BET because she says that's the garbage that ruined you. Londa, what does she mean when she says you're ruined?"

Shalonda thought for a minute, but couldn't come up with an answer. Maybe she *was* ruined. Maybe that was the perfect description of her life. "It really doesn't matter, Mimi," she finally replied. "What does matter is that I'm going to come and see you as soon as I can. I promise."

"I hope so. I got glasses now, but I don't wear them a lot. I don't like the way they feel on my nose."

Suddenly Shalonda heard muffled voices over the phone. She sat up straight in the tub.

"Mimi, are you okay? Are you still there?"

"No, Shalonda. She's not here. Why would you call her? What's wrong with you! You've already messed up your life. Do you want to screw up your sister's life, too? Just stay away from her! Don't call, don't try to see her, don't encourage her to follow you into the gutter!"

"Mom, why do you always have to —"

"Don't act like I did something wrong, Shalonda. We gave you everything and you threw it all away. Your daddy was stupid and you're just like him. As a matter of fact, your whole generation is fucked-up. A bunch of ignorant niggas bling-blinging themselves to death."

"Mom, I'm sorr—" At the sound of the dial tone, Shalonda threw the phone across the room.

She lay back in the tub and took a deep, long breath. That was her mother, always judging other people. If you didn't do things her way you were wrong — and despite a serious Christian upbringing, there was no room for forgiveness. So high and mighty, yet Ben, Mimi's father, her second husband, was a hustler from way back. He kept a string of women throughout their marriage. And each time, her mother wouldn't forgive, but she would turn her head and let him in the back door. Ben had two other kids by two different women. One was the same age as Mimi.

Shalonda lifted a vase of lavender and vanilla potpourri up to her nose. The scent was almost gone. In the beginning it was all fabulous. Juice was like a local celebrity in town. He was treated well wherever he went and that meant she was treated well when she was with him. It was easy to get caught up in such an exciting lifestyle. Riding around in his hundred-thousand-dollar Hummer, attending private parties with politicians and popular media folks she had seen on television. When Juice asked for it, she gladly gave up the only thing she had to offer: her virginity.

When things started to change, she wasn't paying attention. Shalonda sometimes blamed it on the Baker blood, a family myth on her father's side. The blood of Baker women ran a few degrees higher than normal and as a result they loved much too hard. There was an aunt who stayed with an abusive husband for twenty years until he eventually beat her to death. And a cousin who died of AIDS a couple of years ago found out that she got the disease from her unfaithful fiancé, but married him anyway. Shalonda knew that Juice used women, but she truly didn't know how she had become one of them. Maybe it was the Baker blood.

The appointments were supposed to be a temporary thing. Juice said he was having financial difficulties and he needed her to show him how strong her love was. He said only a strong woman could stand by his side. Shalonda slowly waved her hand through the rippling water. It sounded like bullshit now, but somehow it didn't then.

The first time a stranger mounted her for money, Shalonda had held her breath. Now it was as if the act of not breathing could move her out of her body and into another realm. Weeks later she welcomed the fantasies that came. Fields of flowers were followed by deep blue skies and then sandy white beaches gave way to vast ocean waves. In her own mental paradise the men became a blur of contrasting sizes, peculiar smells and distinctive sounds. When temporary turned into permanent, one day she begged Juice to stop and was stunned to hear Mimi's name come out of his mouth. She watched the curve of his lips as he talked about how pretty Mimi was. And her heart sank when he clearly described Mimi's purple lace dress blowing in the wind on their backyard swing set.

A knock at the door alerted her to Rodney's arrival. He always used one hard rap, then four quick ones. Shalonda jumped out of the tub, bypassing her towel. A light spray of Fendi, followed by a soft, silk robe clinging to her wet body, was all the preparation she needed. When she opened the door, she smiled softly. Rodney was holding a single red rose in his hand.

"For you," he said, handing her the rose.

She giggled and took it. "Thank you."

Rodney was an average-looking man. He had big ears, big feet and a big smile. He cared about her, and Shalonda needed someone to care.

"What you got for me today, pretty lady?" he asked with a wink.

She opened her robe and allowed him to survey her thin, tan body. The smooth caramel skin and full red lips beckoned for him to take all he wanted. As he picked her up with little effort and carried her to the bed, Shalonda let it all go. This was one of the few times she would open herself up to enjoy a man's love. Rodney's kindness and compassion was as close to true love as she had ever been. Afterward, they lay together, her head on his chest, the palm of his hand on her hip and he talked about the wonderful places he wanted her to see. San Diego, Phoenix, Atlanta, the Bahamas, Belize, even Costa Rica. The first time he talked like that, she remembered waiting for a punch line, but Rodney continued to shape a dream of the two of them together until she kissed him passionately. Now Shalonda could see a life traveling with this man. She dreamed that someday he would ride in on a white horse and prove his love just like LL Cool J in *Deliver Us From Eva.*

Before he left, Rodney paid the thirty dollars, then he pulled out a twenty-dollar bill and handed it to her. "This is for you," he said, and with one last kiss he was gone.

Shalonda lay across her bed, imagining the possibilities until the slamming of a door next door followed by Snoop Dogg rapping about his ability to turn bitches out, snatched her back. She was irritated. Not because of the song, but because she used to play that kind of music. She used to love that kind of music. When her mother once asked how she could support the negative things they said about women, she would shake her butt to the beat and reply, "They're not talking about me."

She covered her head with the pillow, but the obtrusive beat forced her to get up. Stuffing all of the money from the drawer into a brown envelope, she pulled on a pair of jeans, a wrinkled T-shirt and jacket to start the short walk down the street to Juice's apartment. The extra twenty went into the side pocket of her purse.

Juice actually owned three apartment buildings on the block and was trying to buy a fourth. Shalonda lived and worked in one of the efficiencies along with about twelve other women. Juice called them his rainbows, and the money they made between their legs went into his pot of gold.

She rode the elevator to the third floor, also the top floor of his building. Juice had knocked out the walls between three apartments to expand his living space to the entire left side. He did everything big: oversize black leather furniture, a big-screen television with surround sound, and a huge master bedroom that included a Jacuzzi and sauna. His newest recruit, sixteen-year-old Kristine, opened the door when she knocked. Shalonda handed over the sealed envelope, turned and walked away.

"Shalonda!" Juice called down the hall after her.

"What?" she answered reluctantly. The tears were right there just behind her eyes, but she cut them off with the skill of a samurai warrior.

Juice stepped out of the doorway. "Come on back for a minute."

Trudging up the hall, Shalonda stopped outside the door listening to the macho swagger of his wannabe-playa friends in the back room. Her body suddenly went limp. She didn't feel like dealing with the bullshit tonight.

Juice stepped closer. "What's wrong with you?" he asked. "You don't want to see me? You don't love me no more?"

"I'm just tired, I wanna go back home." She turned to leave.

He grabbed her by the arm. "Excuse me, but I'm talking here. Don't forget I'm the one paying for your home."

Shalonda yanked her arm away. "What do you want, Juice?"

He thought for a moment. "I want you to go to my bedroom, get in the shower and wait for me," he finally replied.

When she heard his request, Kristine leaped up from the nearby chair where she was eavesdropping.

"Juice, what are you doing?" she whined.

He scowled in her direction. "Sit your stupid ass down and shut up!" Then smiling at Shalonda, he continued. "Go on. I'll be there soon."

Shalonda moved slowly down the hallway, choking back determined tears. His bedroom still looked the same. A custom-made king-size sleigh bed with a brown and mauve comforter, two dresser drawers and a matching chaise longue. It was in this bedroom that she first read *The Coldest Winter Ever* by Sister Souljah sitting on that same chaise longue. It was in this bedroom that she gave away her virginity to the man she wanted to love forever. It was in this bedroom that her life had changed drastically.

Shalonda undressed and stepped into the warm shower. The water cloaked her head and back and legs like liquid fire. She watched through the glass as he entered the room, then sucked in a deep breath when the door slid open and he took her in his arms.

"You need Daddy, don't you?" he asked seductively.

Her body shivered, remembering how she used to feel when his hulking muscles engulfed her.

Juice moaned in her ear. "You want some of this good lovin' I've been saving for you?"

Before she could answer, he pushed her up against the wall and licked the trickling water from her neck and ears and back. Then, as if on cue, he bent her over and entered from behind. This was what she used to think love was all about: embracing the heat from his pulsating body; absorbing as much as she could of his powerful presence; inhaling the very essence of him. There was a time when she thought all she needed was this man's love to sustain her, to satisfy her. The head will only hear if the heart listens.

"You like this? Is this what you needed,

baby? Is this what you needed, baby? You like this, don't you?" he repeated the lines as part of his sexual motion.

Shalonda told him exactly what he wanted to hear. "I love it, Daddy. You know you're everything I need."

As the water flowed in a steady stream down their bodies, Shalonda tried to resist, but the rhythm of their movement became so succinct that she climaxed with him. Before he left, Juice kissed her gently and whispered, "I don't want you to ever forget how much I love you, Shorty."

Shalonda stood in the shower and cried violent tears when he was gone. She wanted desperately to understand what she did wrong. Everywhere she looked, she saw it. How could she not eventually buy into it? Images of hard, black men and their sexy, hoochie mammas were a normal part of black culture. In music, on television, through movies and magazines, the thug life was the life to choose. With a deep, painful breath, Shalonda realized that she hated that life now, as much as she had loved it then.

Dressing quickly, she headed to the front door only to be met in the entryway by Juice and Kristine.

"Your tally is short," Kristine blurted out.

Shalonda stepped back. "What? It can't be.

I put it all in there."

Kristine spat at her. "You calling me a liar?"

"I don't know, maybe you are." Shalonda turned toward Juice. "I brought over every dollar. I swear."

Juice shook his head. "I counted it too, baby. It's short."

Shalonda pointed at Kristine. "Maybe she took some out. I don't have any more."

"You lying bitch!" Kristine grabbed at Shalonda's hair and wrestled her down to the floor. As Shalonda's purse was ripped from her shoulder, most of the contents fell out including the extra twenty that Rodney gave her.

"See, there it is." Kristine pointed. "I told you the ho was holdin' out on you, baby."

Shalonda's heart pounded and her body trembled as she stood up. "I didn't take that from you, Juice. Rodney gave me that twenty, plus the thirty for his appointment."

Juice reared back when he heard another man's name come out of her mouth. "Rodney? Who the fuck is Rodney?"

Shalonda backed up against the door, realizing too late the huge mistake she'd made. "He's nobody. Nobody, baby . . . just that guy who's been coming almost every week."

"So you taking money from some motherfucka on the side?"

"He . . . I —" Shalonda couldn't get it out before Juice's fist struck her hard across the jaw. She grabbed the aching spot and slid down onto the floor.

Several of his crew joined Kristine and they watched as Juice demonstrated his title, "Daddy," in a literal sense. Taking off his long leather belt, he swung viciously, hitting Shalonda across the back, shoulders, legs and behind.

At first Shalonda held up her arms for protection and tried to crawl to the door, but ultimately she gave up, pulling herself into a ball of confusion.

"I don't know what the hell you think you're doing!" Juice screamed after one swing and before another. "You don't take money from nobody but me. Understand, bitch?"

Shalonda's head filled with an intense pain each time the tip of the belt struck different parts of her body. She silently prayed for the nightmare to end, and finally Kristine sashayed over and opened the front door.

"Get the fuck out of here before I kill you," Juice hissed.

As Shalonda attempted to drag herself toward the opening, he snatched the twenty-dollar bill off the floor and ruthlessly kicked her in her side.

"Juice . . . Juice, man, come check this shit

out! Our boys are doing that song on TV, man," one of his crew called in a frenzy.

In the midst of the commotion, Shalonda quietly gathered as many of her things as she could. She slowly lifted her body up and limped out the door. Moving cautiously toward the elevator, she allowed the tears to run, wishing she could do the same. Fifteen minutes later she fell into her apartment, spirit crushed, and lay listlessly across the wrinkled cotton sheets.

When the silence became too much Shalonda turned on the radio and listened as a woman's soothing voice washed over her. The voice asked listeners to call in and share their problems. "The only way we can discover new oceans," the voice explained, "is if we have the courage to lose sight of the shore."

Shalonda closed her eyes. She could feel each individual welt as it formed on her body. She listened to the inspiring words gently pulling at her soul: advocating change; promising something better; creating hope; encouraging the first step. With a deep, resolved breath, Shalonda picked up a pen and paper and began her story. "Please help me," Shalonda whispered as the words poured onto the page.

When I finish and look up, tears are streaming down Dallas's face. The audience is stunned into silence. The only sound I hear is the beating of my own heart and the soft sobs coming from the audience.

My own eyes are filled with tears as I relive those terrible years that was once my life.

"Shalonda wasn't some random letter," I say. I lift my head, no longer ashamed of who I am. "Shalonda was me." I look out at the stunned faces.

Dallas gasps. "We'll be right back after a commercial break."

CHAPTER 23

The minute the cameras are off, Dallas turns to me. "Are you okay?"

I nod my head. She signals somebody and a tissue is thrust into my hands.

"Is that story true or some incredible publicity stunt?"

"It's true. Every ugly word." I sniff real hard and wipe my eyes.

Dallas flops back into her seat. "Good thing this wasn't live. We'll have to do some major editing."

I take a glance and see Randy standing in the wings. When we make eye contact he turns and walks away.

"Ten seconds," one of the cameramen shouts.

"Ready?" Dallas asks.

"Yes."

She turns to the camera. "I know you all are as stunned and as touched as I was by the revelation made by Joy." She focuses on me. "Why did you decide to bring your story to the public's attention?"

"I've spent the better part of my career living off of the pain and confusion of others, and now I'm on the threshold of making a lot of money as a result." I sit straighter in my seat. "I want anyone who picks up my book to know that I'm just like everyone else. And that maybe what I was doing all these years was hiding behind the problems of others so that I wouldn't have to deal with my own. I intend to include my story in the book as well. Yes, you heard it here first. And I plan to donate a portion of the proceeds to start the Joy Newhouse Foundation that will help those who are in need of counseling and support services."

A roar of applause fills the room.

"And if there is anything that I can do to help with your cause, I'm here for you," Dallas says. She turns to the camera. "This has been an eye-opening show. I want to thank Joy Newhouse for being our guest and for being so brutally honest about her own life. Be sure to pick up a copy of *The Best of On the Line* when it hits a bookstore in your area."

The red light of the camera goes off. Dallas gets up from her seat and comes over to me and gives me the biggest hug. "That was a brave thing you did. I wish the best for you. Your book is going to be a blockbuster."

"We'll see. Thanks again." I walk offstage where Macy is waiting. She puts her arm around my shoulders.

"You okay?"

I look into her questioning eyes. "For the first time I really think I am."

We head for the exit and Randy is standing at the door. I can't begin to imagine what must be on his mind. I walk up to him.

"I won't blame you if you never want to speak to me again."

"Why wouldn't I want to speak to you again?" He tilts my chin up with the tip of his finger. "That took guts. I don't know if I could have done it. Our skilled PR staff couldn't have done better. The minute you were done, my cell started ringing like crazy. They want you in the office tomorrow so that they can get the story added to the book immediately. Tanya can't keep up with the requests to have you on as a guest on every radio and television show in the English-speaking world." He starts to laugh then looks me fully in the eyes. "We all have a past, Joy. Some are more drama filled than others. What happened to you happens to so many other women every day. And now that they've heard your story, maybe they can find a way to free themselves, too. I am so proud of you."

I don't mean to start crying, but I do anyway. "You don't hate me?"

"How could I hate you?" he whispers. "I'm in love with you."

My heart feels like it's exploding into a million tiny pieces. No one has ever loved me. Well, except for Macy. I'm not even sure if I know how to give it in return. But I want to try. I want to try and see what it's like to give of my real self and have someone know and accept me for who I am. And maybe I'll even get up enough nerve to tell Randy how I feel about him, too.

With Randy on one side and Macy on the other, we step out into the warm afternoon sunshine. Life is good, ain't it? And a fat bank account sure helps!

"Hey, Joy," Macy says as we walk to the waiting car. "I was thinking for your next book . . ."

Me and Randy look at each other and crack up laughing.

ABOUT THE AUTHOR

Essence bestselling author **Donna Hill** began her career in 1987 with short stories, and her first novel was published in 1990. She now has more than fifty published titles to her credit, and three of her novels have been adapted for television. Donna has been featured in *Essence,* the *New York Daily News, USA TODAY, Today's Black Woman, Black Enterprise* and other publications.

Donna lives in Brooklyn, New York, with her family. Find out more about her at www .donnahill.com.